Bread, Wine & Angels

a novel by

ANNA P. ZURZOLO

TURNSTONE PRESS

Turnstone Press
607–100 Arthur Street
Artspace Building
Winnipeg, Manitoba
Canada R3B 1H3

Turnstone Press gratefully acknowledges the support of the Canada Council for the Arts and the Manitoba Arts Council for our publishing program.

Cover art: "View from Fiesole" (1992), by Margaret Berry. Collection of David and Beverly Baird.

Design: Manuela Dias

This book was printed and bound in Canada by Friesens for Turnstone Press.

Canadian Cataloguing in Publication Data

Zurzolo, Anna P. (Anna Paletta), 1952–

Bread, wine & angels

ISBN 0-88801-213-6

I. Title. II. Title: Bread, wine and angels.

PS8599.U79B74 1997 C813'.54 C97-920075-X
PR9199.3.Z87B74 1997

To my husband Sal
and children Cara and Samuele, the dreamers.

To my sisters and brothers,
Rosa, Sal, Joe, Francesca, Viera and Silvano.

To my father, Antonio Paletta, the lover of learning.

And to the two most extraordinary women of all,
my mother and my aunt,
on whose lives this whole house stands.

Acknowledgements

I owe many people for their encouragement and support during the writing of this book:

Nancy Trites Botkin, who meticulously read and edited the manuscript, who saw it through from the very beginning—when it was just an unclear thought—to the very end. For the innumerable hours of standing by me, a million thanks.

David Arnason, Joe Bova and Carmelo Militano, who believed in me. Wendy Raber, Stephen Raber and Marion Kitz, my confidence builders. Marilyn and Art Redekopp for praying. Carol and Don Shields for their gentle guidance.

The many wise women both here and in Italy who never tired of telling me yet another story.

And my friends, who cheered me on. I love you all.

Table of Contents

Minestra

of potatoes, beans and dandelion greens

Bring some water to a boil in a pot (not too much)

Add washed and chopped dandelion greens

After a few minutes, throw in potatoes, cooked beans
and of course a few bay leaves

Simmer until the potatoes are soft

Top with a mixture of garlic and hot chilies
sautéed in some very strong-tasting olive oil

Between mouthfuls, bite on a hot pepper
(the red cherry variety, the ones
preserved in strong vinegar)

Roots

I REMEMBER STEPPING down from the creaking wooden platform where Mr. Ficosecco's desk stood, angry, confused and in a hurry. No, no, I am not going to redo my drawing, I resolved within myself by the time I reached my own desk. I will take the lousy six he gave me but I won't redo it. Besides, I thought, I am not going to be an artist, and my aunt . . . Aie, there was my aunt to think about! Well, my aunt, if my aunt doesn't like the six Mr. Ficosecco gave me on my artwork, then she will just have to pull my hair. Damn pulling. Yes, pulling. It had been this stupid notion of pulling and stretching and wrapping around like a ball of wool that tempted me to include the tree in my picture. Mr. Ficosecco's assignment demanded that I draw a picture of myself, and I did draw a picture of me. But something happened on the way to school that caused me to complicate the drawing.

That morning on the escarpment, I had witnessed the most beautiful scene of disaster ever. The rain, the thunder and the lightning had beaten heavily on the mountainside overnight. The very earth had shaken and moved. It had crumbled like stale bread and exposed naked the roots of the gigantic pine. The tree still stood tall though, and gave no sign of worry. I had seen roots before, and I knew that trees and all living things had them, but I had never stopped to look at them so close up and with such interest before that morning. Why would I? Roots were roots. Uninteresting roots. Uninteresting, that is, until I saw the tree naked before me. There was something about these roots, something so special it kindled my imagination, and soon it was a blazing fire.

So that's what roots were, they were merely branches. They were thick branches, only inverted, with no green, hidden underneath the earth. Hidden until now. Until last night, I should say, when the elements conspired against the tree, against the whole side of the mountain, and stole its cover. The deeper the roots went, the thinner they got, and the thinner they got the stronger they were. They hung fragile, like hair, yet strong. I imagined them very strong. Hair is not strong. The roots of hair don't go down deep enough.

Ha . . . hair!

That is when the idea of pulling really came to mind. I sat there on the edge of the newly formed ravine where my tree stood proud for quite a while, thinking, digging with my eyes in search of the roots' final depth and strength. I concluded that for sure they were so strong and so deep, perhaps even elastic, that if I pulled that tree, if only I could, right out of the earth and dragged it with me all the way around the world, its roots would give and stretch until the tree ended up safe and full circle where it belonged, right here next to me. Not like when my aunt pulled my hair and I pulled my friends' hair in the schoolyard, or not even like when grown women pulled each other's hair in full litigation.

Take for example when Professor Ciano's wife found out about her husband's little affair with the woman who lived above Mancuso's grocery store. I don't need to mention the woman's name. She didn't go by a name that I could recall. She was known as the woman who wore lipstick and rouge. You couldn't miss her. She was the only one on the street with ruby lips.

Once, when cherries were in season, my lips and cheeks were ruby almost like hers. When my aunt saw me so healthy-looking next to a bowl of cherries I had just maimed, she squinted to get a better look, as if I wasn't me. Then she pinched my cheeks very hard and wrung my lips between her fingers until her elbow almost went out of joint. As I screamed, she said, "You want red cheeks? You want red lips? Is it red you want? I'll give you red!"

Professor Ciano's wife wanted blood from the rouge lady. She set out in a rage to find her, and when she did see the beauty from far away, she ran towards her with her hands fully opened, ready to launch herself straight for the well-kept, perfumed hair. There was such a great howling the whole street was alarmed, and in no time at all, every window was crowded with people squirming and fighting for an opening to poke their heads through to get a full view of the spectacle. The rouge lady was at a disadvantage. She wore high spike heels and a tight, very tight skirt, with only one slit, at the back. She couldn't walk and she couldn't run. Professor Ciano's wife dragged the screaming rouge lady by the hair for a good block. When the professor's wife was done, I saw her shake the hair off her palms with satisfaction, and then she waved at the cheering onlookers.

The professor didn't say much. At least not that I

heard. And why should he? This was between women, and then, it wasn't his hair that had been pulled. No, hair didn't come full circle. It simply ended up in the grip of your hand and that was all you were left with: a mass of hair, useless hair. Hair was useless. Roots were not, and that is why I included them and the tree in my picture. And I thought they looked just fine on my paper. If only Mr. Ficosecco had minded his own business it would have been all right. On the other hand, maybe I should have minded my own business too. If only I wasn't so interested in neighbourhood skirmishes and naked trees and wild imaginings of wrapping trees by the roots around the world, I would have probably spent more time drawing myself on the sheet of paper that Mr. Ficosecco handed out. Oh well, I knew it now. If I went home with my artwork the way it was, with Mr. Ficosecco's remarks in red pen all over it, I would lose a few hairs myself. But I couldn't go back on my decision, no, I couldn't. That was a picture of me, and redrawing it to please Mr. Ficosecco would be like denying myself. And anyway, like I said, I was not going to be an artist. In fact, I was going to be a doctor.

Aaah . . . doctor!

Maybe things would not be so bad. Doctor was a long ways off, and drawing had nothing to do with medicine, so maybe my aunt wouldn't care much about the red scribbles and the big red six on the top right-hand corner. That's right, doctor. I had said I wanted to be a doctor someday. Why, a child can't even dream out loud these days!

I had once heard some wise women say, "To saints make no vows and to children promise no dainties." And to parents and aunts, I might add, ditto. That, too, would be wise. You see, my aunt mistook my wishful thinking for a promise. To her it was a promise. A big promise to her and a big mistake for me! From the day I wished my wish, I am sure from the very moment I did, my aunt pictured me among vials, Petri dishes and microscopes, walking about in a white lab coat. She imagined me rich and famous, having discovered a cure for tuberculosis or typhus, although I must admit my aunt was humble enough to settle for a new formula for a revolutionary powder to combat lice and bedbugs. That stuff was expensive! The fulfilment of my promise, or I should say the realization of my aunt's dream, was going to involve a lot of work, most of it on my part, of course. That meant study, study, and then study some more. And when my marks were not up where she thought they ought to be, she would pull my hair, or worse she would pull out her own hair in frustration and desperation. That made me feel very bad because after she finished punishing herself she would sit very silent and hopeless, as if I had just broken a precious crystal vase or shattered something else of value, which we didn't have by the way, or even dream of having.

I worked hard. I think I even tried extra hard. Mr. Ficosecco had said, "Draw a picture of yourself." That's true, he had said those very words, but he hadn't said, "Draw a picture of yourself, only." So I drew a picture of myself. A stick child, you know, a round face with stick hair, stick arms, stick legs, hands all stretched out with stick fingers. I did give myself a heart-shaped torso and a triangle for a skirt. I placed myself in the picture next to my naked tree on the escarpment, and for more effect, I placed us in a vineyard with a cluster of grapes on a vine, and yes, I even added church bells in the corner because where there are bells there are people, and I am a people too, am I not?

I didn't think just then of spending time giving flesh to my body the way Maria Pia did. I shared a desk with

Maria Pia. Maria Pia. Imagine calling your child Pious Mary. Mr. Ficosecco kept pointing to her drawing when he scribbled in red all over mine. When I reached my desk I wanted to call his name out loud. "Hey, Mr. Ficosecco," I wanted to shout, just to get his attention. Then I would have added, "Va fa n'culo, Mr. Ficosecco."

Oh, why wasn't I born a boy? First, because if I were a boy, my aunt would not have taken my wishful thinking as a promise. My brothers, for example, wished and dreamed out loud all the time and all my aunt did was shake her head. And then the second reason I wished to be a boy was that if I was a boy, like my brother Ceci, I could have told Mr. Ficosecco to "va fa n'culo," no problem. I would have taken a good dozen whacks of Mr. Ficosecco's ruler for it and then it would have been all over. But, no, I was a girl and saying something like that would have been enough for Mr. Ficosecco to recommend I be sent to a reform school, if there was one, or worse, to a convent. There were plenty of those, where I would learn about life from a few dozen bitter old spinsters who tiptoed their life away.

No thanks.

So I muttered the words only to myself as I bent over and, with my hands hidden under my desk, gave Mr. Ficosecco an arm's length, never mind just the finger. Just what he deserves, I thought. Maria Pia, Maria Pia. Mr. Ficosecco measured everything against Maria Pia as if she was a yardstick or something. Well, stiff as a yardstick she was. Pious Mary wasn't interested in naked trees. In fact she didn't even take that route to school. She would have scuffed or maybe got mud on her pretty shoes!

Maria Pia's father was an Americano. He was an Americano because he had made it to America. Yes, he had travelled halfway around the world and being called an Americano was part of his reward. He made his appearance from America every second year. I knew it was her father. He was tall and dark and very well fed, and was the only man to wear chessboard pants in women's colours and a white wide, extra wide fedora when everyone else wore French berets.

My father was an Americano. In fact, so was my mother. They were both in America, well, really they were in Canada, not America, and once or twice at first, when someone asked where my parents were, I did say Canada, but they gave me a blank stare as if I had said, "My parents? Oh yes, they live on the moon!" And I wouldn't have minded having to explain that Canada was not in America if it wasn't for their stupid answer every single time: "Ooh, Canada! Yes, yes, Canada, the poor America!" So now when someone asked where my parents were, I simply answered "America." They were in America but I didn't have Maria Pia's pretty shoes to worry about. I didn't care anyway. The bottom of my feet had become so hard I could have walked on glass, and I did. And then, if my feet got dirty, I would wash them in the stream and my aunt wouldn't guess that I had taken the long way up through the basin of the mountain to get to school.

I peeked at Maria Pia's drawing when she returned to our desk. She had paid careful attention to the assignment. She had added muscle and flesh on the stick frame of herself. Her hair, for example: she drew it smooth and close to her cheeks, not in spikes all around the head like mine. I looked at my drawing again. I didn't think of doing any of those things. Besides, my hair was unruly and all over the place. But goodness, tell me, what's wrong with a tree and a cluster on a vine and some bells instead?!

Just as I thought, when I got home my aunt took a look at my work and didn't like it. No, maybe I should clarify that. She would have said nothing about the quality or quantity of the work on my paper had it not been for the red pen markings on it and, most of all, that loud number six. She crumpled it and then nervously worked it between her hands as if she were scrubbing a stain off my clothes. I didn't mind. It was better than having my hair pulled.

She meant well, my aunt. Everywhere she looked, the rich got richer and the poor got poorer. Money made money and lice made lice. She just wanted me to take my schoolwork seriously. She had it all figured out. If you weren't born rich, the only way out of misery was an education or marriage to a prince. Since there was little chance of royalty ever noticing me, my aunt voted for the other option—an education. Not because I was not pretty. Oh no, my aunt called me beautiful all the time. In fact, she hardly ever called me by my name. When she was in a good mood she called out to me, "Bella, bella." That was my name, bella—beautiful. She called me bella, even the time my whole right eye was almost invisible, buried in a thick yellow crust. "Chronic conjunctivitis," I remember Dr. Rafaelino said while with his fingers he attempted to pull my eyelids apart. My aunt sold two quart baskets of wheat to take me to Dr. Rafaelino. As a rule, she would have showed up with wheat just to get the appointment, and then with money for the visit, and then maybe a chicken or some other live offering for the medicine. But Dr. Rafaelino handed her the tube of white paste and shook his head when my aunt insisted he take the money. "For what? I did nothing. It is nothing," Dr. Rafaelino said. I saw her blush as she put the money back into her skirt's pocket. She kept her head down when she said "thank you." "Thank you," she repeated. Then she swallowed quite visibly and took me by the hand.

I didn't keep my head down, no, not at all. I looked straight up into Dr. Rafaelino's face. He was close to me.

His hand rested for a very short while on my head. No, no, not my head, my hair, only my hair. His hand was so gentle that I did not feel it on my head, only my hair. He was tall, almost as tall as the pine on the ravine. I think, if I was not attached so tightly to my aunt's hand, I would have stayed there to look at him for a long time. But then what? What would I have done with Dr. Rafaelino had I stayed? I know, I would have pulled him along with my tree and I would have wrapped him, no, I would have dragged him with me on an imaginary trip around the world.

Oh Lord, no. No more wrapping and dragging and pulling. I was in enough trouble already. I felt my arm almost leave its socket and that helped me to leave the doctor's office quite willingly. You see, my aunt wanted me to get serious about my studies and become a doctor or something or somebody, because "somebodies" had power. With nothing but your eyes and nothing but your words you had power to decree: "It is nothing. You will live," or "It is serious. You will die." And people would believe you because you had read all the right books and had done all your assignments properly. She also wanted me to work hard because other than Dr. Rafaelino, who did not follow the rules, life had many rules, very strict rules, in fact, and one of these rules is that, beautiful or not, a prince will marry a princess one hundred percent of the time. Lice will produce lice. Everything will produce its own kind.

My aunt was young and pretty and she still wasn't married. She didn't think she was pretty. When I said to her that she was pretty she lowered her head and just pointed with her eyes to the patches on her skirt. I thought she was very pretty, even if she did have cat's eyes. I didn't ever call her "cat's eyes." I wouldn't. Others did though, in secret. You see, my aunt's eyes were not the normal dark brown, they were bluish green and, depending on what colour dress she had on, sometimes more blue, sometimes more green. And also depending on if she was crying or not. That made a difference. When my aunt cried her eyes were blue, very definitely blue. She cried at the end of the school year, every year, when the report cards were handed out. With five of us, if it wasn't one, it was the other who didn't do too well in a subject here or there. My aunt also cried every time a letter came from America. My parents promised they would be gone only for a short while, just long enough to make money so we wouldn't have to swallow empty. But the years were dragging by, one after the other. My aunt cried when each letter arrived. Even when the letters had money in them, she cried. She cried when my father wrote to say we had a new sister. The only time she didn't cry was when she read that we had a new brother in America. But then, later, she cried about that too, because, she said, first we were six and now we were seven.

It's not that she minded the hard work. No, it wasn't that for sure, because when she washed the clothes or swept the floor and I asked to help, she would push me away with her hand or with the end of her broom. "Have you got no studying to do?" she would ask. "Study! If you make something out of yourself, you won't need to wash and sweep. Someone else will do it for you."

Fancy, very fancy ideas for a simple woman like my aunt.

She did let us help with food though, because food was living and living was life. People wandered and moved and trekked and trotted around the earth, and for what? For survival. That's the cost of life. She allowed us to help with food also because she believed that if you were rich and had all the finest ingredients but you didn't know how to prepare or when to prepare, and for what occasion to prepare what, you were indeed poor. Other children embroidered sheets and doilies and knitted sweaters. We were not allowed. She had no use for pretty things like that, not because she didn't like them, but because in reality it was life itself that had no use for them. It was not an education. There was no money in these trades, fine as they were. They were pits, nothing but pits, with a bold sign posted right at the mouth of them. "Women Only," my aunt said, that's what the sign read.

We were allowed to sit from time to time with the women who gathered around the clearing at the edge of our street, passing time performing these arts. She let us because these women had good qualities about them. They were old and wise and had much to say about life. They said it just like it was—"pane pane é vino vino." It was their job to see that the young never got the two mixed up; bread was bread and wine was wine.

My aunt, of course, never joined them, or us, I should say. God forbid, not even in the antechamber of her brain would she entertain that idea. There were far too many children at these gatherings around the wise women. After all, it was here at their feet that little girls learned to pull thread and knot wool. My aunt was already raising five children, not her own, and worrying about two more in America, also not her own. She did not need to see or hear any more. To tell you the truth, I heard my aunt say that the whole idea of living a saintly life seemed futile and pointless. She had lost, it seemed, her interest in paradise, the reward for such a life, all on account of children. It's not that she didn't want to go there, but she did not know whether it was a desirable destination for her any longer. She had started to doubt this destination ever since Bernardo, the preacher, one Sunday night during his sermon alluded to the fact that paradise was primarily for children. The place was full of them and anyone who planned to be there had to enter a very narrow door, which meant you had to become small too. This is all I remember. I fell asleep, but not because I was bored. Oh no, I loved Bernardo. It was just his voice that lulled me to sleep.

When he told his stories of laughing demons and blazing fires, he told them in a deep dark voice, different from his usual voice. When he told of once-proud people reduced to walking on their knees with their mouths forever open and their eyes looking on high, longing for precious drops of water, I did not fall asleep. I couldn't! Bernardo's own body reached for the ceiling as if it was the sky, and with his voice, with his deep dark voice, I remember, he told us that the fire was so hot, the drops of water became nothing but hot air by the time they fell into the people's open mouths. How could I not be alert when he told such stories? But when Bernardo spoke of children and paradise his voice was so soft that my tired body slowly slid across the empty seat next to me, and before I knew it, singing voices woke me and then everyone said "peace" to each other and my aunt took me home.

I remember that no peace came home with my aunt the evening that Bernardo told of children, lots of children, being in paradise. I couldn't figure what her fuss was about. Everyone knew that children became angels when they died. Where did she think angels lived anyway? What was so new about what Bernardo said? But to my aunt it was all new, brand new, as if she had never heard it before. As if she had received a new revelation. And from that night on, I often heard my aunt sigh, "Lord forgive me." She'd say with such meaning, reverently, looking towards the ceiling, "But the place is full of children, children." And then she would shake her head in disappointment, still looking at the ceiling, of course.

That there were children in heaven was a fact. It was not hearsay. She had not only heard Bernardo tell it from the pulpit. If she had heard it from Bernardo only, it would not have been so bad. He was a man, just a man, and she would have challenged the issue because my aunt was not scared of men, in fact I could tell you a million stories that would prove they were indeed scared of her! No, she had read about this paradise and children stuff herself. I remember that she read and read those words in her little black Bible when she came home that same evening just to make sure. Yes, the words about children and paradise were true. There was no denying the fact. The words she read were clear and the message was clear too. But it sure seemed unfair! Children, children. She had not had the pleasure of producing them. She had taken the punishment of raising them, and now the prospect of future peace and rest included them, forever.

My aunt had plenty of time to deliberate about her trip to paradise. She was still very young, and even if she wouldn't admit it, I think she loved children. Look at the way she worried about us. She wanted no disappointments in our lives. She was determined not to see us struggle and wrestle with life the way she did. I think this is why she screamed and threatened so much. "Look around you, observe, observe, listen and observe." Although, as much as my aunt revered studying and dreamed of high prestigious degrees for us, she always said, "A theory without the praxis is worthless." I know, Professor Ciano always rolled his eyes and said that it was not flour out of her own sack whenever my aunt said things like that. I think she heard it during an interview at school with Nina's professors but my aunt was smart. Smarter than some professors I knew. She said that an education, and the highest degree, when it does not include respect and knowledge of your environment, its rules and traditions, is a waste. It would be more useful hanging in a bathroom next to the toilet.

I didn't have to worry about such waste. We did not have a bathroom or a toilet. We had a pisspot. Dr. Mauri's wife had a beautiful toilet of shiny marble in a marble bathroom—that's what everyone said—yet behind her back she was called the pisspot lady. My aunt was the first to call her the pisspot lady. I heard my aunt call her that out loud once when I was just a little girl. I heard her because I was there.

I always used to linger on the little landing of Dr. Mauri's house. Dr. Mauri's wife hung the rugs outside and beat them with a stick. She hung them on the railing of the landing and I sat there to watch, and sometimes, when she wasn't looking, I even caressed the velvety colours and, with my fingers, traced the paisley and flowers that spoke of places, far-away places, where only the wind had been on its journeys halfway around the world. I don't remember, but my aunt tells me that one winter, because our wheat crop had not done well, we ate more, many more, dandelions, figs and beans than we usually did, and for sure, then, we should have had a bathroom. Well, a toilet, an indoor toilet would have been sufficient too because figs, beans and dandelion greens did not take long to digest and I never quite made it to the bushes on San Giovanni's mountain.

The day I first heard my aunt call Dr. Mauri's wife the pisspot lady was one of those days. On that morning, I never even made it past Dr. Mauri's house. In fact, I remember that his wife had just spread her silk window coverings, the ones I had looked at once through a crack in her door, on the railing. More than anything, I wanted to touch what looked to me like the shiny waves of a purple sea. I wanted to touch this sea and I wanted to make it badly to the bushes. I really wanted—I really tried to do them both. I squeezed my buttocks real tight with all my might, but the half-digested dandelion greens didn't let me, and before I knew it, they burst out of my body and trickled down my legs and onto Dr. Mauri's landing and some even, because I panicked, ended up on her silk coverings.

I'll never forget that woman's face, the way her pale cheeks suddenly became red, as red as the rouge lady's lips, and for sure I will never forget her screaming and shouting as she chased me off her stairs. "Buy this child a potty, a potty," she screamed towards my aunt. The way my aunt was rushing down the stairs, I thought for sure she was running to pull my hair, but she didn't. She stopped and stood by my side. With her hands firmly on her hips she mimicked Dr. Mauri's wife, shouting, "A potty, a pisspot, says the lady, the pisspot lady!"

Dr. Mauri's wife was not a doctor herself. Dr. Mauri married her because her parents gave her as much land and nightgowns and carpets and silk as Dr. Mauri's degree could buy. But had she been a doctor, and had she read all the right books and done all her assignments properly, my aunt would say for sure that her degree would do better hung next to the shiny marble bowl, that fancy pisspot in her bathroom.

Now, since my aunt did not pull my hair after she saw that I had not done my assignment properly, and after she even saw Mr. Ficosecco's big red six on my art-work, I decided for sure I would leave the drawing just as it was, of me and my tree. I also decided I would make it up to my aunt, and myself too. From now on, I would make a real and genuine effort to listen, to observe, and then to listen some more. And yes, I also decided to save and treasure, because "Someday," as my aunt would say, "you never know where on earth God may lead or pull you, and then you might need to remember."

Bread

Yeast, water, salt and flour

Let the yeast bubble in the water

Make a well in the flour

Sprinkle the salt around the edges of the well

Pour the yeast water in the well

Pull in the flour, as much as the water will take

Squish it, then knead it all you want but only
until soft and smooth like a baby

Let it rise

Shape it

Let it rise

Place gently in the oven

DON'T SLAM THE DOOR

Tap the bottom of the bread

If the sound comes back to you live, it's ready

Bread

BY SIX IN THE MORNING my aunt was always up and awake. In the summer she opened the windows to let the fresh air in. The morning sounds of life—roosters, goat herds and people wishing each other a "buon giorno"—woke us. In the winter she did not open the windows. The wind tried by rattling the shutters. In the winter she made a fire, and the fragrance of fresh-ground coffee, spewing out of a little contraption among the coals in the fireplace, did the job. "Up, up," my aunt always said. "If you sleep you won't catch fish."

And where was I to find fish at 1400 metres above sea level? Although once a week, I don't remember exactly when, most likely Fridays though, to enforce some holy law, a woman showed up and wailed through the streets, "U peesciu, u peeeesciu, u peeeeeeeesciu friscu."

The fish lady was in town advertising her fish and I was sleeping and my aunt was nowhere to be found. Damn, she must have snuck out again. She always did this to me the day she made bread. I just didn't understand my aunt sometimes. If I was supposed to learn how to make bread why did she not wake me? Why did she leave me behind? Bread was the one essential in life. It was the one thing no one could live without. That is what she herself had said. "As long as we have bread." Mammarosa would tell you the same thing.

Mammarosa was not my mother. She was my mother's mother so she was still my mother and she lived with us. If by chance you met my Mammarosa on the street and you were polite, and would say more than just hello and good morning, you would say "ziaco." If you asked her or any of the old women, for that matter, "How are you, how are you?" you had to add "ziaco." It means aunt of my heart. I called every old woman ziaco, even if they were not my mother's or father's sisters. It was the polite thing to say. And if you were polite and called them ziaco, they certainly made it worth your while. Right away they volunteered all kinds of information and told you story after story without you even asking.

My Mammarosa would reply, even if she had never met you before, "How am I? I'll tell you how I am, dear child, I am consumed. Every bone in my body is consumed. . . ." Mammarosa always said she was consumed. Every old woman said, "I am consumed. . . . People in my condition should be in bed." She would say, "But life has to go on. The fields are tired, the harvest is meagre and the pests multiply. Yet, we carry on just the same. We eat, we drink and keep on going. As long as there is bread we live and keep on living. Sometimes we smile and sometimes we cry. Of course, we cry more than we smile. And then, if we are lucky, we have a good death and then we finally rest. There is no rest here and now. We sweat for the bread we eat. It gives life all right, we couldn't live without bread, but bread demands it back."

I wouldn't know because I never took Communion. But I did overhear children say that the little thin white crust handed out by the priest at mass was really bread. And here, bread was paid its highest respects. It was never chewed because it must not be harmed. It was swallowed whole, just as it came. It was Life.

Bread, if it had to, only if it absolutely had to, could be thrown out—if a mouse had made a home in it or because it turned blue and green with mould. However, my aunt did not throw this bread out. She simply cleaned it up and we ate it just the same, because she said to life's problems one had to find solutions, not give up and throw it all away.

Bread was sacred. I remember even the professor's wife kissed it before she crumbled it for the chickens or dumped it in the pigs' slop. And they had lots of bread. It wasn't every day you would make bread. Not even every week, only once a month was bread made. And then you wouldn't just make a few loaves. Of course not. I heard my aunt speak of a hundred pounds of flour! That sounds like a lot, doesn't it? But it was not much considering we ate bread and figs and bread and nuts and bread and olives and water-soaked hard bread with sugar and oil, or just plain bread for dinner.

Bread was not baked at home. Not even the rich baked their bread at home. There were public ovens here and there around town and a woman baker, always a woman. Making bread was a woman's business. She was called the "fornaia" because she was the keeper of the forno (not the bakery, by the way—the forno, the oven). She did not make pasticcini, panettoni, cannoli and those kinds of good-time goodies. Men did that. The fornaia just made bread. Women said the fornaia's job was to supervise the bread-making, but from what I saw, she did most of the work herself. She was paid with bread. She sold the bread and that's how she made her living.

If bread was so important, why did my aunt leave me at home again? Every time she said, "Next time, next time." By the time the fish lady sang another round of "Fish, fresh fish, come and get your fresh fish," I was awake and on my way, running towards the oven. Damn, I ran so fast I was almost out of breath and nearly tripped on the cobblestones. If I ever tripped and hurt myself, my aunt would pull my hair. I didn't know if she did it because she did not want me to injure my body again or because she was angry, since stitches cost money.

I was angry. What kind of nonsense was this? I was expected to catch fish on the mountain and make bread someday without instructions. Didn't my aunt know that fish need lots of water and we did not have lots of water? There was such a lack of water, in fact, that Don Antonio, the priest, was worried. He was worried because the Christian Democrats were losing ground to the Communists who promised to dam the streams and form a lake, one full of trout to fish. Don Antonio was worried because good churchgoers like Tata wore red skirts and chanted "Sickle and hammer" while punching heaven, it seemed (to Don Antonio anyway), with tight fists. And Tata, of course, was there at the very front, pulling bystanders onto the street to join the march shouting "Sickle and hammer." And they did, because all they wanted was water, a simple thing like water, gathered in one huge place. A promised lake. Even if it would never have fish in it. And now that I think about it, the Communists had their turn at the town hall and we still had no dam and no lake, not even a pond. So how could I catch fish?

Oh, I know, Mammarosa said that nothing was impossible. I remember that she said it to me in a riddle and she recited this same riddle every time I turned up my nose and said "I can't" at something new I was expected to do. "Chine vo filare fila a nu scuerpuru," she said. But I knew what it meant. It was no new revelation to me. I had heard old women repeat that riddle over and over again and I listened and I observed and I remembered. It meant that if I was real serious about knitting, not having needles would not be a problem, because if I really wanted to knit, I could knit with two sticks.

Well, I did not want to knit with sticks, I wanted to learn how to make bread. My aunt had said a million times that I could watch and now, as always, she had broken her promise. She had said it was important to observe and then she left me home! I ran and ran, and when I ran out of breath, I ran out of anger too. That was a good thing on my part because when I reached the threshold of the oven, there, in front of me, was my aunt sitting on a bench nervous and impatient, waiting for the dough to rise. Too bad for me, the fun part, the most important part, was over. Although, with making bread, nothing was unimportant. Every little detail mattered and counted, from the feel of the water you added to the flour, to the way bread was rotated on the hot oven floor. Everything mattered. The water had to be just right. It had to be tepid, as if it had been sitting in a basin in the sun for a while. Not cold, not hot, just right.

I knew all about tepid water.

I let it sit in a basin in the sun several times every summer and my aunt washed my hair in it. Only in the summer did she work my hair, never in the winter. The bugs and lice didn't mind. I didn't either. The blood that squirted out of the little crawlies when I squished them between my fingers was nothing compared to the red stuff that came out of the rouge lady's mouth because she had been foolish not to let a few bugs suckle on her head and wanted her hair in water, not tepid, in winter. The women pointed their fingers and said "ha ha."

Well, ha ha. The rouge lady didn't die because she sent for Dr. Rafaelino, who looked into her eyes and said, "Nothing. It is nothing." But if she had died as the women (especially Professor Ciano's wife) thought she should, then in no time crawlies and bugs and mice would have eaten her whole perfumed body like a loaf of bread. "That's life," my aunt said.

Oh yes, bread. Bread, while it baked, had to be rotated gently because the yeast bubbles inside had to burst and not collapse. The little burst bubbles became chambers in the bread and they had to bake intact. That's what gave bread its special texture and taste.

Oh well, I didn't say anything. I didn't appeal my case. What was the use of arguing with my aunt? Especially when she was nervous. It served no purpose. I was destined to learn how to make bread "a singhiozzo," hiccup style. One hint, one tip, one step at a time, here and there, depending on which time in the bread-making process I arrived on my runs to the oven. If only she would have awakened me, if only she would have let me help, I wouldn't have messed around with the flour or the dough in the trough. All I wanted was to squish a piece, a little piece, of sticky dough.

Bread was such fun before it became bread. Soft and pliable. I would squish it with my fingers and pat it with my hands and then I would shape it any way I wanted, and if I changed my mind, I would reshape it as often as I wanted. Well, not too often, because after you make up your mind what that piece of dough is going to be, you have to let it rest and rise and affirm itself. And then, at the right time, it has to bake, otherwise it would end up being nothing but a sour lump, fit for nothing but the garbage.

I don't know why my aunt didn't call me when she made bread. I wouldn't have pestered her to let me knead or do anything like that, even though I knew how. I knew I had to be gentle. I knew how to make a well in the flour and then pour the water with yeast and then pull the flour in a little at a time and then add more water, as much as the flour wanted. And the salt, I almost forgot the salt! Salt first had to disappear in the water but not with the yeast water, a little sugar was better than salt in the yeast water. See, I could have made bread. But she just didn't wake me.

But maybe it was a good thing after all, because that day my aunt stood, and then she sat, and then she walked around, and then she stood again. She was not just nervous, she was very nervous. She made people around her nervous too. Her anxieties were like a fire. It radiated from her body with such intensity that sometimes, without meaning to, it burned those around her. When she didn't burn so hot, she was very warm and very nice to be around, like a fire in the hearth in the dead of winter. She had mixed one hundred pounds of flour before and she knew how many loaves a hundred pounds of flour would yield. But no, every time while she waited for the rising, she would lift the covering blankets and peek and poke. When the fornaia saw my aunt fidgeting she gave her a push to get her out of the way. "I just, I just . . . ," I remember I heard my aunt say. "You just, you just want to ruin my reputation," the fornaia spat. I'll never forget the fornaia's strong hands, determined on her large hips. "Bread takes time, you know that." The fornaia meant it. Since I had missed the fun part of making bread, and the only part left was where my aunt would argue with the fornaia, I went outdoors.

There was a fountain next to the oven. It was the fountain of San Giuseppe on Via San Francesco of Assisi.

This was not like the ordinary fountains, you know, the ones with the hand-carved iron base with gargoyle faces that spewed water. These fountains were very common on the street corners of San Giovanni. San Giovanni is the name of my village. San Giovanni was known at the very, very beginning as Universitas Florenz. It was never meant to be a village or a town or a city. It was a universitas where the abbot Joachim came with his students in the year 1190, to contemplate life. Even when it did become a town San Giovanni was not a very big town. Its real name is San Giovanni in Fiore. Visiting Americanos, like Maria Pia's father, call it "Blooming St. Johns," but I just call it San Giovanni. San Giovanni blossomed up the side of a mountain facing south, with a whole ring, a gigantic cradle, of mountain peaks and hills in full beautiful view. San Giovanni had two main streets. They hugged the mountain like a set of arms. One street went down the east side and one street went down the west side. After much winding and contorting they clasped at the place where it had all begun, where the Abbey of Contemplation was, at the meeting of two rivers in the valley, the Neto and the Arvo, and that was the end of San Giovanni. Past that junction it was forbidden to build. There was a curse placed there by the abbot himself which dated back to his arrival in 1190. The abbot had pronounced a curse on the rising town of San Giovanni and its inhabitants which would come to pass should they build and extend the town limits past the point where the two rivers met. The curse involved a heaven-ordained disaster of total destruction should his order to keep the town contained within his prescribed boundaries not be obeyed. But someone, thank goodness—not the abbot—came up with a very bright idea. This person, probably a wise monk, suggested, so as not to annoy the inhabitants with constant warning of the impending disaster, that they make the forbidden site San Giovanni's cemetery. That was that. No more worrying about San Giovanni's expansion past the rivers' junction after that. No one would ever build next to, or near, or in view of, the cypress trees that were planted there as a shelter and border for the new holy site. No one would dream of building near the dwelling-place of the dead. Because once someone was dead, he was dead, and no matter how much he was loved, death and life would not, could not, co-exist. Life and death have always, and will always, war against each other, one claiming to be more powerful than the other.

The people of San Giovanni had already decided who the winner of the two was. It was an easy decision to make. Since no one had come back from the dead, and since people died every day, it was not hard to conclude that death was stronger. Therefore on their own, without anyone's prompting, the people of San Giovanni willingly respected the abbot's boundary, simply by staying away from death's resting-place. The cemetery would be where the dead of San Giovanni lived and San Giovanni the town would be the place where the living lived. And for good measure, to keep both the abbot's curse and death away for as long as possible, they prayed and enlisted the help of many saints.

To remind themselves to pray to the saints, the people of San Giovanni had streets dedicated to them all over the place. The street that the fountain and the oven were on was called San Francesco of Assisi because of the abbot Joachim's and Francis' shared ideals. The fountain itself was called the fountain of San Giuseppe because Joseph was a model husband and a model man, and his wife paid him much respect and she probably washed his clothes in a fountain just like this one.

The fountain of San Giuseppe was no ordinary channel of water, no ordinary fountain. No, not this one. This one did not even look anything like the common fountains, although it too had a gargoyle face. The mouth of San Giuseppe's fountain was gigantic and wide open, not small and narrow like the mouths of the other fountains. Out of this fountain, water continuously gushed. It poured directly into a massive stone tub with a hole in it which allowed the water to travel to the other stone tubs arranged around the fountain. This was not a fountain where you might stop and drink water if you were thirsty. You could do that, but if the women gathered there were busy, they might resent you. Here, the women came to scrub and wash clothes. But from what I heard and saw, there were more than dirty linens laundered at San Giuseppe's fountain.

It was here at this fountain while I waited for our bread to rise that I first heard of bread and life. "I am convinced . . . ," I heard a woman say. I don't recall exactly who this woman was, but there is really no need to remember who she was, because in San Giovanni every woman held the same conviction regarding this argument. "I am convinced," she said, "that when a woman knows a man, you know, after she has lain with him, she acquires a craving for it. You know what I mean." She kept on repeating "You know what I mean, you know what I mean. . . ."

How was I supposed to know what she meant? Although she wasn't talking to me, I was listening in, but I wondered why she had to complicate things so much. "And with this immigration, with men leaving their women behind for so long, God knows, mark my words, no good will come out of this. There are sad times in store for the senseless."

Sad times did come. Sad for Filomena. Someone had called the police on Filomena. Filomena lived smack right on the Avenue, almost at the very beginning of Via

San Francesco, close to the wash fountain of San Giuseppe. She sat outside her door pretending to be honourable and homey. She never embroidered little items like hankies or doilies, oh no, she embroidered big things like sheets, tablecloths and blankets. She gathered the bulk of her work on her lap. While she pulled on her needle, Filomena kept an eye on what was going on in town, you know, who bought what at the market, who walked with whom, who entered whose house and who said what. What Filomena didn't count on was that others were keeping their eyes open too. Open wide on what she was up to.

Filomena would not have made good bread. She was not good with details. Details that seem so unimportant, like melting the salt in the water but not the yeast water either, before you added it to the flour. She had no salt to add. In fact the other women thought her head was totally lacking salt. And if she ever had any, she lost it suddenly, the very day her husband left for America.

America is a far way off. Husbands that emigrated to countries like Switzerland or France or Germany came to visit a few times a year. But America was too far for that. Filomena was soon spending dollars. She ate well, and because she liked to dance, she bought herself a phonograph. Filomena would never have succeeded in making real good bread. She didn't know when enough was enough. She didn't know when to stop shaping and reshaping and beating the dough. I don't blame her, it is too much fun. She was having fun and so far what could anyone say against it? That she squandered a little? That she didn't respect her husband's hard work? What could they say? That the poor bastard in America didn't earn the dollars sitting at a desk pushing papers? That he earned the money with either a pick or a shovel above the earth or in its bowels below? So far—so what? Mind your own business, one might answer, and rightly so. But when young men started to swing Filomena around her living-room floor to hot new tunes from the phonograph, that's when everything changed.

Life was fun. Just like dough in a child's hands is fun before it becomes bread. But you can't play with dough after it becomes bread. Bread is life and bread is holy. For sure I would have been in deep trouble if my aunt ever caught me playing with bread. It may as well have been another commandment, "Thou shall not play with bread."

I heard from the women at the fountain, while I was waiting for our dough to become bread, that Filomena's belly often rose like bread dough in the trough and then just like that—poof—it was flat again. No more bread. If you did that with dough too often it was good for nothing. It turned sour and foul smelling; you would never have bread.

Someone called the police on Filomena because someone had a good conscience, the women said. When the police showed up at Filomena's door she was sitting there in her favourite chair embroidering a sheet. Of course the sheet was all crumpled and fluffed on her lap as usual. The police officer lifted the pile of fine linen with his stick and, oh my goodness, it was true, there it was, a bulging, firm, well-rounded loaf, oh no, stomach, I mean. It was not the direct result of good food and good wine, either. More like the indirect result of such luxuries. My aunt said that when lice have their fill of blood they start wandering to open spaces.

"This bread you will not break and throw away," the police officer said while he ran his stick up and down the bright red stripes of his uniform. The officer came with a witness, a woman, who nodded heavily in Filomena's direction at each syllable of the warning. And you should have seen the officer's face! The women at the fountain said his eyebrows raised so high they pushed his whole forehead right out of existence. Erased, it seemed, just gone.

He pointed and shook his finger sternly at Filomena's belly. "This dough has risen," he said, "and now it will bake and I will see to it! Defy my order and I will charge you with murder." Filomena was in trouble. She was in shit is more like it.

And then one day Filomena had a little boy. "Imagine, a boy," the women said scornfully. Personally, I had always believed, because this is what I was told, that boys were special miracles. And aren't miracles from God? With whom she had the child no one really knows. Any one of a dozen could have been the father. No one made claims. Vullarina, San Giovanni's head whore, really put on a show. Vullarina and Filomena must have had some contention over a man or two, so Vullarina was determined to relish this happy event. She came out of her house as proud as hell. She tried hard to balance an immense tray of glasses filled with Strega liqueur. I loved the sweet yellow syrup even if it had a witch's profile with loose, very loose, long hair picture-wrapped around the bottle. My aunt warned us about magic and witches. The tray shook in Vullarina's hands. Her whole body shook with laughter. Her red mouth appeared larger than life. As large as the mouth of the gargoyle that spewed water out of San Giuseppe's fountain. "Come, drink, celebrate," Vullarina shouted up and down the street. "Filomena, congratulations Filome," she cried towards Filomena's window.

Every balcony on Via San Francesco was soon crowded with curious people roaring and laughing at the invitation. "A boy, Filomena had a boy," Vullarina went on and on while she offered her Strega liqueur. I remember the commotion. I did not know what it was about just then.

I went to see the baby because it was the thing to do. Children were allowed to go and see a newborn. I don't even remember being asked to wash my hands, yet I was allowed to get real close. I went to see Filomena's boy. He was warm and smelled fresh. He was sucking on Filomena's breasts. Filomena's nipples were big and round like a wine bottle cork. They looked like they had been suckled on a lot, yet this was only her first *real* child. The baby smiled. "He is speaking with the angels," I had heard the women say when babies smiled.

My aunt says that once I too was a baby and that I smiled a lot. But I can't remember speaking with angels. I asked her once why I couldn't hear their voices anymore and why I wasn't smiling or speaking with them. She said that you cannot keep two conversations going on at the same time. Once a baby says its first words, the angels know it is time to end theirs. Their job is done, they have accompanied us on the journey down the dark tunnel, they have lit the candle and now they let us get on with our lives on our own. You know, like when a little bird first tries his wings? The mother just lets him be. She watches from far away. They are still there, my aunt says. The angels too watch from a distance, and sometimes, in emergencies, they even come close. But they don't get too close. Remember, they want you to make it on your own. That is why you don't hear or see them anymore, that's all, my aunt said.

I thought angels must be sad. Angels must be very sad creatures, because they must feel like abandoned friends. They are there, and we know they are there, but we hardly ever think about them and never try to speak with them. I don't think too much about angels either. Imagine—I used to speak with them! After my aunt explained this to me, about angels, I went to see babies, just to see them smile, because if babies smiled, then the angels must be right there, standing in that very room. I even remember taking cautious steps because I didn't want to accidentally bump and hurt any of them. If babies could answer I would have asked them what angels said. And then I would have also asked them to tell me what God was really like because angels and babies come from where God lives, so they would know.

Don Antonio didn't know and Bernardo didn't know. In fact they couldn't agree. Don Antonio gave children pictures of a very very old man with a very white long beard, as white as the clouds he sat on, and he said that was God. Bernardo said God, although He had lived from ever to ever, was not an old man. He said that He was more like the wind, everywhere, always, and everyone could feel Him at the same time. I didn't know who to believe. Angels, though, would know. I would believe what they had to say.

"Sometimes I wish I had never stopped talking with angels," I said to my aunt once. And she replied that life must go on and she told me not to be sad because when we die they have permission again to talk to us and they take us by the hand on the journey back. The journey back is dark.

There was a time I doubted what my aunt said about angels. I had my own ideas. I thought that since the silence was so strong, maybe angels were not here next to us at all. I thought maybe their job was to bring us here to San Giovanni, and then they went back to heaven. Then another time I thought the reason I couldn't hear them was that their voices were too faint, or perhaps my hearing was not good enough. And then another time I thought that maybe the reason I did not see or hear angels was that the distance between heaven and earth must be greater than the distance around the earth. This is why I could pull and drag something like my huge pine tree by its roots anywhere on the earth with me but I couldn't pull or drag an angel along. Maybe heaven where angels lived was just too far. Nah, I think now my aunt is right about angels. My Mammarosa agrees with my aunt too.

Filomena's baby smiled a lot and there were women in the room but no one said that he was speaking with the angels. I don't know why, because of all the babies I had ever seen, and I went to see them all (I even went to see one baby that was blue, dark blue, like the midnight sky), never was a baby's smile ignored. And every time, at every birth, women talked of pain. They said, "No more pain, as water gone over, no more pain. It is forgotten."

No one said "No more pain, no more pain" to Filomena. No one dared. I think they were there for curiosity, to scratch an itch on their ears, and soon they would bite, real hard. Soon they would make sure Filomena's pain would not be gone as "water gone by." They would make sure. Life itself would make sure. And another thing, I didn't feel salt in the baby's swaddles either. That was an important first thing to do: wrap a small salt stone and hide it close to the baby's heart. The baby's heart and mind had to be guarded from evil. Evil does not like salt. And there is yet another thing I remember noticing when I went to see Filomena's baby. There was no soup on the stove and no one brought any either.

Chicken brodo was a tradition. The women knew that. What was wrong with them, breaking tradition? Even if it was a weak meal, simple and weak, fragile like life itself, it was most important, because it served for the cleansing of the mother's insides. The brodo had to be simple and clear. Not clouded by excesses. Not too much celery, not too much onion. It had to be simple and clear, almost like water. The baby was washed with water, and the mother, for her cleansing, drank brodo. So why didn't anyone bring Filomena brodo? Was life paying her back?

Filomena had not washed her other babies, the babies that didn't make it, the dough that had risen inside of her, time after time, but never became bread. She buried them in their filth in the earth under the oak tree at the basin of the mountain. Poor Filomena. No one lent a clean hand. No one.

Had my aunt lied to me about the value of friendships? She had said many times, "Meglio un amico vicino che un fratello lontano." Indeed, better a close friend than a far-away brother! These very words were the measure of friendships in San Giovanni. The old wise women said the same thing. They agreed with my aunt. I think my aunt first heard it from them. In fact, the word neighbour and the word close are the very same word: "vicino." They are used interchangeably. It was your vicino who ran to help when you were in trouble.

I don't know why Filomena was the exception. I don't know why no one ran to her with brodo. Piperella's wife would have got brodo. When her husband chased her with a knife in a drunken stupor, and he did that often, she did not run to her mother's house, oh no, she took refuge in her vicina's house. Poor devil, I remember once she was pregnant, very pregnant. She could hardly walk never mind run, yet she tried. She knew that, if need be, she could even deliver her child at her vicina's. I sure wouldn't have minded if she delivered her child in our house. Even if it meant giving up my spot in our bed (mine was the left end corner at the foot of the bed). You see, if she did, then immediately some other neighbour would show up with the brodo. It was the custom, a timeless tradition. Your friends, your vicini, would bring you the brodo. Brodo bypasses the digestive system and flows right into the breasts to make the very best milk for the newly arrived angel. Who wouldn't feed an angel! Wasn't Filomena's baby an angel too? He smiled, although, like I said, no one paid attention. Bringing brodo was the true test of a friendship. In San Giovanni people took pride in how much they valued a friendship. I guess Filomena had lost her value.

To kill a chicken for someone is no small thing. Poor folk like us didn't make brodo every day. Not even once a week or once a month. Chickens were supposed to lay eggs. A good and steady source of food and income. They were not to be eaten, unless of course they stopped laying or did something to deserve death. I'll never forget the last time we had brodo. No one had had a baby. No, no angels had arrived. In fact a devil, I am sure, was out to test my aunt's patience, again!

La Casinise had her chicken coop right under her son Piperella's steps. Since we lived across from each other, that meant her chicken coop was right across from our pigsty–chicken coop under our set of stairs. My aunt knew her few chickens very well and the chickens knew my aunt. The hens never knew when she would stick her finger up their bum to check for eggs, but they still came when she called. The hens squawked yet they came. Well, all except one.

Lately, a nice layer, the colour of a tender chestnut with a bright red crest, decided to follow her chicken friends into La Casinise's coop. That was no problem. La Casinise and my aunt were friends so there was no reason why the chickens could not be friends too. And I should mention that what took place did affect the relationship some, but only for a limited period, because not only were these two women friends but the location of their coops made them vicini and one must keep sweet the relation with a vicino, because one never knows! See, look at Filomena! She should have thought about it when she closed the doors to play her phonograph and dance with people who were not her neighbours.

Anyway, the fact that my aunt's little chicken spent time with La Casinise's chicken was no problem. It was no problem until my aunt noticed that not only had her little chicken rebelled but she had started to lay her eggs there too. La Casinise did not think so. "And how can you tell which is your chicken's egg? I have chickens too, as you know." Some friend and neighbour La Casinise had turned out to be! But it was true. Who could argue with what she said?

Early one morning my aunt entered the chicken coop. She closed the door behind her. It was time for an inspection. She grabbed the little rebel chicken and held her firmly by her legs upside down and then stuck her finger up her bum. My aunt smiled when she let the chicken go. This would be the day. There was a giant egg in there and it was ready to come out at any moment.

Sure enough, the little chicken went her own way and entered La Casinise's coop. As expected, there she laid the precious egg. "It is my egg!" my aunt said. My aunt did not anticipate an argument from La Casinise because if there was one thing that shined about my aunt it was her integrity. It ranked almost as high as her secrecy. The neighbours said it themselves. "For honesty no one surpasses Saveria!" they said of my aunt. So when my aunt insisted "It is my egg," and La Casinise persisted "It is my coop," quickly, real quickly, my aunt lost her patience. In no time she had her fill of "My egg!" and "No, my coop!" Her fury ignited like pitch-covered pine.

Even the little chicken sensed there was trouble. I think she tried to plead her own case as she squawked and squawked in despair. The little chicken was trying to locate an opening in every possible direction, but everywhere she turned, there was my aunt running in a squatted position with her arms out, reaching for her. Finally my aunt grabbed the chicken and held her securely upside down by the legs. I think the poor chicken would have had my aunt's finger up her bum a million times rather than be subjected to what followed.

I knew as I watched from a safe distance that this was not what my aunt wanted to do, but some devil inside her won. He won and was for sure smiling when my aunt with one furious swing bashed the chicken against the coop. "No more eggs for you!" she said. She was on fire. My aunt was flushed and her breathing was heavy. She was so nervous her body started to do involuntary funny movements. This is how I could tell on any occasion, even from far away, that something bothered my aunt. Her lower left arm would spastically move in quick rubbing upward motions against her abdomen. I often wondered why she didn't pass out, her breathing was so intense when she did this.

My aunt removed the chicken from the boiling water. I knew that she was strong, I had watched her load a whole sack of potatoes on her back once. But what was the meaning of plucking the hell out of this little chicken? You can't cry over what is done. The chicken was dead and there was nothing she or anyone could do about it. What was done was done and my aunt may as well have enjoyed the soup. I was going to.

I hopscotched extra high that day and I knew it had to do with the chicken in the pot. My aunt covered the chicken with water in another pot and when the scum started to surface she skimmed it off with a slotted spoon, again with a little too much strength. And if any of us came too close she'd say, "Out, out, clear the way, out of the way." She threw in some onion, celery, garlic and parsley and covered it to simmer for a long time. She cooked the pasta, "capellini d'angeli," separately. Some people threw it in. Not my aunt. The starch interfered with the delicate clear taste of the brodo. That is why she cooked the pasta separately and then added it in at the very end. And yes, one more thing, capellini is long pasta so she cut it very small because one shouldn't eat soup with a fork.

I remember we didn't talk much. The slurping seemed louder than usual. My brothers Ceci and Peppe did make us giggle, but not a lot. They knew how far they could go. Even if they were boys, this was not the time to have one of those roll-on-the-floor-with-laughter days. "A good layer. A damn good layer," my aunt muttered from time to time. Now that I think about it, I remember being thankful that none of the neighbours had a baby on that day or we would have had to share our brodo. Even if La Casinise herself had a baby, my aunt would have sent the brodo, such were the strict rules of friendships and neighbours.

Now, I wished Filomena had birthed her baby on that day. I would have snuck some brodo out to her place even if she was not our neighbour. Poor Filomena! What is the use of living if you don't even have a friend or neighbour? She would have been better off if someone had grabbed her by the legs, like my aunt grabbed the chicken, and smashed her against a wall. Then it would have been the end. No more eggs, no more bread, no more friends and no more neighbours. Poor Filomena, to make matters worse there was a rumour circulating in San Giovanni that her husband was returning from America. "Thank God America is so far away," Filomena said.

Piece by piece, day after day, Filomena emptied the house of all its contents—phonograph and all. Even the lightbulbs. She unscrewed them and carried them, carefully wrapped in the linen, to her mother's house. Filomena took her son and went to her mother's house because even if Filomena had covered her mother's face with shame (the women at the fountain said shit) she knew she would be welcomed there, and if not welcomed, she would at least be tolerated. Filomena's mother would forgive and would take her back. She would, because her honourable family needed no further disgrace or more stories to be told of them. It would not be an easy decision. If she didn't take her daughter back, the townsfolk would shake their heads and say, "Heartless mother." If she did take her back they would say, "She too must be a whore to take in a whore."

Filomena's mother decided to take her daughter back because she was old enough to know that you can never please people. She said, "What has happened has happened and nothing will change that. Feathers blown in the wind cannot be recaptured." For now, her daughter Filomena had no place to stay and no more dollars to spend. What was she to do? Was she to throw her away? Was she to force her daughter to sell her body to survive? No, a mother would not allow that. Only a mother will always forgive, and only a mother will always love.

The rumour was true. One day Filomena's husband arrived.

He looked like any other Americano. Who in San Giovanni didn't remember the day he left? He looked so small, slouched by his bundles. To look at him there you would mistake him for part of the baggage. Now, as he returned, he didn't even carry his own luggage. The old luggage he took from San Giovanni he had left or discarded in America. It was obvious. His new bags were handsome, sturdy, leather-bound instead of roped. Filomena's husband handed a young man a crisp green bill to carry his new luggage. He didn't carry his own bags! That was unheard of in San Giovanni. What is yours is yours. You carry what is yours, no matter how heavy, no matter how humble, and no matter how small. Your baggage is you.

Filomena's husband came back brand-new. He carried a camera, all wrapped in leather, and it dangled from a strap, also of new leather, around his shoulder. I don't think I liked cameras. I know, you will probably say it is sour grapes. That my feelings towards this gadget were nothing but envy. You will say, maybe, that I didn't like a camera because I didn't have one and probably never will have one. No, I didn't care to have a camera because cameras are deceiving. Cameras give you the feeling that you really possess something. A camera makes you think that you really have it, that it will be there in black and white forever, and that you will never lose that something. But what the camera captures is stilled and killed. Dead memories. As soon as the camera flashes on something, it dies. It dies and you don't even know it because when you entrust something to someone else, it leaves your care. It leaves your mind, and soon enough, it will leave your heart.

I was not envious. I didn't even want a camera. If my father showed up from America with a camera, I would find a way to lose it or break it. The best camera is a well-kept chamber in your mind, one connected to your heart. I had one. And wherever and whenever I wanted, I could walk to school the long way, and I could stand a long time to watch a willow or my pine, and it would be so real I would even flinch if a twig or pine needles pricked my fingers. Let me tell you something, I don't want a picture of San Giuseppe's fountain. I have San

Giuseppe's fountain. I have San Giuseppe's fountain, I have San Giovanni and all my things in my safe chamber. Even if the abbot's curse came to pass, and the whole village ceased to be, I would still drink water from my fountain. And let me say this too, with my camera, in my secret chamber, I could cross forbidden boundaries and no one would need to know. Cameras make you forget, and what is there to envy about a man who forgets himself?

Americanos showed up brand-new all the time. They stood proud and tall. But proud of what? Filomena's husband too showed up brand-new. Even his ideas were brand-new. "Don't worry," Filomena's husband said to her. "In America this is an everyday thing. Come, come back home. We will start over again. We will raise the child and we will be together."

America, America, God bless America, Filomena thought as she carried her linen back from her mother's home to her house on Via San Francesco of Assisi. "Maybe we will go to America," she said to her husband. There was a shy longing in her eyes. She looked towards the floor when she spoke. "America, what a beautiful place America must be." "Maybe, maybe we will," he answered smiling. Unbelievable!

The unbelievable thing is that Filomena actually believed him. That she actually believed going to America would make someone an American. "You are who you are," said the old women. Had she not paid attention when they spoke? Did not even her own mother tell her that a wolf is a wolf and a lamb is a lamb? Did she not know that a wolf will not become a lamb just because he wanders in pasture and grazes among the flock, or just because he puts on a coat of white wool? A wolf would remain a wolf unless someone was brave enough to plunge into his insides and tear out his old heart. And then too, he would have to reach into his skull and put in a new mind. And then you would still have to worry about claws and teeth, oh it was too complicated. A wolf should just stay a wolf and a lamb should stay a lamb.

When Filomena finally settled in, when all the possessions were in their original, rightful place and order, even the phonograph in the living room, Filomena's husband locked the door. She and her child, her boy, were on the outside. Filomena cried and the child cried.

If only the little child was still on talking terms with the angels. Oh, if I was him, I would have called a whole million of them to my mother's rescue. I would have asked the angels to burn the house down, even if the Americano was in it—especially if the Americano was in it. I remember that I told Mammarosa about this, and for sure, I thought, she would agree but she shook her head. "Calm down, calm down. You don't know what you are saying, child. You don't need a million, only one would do." And then she smiled. I don't think Mammarosa would have asked the angels to burn the house down, but I don't think she would have rushed with her water buckets either, in case it did.

The police officer never came to the door. He did not shake his stick at Filomena's husband and say, "See this loaf, now that it has risen and it has baked and it has become bread, it is unlawful to throw it away. Do it and I will charge you with murder."

No man, no woman, no witness ever came. Filomena left naked, the way she had come into his house, with nothing.

Even the women at the fountain felt sorry now for poor Filomena. Filomena's husband threw her out and he even threw out the child. Sour. Poor Filomena. Her life had turned sour. The women felt sorry but mostly for the child, because no child should be thrown out. Mouldy, hard, stale, worthless bread was not thrown out that way, and worse, what was worse, never a fresh loaf! To throw out a fresh loaf was a mortal sin! Even men in San Giovanni knew that bread is kissed and crossed and blessed before it is thrown out, if it absolutely must be thrown out.

My aunt called. Our loaves were ready. The fornaia paid respect to bread even if it was not her own bread she made. She crossed each loaf with as much pomp and ceremony as Don Antonio, the priest, when he crossed a baby at a baptism, or when he crossed a coffin before a burial. The fornaia crossed each loaf as she slid it off her paddle onto the hot oven floor. She kept my aunt out of the way because my aunt had itchy fingers, and with bread, as with life, one must be gentle.

Zuppa di Latte

Fill a bowl with chunks of dry stale bread (preferably crusts)

Sprinkle with tons of sugar

Top with hot milk and a good splash of strong espresso

Latte

I REMEMBER MY AUNT tried hard, real hard, to be gentle with my brother Ceci. Every morning before Ceci headed off to school she would say to him, quite calmly, "Respect, respect your teachers and pay attention, Ceci, pay attention and be respectful." But it did no good. The interviews with Ceci's professors were never good. The principal called her to his office often, and he said what he always said when my aunt went to see him: "Gli manca quel senso psicologico della vita del qual si puo fidare." He is lacking that psychological sense of life upon which we depend, that is. Well, all the principal had to say was that Ceci had lost his common sense. Imagine, such a roundabout way, with all those complex words, said to such a simple woman. My aunt understood what she always understood over the years from the mouth of this academic: Ceci was lacking. Ceci was lacking something, and that something was respect. This was not news to my aunt. She too had seen this lack of respect suddenly blossom and take over like a weed among the vines.

I remember my aunt once pointing to a harmless little leaf next to a vine. When I tried to pull it up I realized this was no weakling. I remember that I pulled and pulled but the roots would not budge. I ended up with shreds and sticky sap all over my hands. My aunt had weeded enough in the vineyard to know that weeds are best pulled out when tender, before they really take hold. She said that if they aren't, they would soon grow and choke the real vine and you wouldn't know about it until you went to look for grapes and noticed that the only grapes there were hard little balls, impostors that not even the birds of the air wanted. She said certain things were not to be allowed to creep up because they would destroy, just like that.

Ceci was innocent then. He didn't know about vineyards and grapes and weeding. He didn't even drink wine yet when it happened, when someone spitefully dropped a seed, a weed seed, right next to him, inside of him, really, inside his heart and soul. It rooted quickly and it grew and blossomed and it was then that Ceci lost respect. He lost respect for teachers, for life, and for everything. This was serious. Who would be Ceci's keeper? My aunt was one of them and she would be damned if she would let a weed choke Ceci. This is why my aunt tried so hard to be so gentle. I remember that she did this so he would take her recommendations seriously, so she could pull that weed called "disrespect" out, before it damaged the whole vineyard. I remember that Ceci tried to be polite. He always replied "yes" to my aunt's gentle warnings, between mouthfuls of morning zuppa—a bowlful of hot latte, macchiato, tainted with espresso, loaded with hard stale bread, sometimes with sugar.

Zuppa was very good. I too ate zuppa, but I think

when I grow up and have children of my own, I will not give them this zuppa. Oh, I will give them zuppa, for sure I will, but plain zuppa, not macchiata. I will make it with latte only. I will not taint it with coffee, because milk is pure and good just the way it is. God didn't taint it when he made it flow out of mothers' breasts. Of all the babies I had seen suckle, and I had seen many, not one of them suckled tainted milk. Milk is pure and children should drink it straight and pure.

Dr. Rafaelino said so. I heard him and I believed him. Dr. Rafaelino said it over and over to the women when they came to his office to inoculate the children. "No old hat shavings and fresh urine on wounds and no coffee in the milk for children, categorically no coffee." These words had become Dr. Rafaelino's song, and eventually, because of the persisting wound infections and gangrene cases, the townsfolk decided to listen to Dr. Rafaelino. They stopped pouring urine and old hat shavings on wounds, they used hot water and soap, just like the doctor had suggested. But not the coffee. They never did listen about the coffee.

It was a plain and simple order. You would have to be either stupid or deaf not to get it. Even after Dr. Rafaelino said that coffee stunted children's growth and it made them nervous, even after all that, the women still poured the black liquid in their children's morning milk. Of course they were deaf. What else?! How else can the resistance to Dr. Rafaelino's words be explained? I was determined to listen to Dr. Rafaelino because you had to be blind not to see that he was right. Have you ever seen a tall person in San Giovanni? I have not. Never. And how could there be? Forever, always, children were given their latte, macchiato, tainted with coffee. Coffee had been, was, would always be. It was life. You started your day with it and ended your day with it. Life, too, started out pure, and the early sky might be clear and bright, but who is to guarantee the remainder of the day? That's just life!

I remember Ceci would raise the bowl of tainted latte to his mouth. He would inhale the last sop and then he would take off like a bullet. In his back pocket was all of a school year's learning, a notebook rolled up and sometimes a pen. Ceci had been polite. He had replied "Yes," but "Yes, I will try" is what he meant. Yet my aunt followed him halfway down the stairs and repeated her appeal: "Be respectful, Ceci, be respectful and listen." Ceci's intentions were good but then as soon as he set foot on the threshold of the school, actually before, even while he approached the schoolgrounds, as soon as the big stone statue of the angel came into his view, it happened. Something happened to Ceci.

The town council had approved the purchase of the statue because of the parents' fixation with angels and children. (And parents, of course, were voters.) This angel had huge wings and he waved a book in his hand, towards heaven. The angel guarded not only the children but the school and the learning. He guarded the future, the very essence of the institution. The angel in the Dante Alighieri school was majestic. It was beautiful to behold, its wings of dark black steel strong enough to fear. But it did nothing to draw respect out of Ceci. In fact, as soon as he came near the statue and the institution it protected, it was as if someone else took control of Ceci, and nothing ever came of his good intentions.

Ceci had no trouble being respectful when he was younger. Then all of a sudden, no matter how much gentleness, and no matter how wise the recommendations, there was just no respect to give. I think, actually I am convinced, this all had to do with the boots incident at school on picture day, a long, long time ago. Now, like a pear on a tree, the fruits had ripened and had fallen to the ground. Or as my aunt would put it, the little weed seed spitefully sown had finished setting up shop underneath the earth and now it poked its head above the ground. When I heard about it I realized why my aunt's efforts were useless. She wouldn't squeeze respect out of Ceci any more than I could pull that little leaf by the vine at the vineyard.

I heard about the boot incident on picture day from other children, long after it happened. They laughed. I lifted my foot and almost kicked the statue. But I didn't. I stopped short. In my mind I heard Mammarosa. I couldn't hear angels' voices, but hers and that of my aunt I heard often and quite clearly, too. "Be true to who you are, always be true to yourself." My boots were still quite new and I didn't know how long it would be before I would have another pair. This too, along with Mammarosa's voice, may have had something to do with the fact that I did not kick the stone angel.

I had new boots because I lied. Usually I didn't feel right about lying. When I lied I usually felt as if I was naked in front of a crowd. I wanted to shrink when I lied. I wanted to make myself fit under some piece of furniture or hide in some dark corner and never have to see my aunt's or my Mammarosa's face. But this one time I lied and I remember feeling good about it. I didn't feel like hiding at all. In fact I remember feeling rather tall and proud. It was the day after the Epiphany, the seventh of January. Mr. Ficosecco did not feel like teaching so the whole classroom gathered around him at his desk. We were all talking at once: "I got a huge torrone," and "I got a scarf," or "I got a new doll." Everyone got something from the Befana on Epiphany night. And then suddenly it was quiet, there was perfect silence and everyone smiled because Maria Pia started her list—a new hat, new lace gloves for Sunday mass, a new coat with a real fur collar, candies, chocolates and a globe! "Ooooh, ooooh," everyone exclaimed. A map of the whole wide, round world that rotated on a gold stand!

The other children turned towards me. They were staring. Their eyes were open wide, so wide that I could see the white of them, as white as the full moon in a dark sky that caused a tide, a high tide, and made whatever it was inside my head start to swim. For a brief moment I thought I would drown. I felt just like the time after I drank glass after glass of a sweet yellow water in a bottle from a cupboard where my aunt also kept the few small dainty glasses she used only when guests arrived.

They waited for me to speak. I knew what they wanted. Maria Pia's father was in America. My father was in America too. They had heard what she got and now it was my turn. "I got a trumpet," I lied, "and a doll with its own house, with its own carriage and a pink dress, and a matching pink organza dress for me, and red and white candies and chocolate powder and strawberry powder and a whistle. . . ." I was on a roll. I was swimming hard because I didn't want to drown and when I saw Mr. Ficosecco smile funny I didn't stop, I just kept on going: ". . . and brand new shoes!" Mr. Ficosecco almost laughed out loud. No one noticed but me. The children's mouths were as open as their eyes. They were all looking at me, not at him. So I didn't care. I knew what Mr. Ficosecco was thinking: If your father has sent you new shoes why do your toes stick out? So what! I had said he "sent" them. I didn't say I "received" them yet. What kind of teacher is this Ficosecco anyway? Does he not know that America is a long ways off? I knew where America was and I didn't even have a globe like Maria Pia.

I don't think anyone else questioned my shoes. I could tell. The children just kept on saying "Ooooh

ooooh ooooh." And if later they asked me where the candies and the goodies and the chocolate were, I would say that I ate them. And if later they wanted me to show them my doll and my other toys I would say that Ceci and Peppe, my brothers, broke them. But my shoes! What would I say about my shoes—the ones that surfaced in my mind out of the turbulent waters at high tide? So I kept on lying. I lied to my aunt to cover up my lie.

My aunt said once that lies are like cherries. You pull one and soon a whole bunch end up on your lap. I had to keep lying. What would I answer the children and Mr. Ficosecco when I showed up forever with my toes out of my shoes?

I started to cry to my aunt that my toes hurt and that my feet were cold. My toes didn't hurt, they wiggled free. And my feet could not feel cold. How could they feel cold if they had never been warm? My poor aunt. She believed me. She grabbed me by the hand and pulled me along down Via Roma. She pulled so hard that in no time we were at the store's front door. "Lallo Shoes," the sign in the window announced. I wanted to struggle out of her hand and leave because all of a sudden my aunt was not in such a hurry to enter the store. I thought maybe she had figured out that I had lied. She paced in front of the door for a little while as if she doubted whether this was the place. If she really wanted to buy me new shoes, this was the place all right. There were lights that flickered on glass and bounced off the shoes. Shoes, shoes, everywhere shoes.

My aunt said that Lallo was her cousin, her first cousin. I didn't believe her. He hardly looked in my aunt's direction. And when she spoke to him, she looked down, as if she were searching for her reflection on the polished stones of his elegant floor, rather than up at his face. When the words finally came out of her mouth they were feeble. "A letter from America is due any time," she said softly. "I will pay you when it arrives." I think he said no because my aunt held me so tightly that my hand almost turned white and numb. We left. We left with no shoes. I don't know why. He had so many of them. The walls were made of shoeboxes all stacked high, so high that Lallo used a ladder to reach them. But oh, watch out Lallo!

The letter did arrive, and when it did, after my aunt cried, as usual, she grabbed me by the hand, and fast, real fast, we were on Via Roma again. My aunt didn't stop at Lallo's store this time. She went down a few doors. She went past Lallo's brother's butcher shop. Now, Lallo's brother was nice. He was on the town council and at election time he always gave us a half chicken hacked up, and a piece of paper that showed my aunt and my Mammarosa where to put their X and how to put it properly next to his name. And Lallo's mother was nice too. When my Papagiuseppe—Papagiuseppe was not my father, he was my mother's father so he was still my papa and he lived with us too—when he was sick once, for a whole summer, Lallo's mother sent a pint of milk every morning. After all, he was her sick brother. The milk, she said over and over, was for her ailing brother. Ceci picked it up. And she always asked Ceci if he had milk for breakfast.

My aunt went right past Lallo's shoe store and then she went right past Lallo's brother's butcher shop and stopped next door. In the store next door, my aunt bought me a pair not just of shoes, but of brown leather boots that were so pretty they looked even better than shoes. They had a bottom that needed no tacks. It was a new material, an American invention. It was thick yet soft, not slippery, and was called "cowchew."

My aunt dawdled in the store, looking out the glass door long after we paid for the shoes. Then suddenly, with the shoebox in her arms, as if she was bearing a gift, she slowly walked out of the door. We walked real slowly. Slow enough to bump into Lallo, who had just come out of his shoe store for a breath of fresh air. Shoes smell. Even new shoes smell bad. He must have smelled like his shoes because my aunt stayed clear of him when she walked by.

I looked at Lallo standing there and I squinted hard. I wanted to look close and deep inside of Lallo. I wanted to dig with my eyes to see him as I saw the naked roots of my tree on the ravine. I thought for a moment I would try and pull and drag Lallo along like my tree, but no. No, no. God forbid, never. Lallo's type are best not even touched. They are worse than weeds. They don't even pretend. They have no roots. If you mess with them, if you even touch them, they fall over and break and then you are in real trouble because you have to pay for them as if they were good and new. You know, like when you go in a store and you break a worthless glass but then you are made to pay for a piece of crystal? In my mind, I did not, I would not pull or drag Lallo along with me on an imaginary trip around the world, because there was nothing to pull Lallo by. He didn't even have hair, let alone roots.

He stood there, leaning against the door, caressing his shiny bald head. My aunt didn't speak to him. She kept on walking slowly with the shoebox displayed openly in her arms and then I saw her smile. A devil's smile! I loved that smile. I had new boots, lovelier than shoes, and I didn't feel bad about lying. But I remember that when I heard of Ceci's incident, I didn't know what I felt anymore. All this time I was wearing new boots while Ceci wore his old ones, and now I knew why.

Ceci himself wouldn't say anything about the incident. Except that a happy carefree child like Ceci had turned strangely quiet after that. It was like watching a healthy plant slowly turn from green to yellow to orange as if something invisible underneath had squeezed the life out of it. Of course, now it all made sense. It was right after the incident at school, on picture day, when Ceci was still young and tender, that he lost respect. He suddenly insisted on wearing his old shoes with holes at the bottom rather than wear the rubber boots that had come in the American Aid Package. That was strange because he had so much enjoyed the boots. I remember when he had those boots on, Ceci was nowhere to be found. Ceci was always on the go. He loved rain and he loved snow.

The American Aid Package arrived at Bernardo's house and his wife distributed the contents among the congregation. My older sister, Nina, received a rabbit-fur coat. It was warm and she wore it even when children laughed and nicknamed her "pelliccietta," the furry girl. We also received our fair ration of yellow cheese. Cinderella cheese, we called it. We stuck cubes of it on a spit and ate the melted gobs even when they were covered in cinders. That's when we had let the cheese drop on the coals, just for fun. And macaroni, yes, Bernardo's wife weighed the elbow pasta, to be fair, and dropped our ration in my aunt's apron.

There were plenty of elegant evening gowns and other fancy dresses in the American Aid Package. Most people laughed at them and left them behind. Not my aunt. She picked up what she was allowed to. She took them apart stitch by stitch, ironed the material and started from scratch.

Then at the very bottom corner of the box, flattened and deformed, was a child's yellow rubber boot, and in the other corner, just as flattened and deformed, was a faded orange child's rubber boot. What a shame! Ceci's shoes were so badly worn that his feet were always wet. My aunt even accused Ceci a few times of purposely playing in the puddles until she checked out the soles. They had holes all through them. "It doesn't matter. We will take them anyway," my aunt said to Bernardo's wife. She was smart to take the rubber boots because it didn't matter to Ceci either. He didn't even notice that one was yellow and the other faded orange.

He didn't notice, until one morning at school. Ceci had been plenty respectful to Mr. Ficosecco up to then. He was respectful, paid attention and didn't turn around. He stood reverently when Mr. Ficosecco entered. Ceci slapped his feet together and dropped his arms rigidly by his sides. Like a little soldier, he even held his head slightly turned away and high. Once he even brought Mr. Ficosecco a basket of figs that Mammarosa baked, and walnuts that Ceci himself had gathered by the wayside on the trip back from the vineyard. And that wasn't easy. Ceci had carried the load on his back for the whole two-hour walk back to San Giovanni.

Well, this one morning Mr. Ficosecco seemed to be in a very good mood. The fluffy cappuccino foam was stuck on his moustache ends. But no one laughed. He bought his cappuccino at the Espresso Bar. Our lattes never had those clouds of milk floating on them. Ours were just plain coffee and latte, goat latte that the shepherd squeezed in front of our door. And the mess the goatherds left behind every morning! I know. But not Ceci. Ceci didn't even notice that part of his breakfast. He didn't have to clean the steps. He was a boy.

Anyway, Mr. Ficosecco's aunt, if he had one, should have shouted at him, "Respect, respect, Ficosecco, pay attention and respect." First of all, because Mr. Ficosecco should not have brought his cappuccino in the classroom.

He didn't come from heaven, you know. He too lived in San Giovanni and knew that some of the children he tended probably had not had zuppa. Not everyone could afford to buy milk from the shepherd on an everyday basis. And then, second of all, there was the piece of bread he dunked in the cup. It was not stale like ours. It was fresh and sweet, you could tell by the maddening fragrance. Mr. Ficosecco had no respect and someone should have pleaded with him before he came to school, just like my aunt pleaded with Ceci, because Mr. Ficosecco didn't even ask the children if they wanted any. He didn't even offer, as was the custom.

Some of the children may have been hungry but they all had manners. They were taught respect and knew the rules of life and living. The children would have refused his offer with thanks even, they would have said no. I, for one, was instructed to respond in this way when someone offered food. This instruction was so sacred it carried a warning. "They will offer you dainties," my aunt said before we left to pay the odd visit to someone, "and I will say to you, 'Take it, take it.' But don't pay attention to my lips; listen harder, read my mind!"

We listened because we understood. We knew that if people were respectful enough to offer, we had to be respectful and refuse. These were not times of plenty, we knew that all too well. But Mr. Ficosecco didn't listen, his mind was busy with other things. He had no time for the rules of life. My aunt always said that for tending a vineyard and weeding you have to hire people who know what they are doing or you might end up with a desolate field of dried-up sticks, never mind grapes and wine.

I wonder who hired Mr. Ficosecco. He didn't understand and he didn't pay attention because he was too occupied. He played with his moustache and ran his fingers through his slick black hair. He swept his shoulders and adjusted his collar. His picture was being taken. His and that of his students, of course. Soon the whole class was frantic with excitement. "Outside, outside," shouted Mr. Ficosecco. It was a lovely day. The class picture would be taken outside.

After all the pushing and shoving Ceci found himself smack right in the middle of the front row. His hands were neatly by his sides and he was smiling, ready for when the photographer, Mr. Chica, stuck his head into the little black box and shouted, "Attenti. . . . Smile." But the show was abruptly stopped. Mr. Chica, who had been going in and out of his black box, decided just then to shuffle and rearrange. "You, over here. You over there." Ceci was respectful. He stood still, like the others, and allowed Mr. Chica to move him where he thought it was better.

It was then, while Mr. Chica was doing his job, that Mr. Ficosecco looked down and took notice of Ceci's mismatched boots. "You, out, out, get the hell behind. Go in the back, back there," Mr Ficosecco shouted while his thick hands directed Ceci to the second row. "You will ruin my picture," he added. (As if there would be much to ruin in black and grey!) Suddenly everyone noticed the little mismatched rubber boots. Laughter, uncontrollable laughter broke out. The yellow one seemed brighter and the orange one began to shine. Mr. Ficosecco and Mr. Chica the photographer, they too began to laugh. Well I say, too bad Ceci didn't even think of shouting a nice "va fa n'culo" to Mr. Ficosecco. Instead Ceci changed after that. He became real quiet. He just shut himself in.

I think it was a little like when Mr. Ficosecco (when he became my teacher) asked me to redo the drawing of myself. I didn't redo mine, but on picture day, when everyone laughed and Ceci said nothing and shut himself inside, I think it was the same as if Mr. Ficosecco had asked him to redo his drawing. And Ceci did. He did and he was not happy about it.

I could have told him that! I could have told him that if you change who you really are, you will never be anyone at all. You are who you are. Once I heard Bernardo say that we are one, as God is one. He said God made us a little like Himself. That is why Ceci should have stayed who he was. Just himself. He should have told Mr. Ficosecco to "va fa n'culo" because changing yourself to become someone else is a complicated thing. You end up with two sets of ears, and listening with one set is bad enough already, I know, just ask my aunt, she will tell you. Imagine trying to listen with four. And what about eyes? Do you think people with two sets of eyes have better vision? Any four-eye will tell you that it is better to have two good eyes. Two are enough.

Ceci was little. He did not know better then. "I just don't want to," Ceci said when my aunt asked why he no longer wore his boots. "Your feet are wet and your socks are always drenched. You will catch rheumatism and then you will walk with a cane when you are old. Why, Ceci, why? They are beautiful, they are beautiful boots and they keep you warm and dry." "I just don't want to," Ceci shouted again and again.

Yes, he didn't say much after the incident, but around this time the battles began. Thoughts, bad thoughts, started to grow in his mind. Thoughts that left him with problems to solve. Thoughts and problems like "Huh, should I puncture Mr. Chica's tires today or should I make a fire in the waste-basket under Mr. Ficosecco's desk?" From that time on, Ceci frowned a lot and was sad most of the time. Then all of a sudden he would laugh and laugh and laugh and then frown and be sad again.

He laughed at me a lot too. The yellow plastic raincoat I wore (it also came from the bottom of an American

Aid Package) was nice and comfortable, with a hood, and left no part of me exposed in the rain. I loved that raincoat. When anyone laughed I just thought, too bad! They obviously laughed because they were jealous. Too bad. I could stay out and play in the rain instead of sitting indoors by the fire to watch my aunt knit and grumble. I wore and wore the raincoat, until Ceci's merciless laugh. "The fasteners are metal," he said between one laughing fit and another. He was laughing so hard it took him a while to say those few terrible words. And I understood what he said only because Peppe retold the words to me. He was laughing too, only not as hard. "Lightning is drawn to metal, you know." Peppe explained what Ceci had meant.

I don't know why my brother Peppe laughed along. I never laughed when my aunt tricked him day after day at dinnertime, when she put his pasta in a big bowl so it would look as if he got more so he wouldn't cry. And when he did cry, I never laughed. But he laughed when Ceci laughed, all the time.

Once when I was playing hopscotch on the cobblestones of Via Monterosa I stopped and looked up because from the top of the stairs of our house I heard words, very familiar words. Well of course they were familiar, they were my own words! Words that I had written secretly in my notebook of poems, and Peppe was laughing while Ceci tossed my thoughts, my very private intimate thoughts, carelessly to the wind. Oooh, if someone had stolen my clothes and left me to walk naked on the streets I would not have been as embarrassed or as mad! I felt my heart pound so hard, as if it was going to explode. I felt the blood flood my body all over, especially my face. I was crying and they were laughing. I ran up the stairs, three steps at a time, and ripped my notebook into a million pieces. I missed my poems. I would sure miss my coat, too. I should have told Peppe, then maybe he would not have laughed. I should have told him that I knew.

I knew even if my aunt had not said anything about it because I saw it all. I knew that my raincoat did not come free from the American Aid box because Bernardo's daughter wore it before I did. I saw my aunt pick up a large basket of clothes at Bernardo's door and I was there when she cleared the ice off the water at the stream to wash them. Her wet skirt became stiff and her hands turned blood-red. They were still red, red and swollen, when she set down the basket of clean clothes and took the yellow raincoat. He would not have laughed if only he knew. Now when it rained cats and dogs, I still walked to school, but without my coat. I'd rather get wet than fry. Wouldn't you?

And yes, angry mothers started to show up from time to time at our doorstep after the picture incident at school. They dragged crying youngsters along. One with a scratch, one with a bleeding nose, one with a black and blue addition to his shin and others with who knows what else. Well, if that is not aggravation to a woman raising so many children in such difficult times. My aunt pulled her hair and she slapped her own face a lot. It was from that time on that my aunt started to plead with Ceci loudly, "Respect, respect, pay attention and respect." But it did no good.

That same Mr. Berlini, the school principal who interviewed my aunt, and who in such a fancy way told her every year, several times a year, that Ceci lacked common sense, called her in again. Mr. Berlini suggested that it was Ceci who organized the three-day strike at the high school he now attended. And he also suggested that it was Ceci who threatened to hit the music professor and drove him out of San Giovanni. As if San Giovanni could afford to lose its only music professor! And now Ceci was starting in on the philosophy professor, a rather academic serious type whom Mr. Berlini did not want to lose.

Professor Pallina, the philosophy professor, commenced virtually every one of his classes with a life application lesson. His words were fluid and pure, like the latte that the shepherd squeezed in our pot in the early mornings.

Ceci knew all of Professor Pallina's life application lessons by heart. And every time the poor man stepped onto the platform Ceci would mimic, "The cradle of duties and the cradle of rights, the cradle of duties and the cradle of rights . . ." The whole class joined in. Professor Pallina had tried to keep speaking but he couldn't go on. And then this very patient, distinguished man lost it and grabbed his stick. It came crashing violently on his desk several times before the mimicking and laughing stopped and there was some degree of order, enough to permit the professor to continue with his lesson. "Life is spent in two cradles," the professor went on, "and a balanced life is a balanced stay in each of them. There is the cradle of duties. Here in this cradle you will develop a sense of what your obligations are to society, to the family and to yourself. You learn here of your obligations to life as a human being, to develop virtues, values and morals. But don't linger in this cradle too long. Self-righteousness and pride, they too live in this cradle, and they will corrupt you. In the cradle of rights you will learn of society and family and what you owe yourself. But don't stay too long here either. You might think life owes you everything. It is in the cradle of rights that habits, defects and deficiencies are nursed. It is in this field that weeds prosper. It is here that impostors dwell. Respect the sacredness of each cradle. Respect the time limits of each one."

Ceci liked Professor Pallina and he wanted to do what was right. He wanted to move on. He wanted to leave the cradle of rights. He knew he had been there far too long. He owed it to himself. But he couldn't. It was as if someone, someone attached to him, played tricks on Ceci. It was as if this someone had put lead in Ceci's boots, which prevented him from moving from the place he stood.

After this final interview of my aunt's with Mr. Berlini, Ceci quit school. A whole company of young men like Ceci followed him. It didn't matter how much my aunt cried after him, "Bad company will ruin you." Sometimes he thought she was right and sometimes he thought not. The same problems, the same wicked thoughts. Who to listen to? Ceci decided he would linger in the cradle of rights for just a little longer. He was having fun and now it was he who laughed. He kicked the statue of the angel in Mr. Berlini's presence when he got expelled, and he laughed, he always laughed. He laughed until he came home, where he sat quiet and sad, and then he would laugh some, then maybe injure one of us some, and then laugh some more.

"Wine, women, songs and laughter." It was Ceci's right to have just a little more fun. "Oh, rights, rights you say," my aunt shouted. "It is your right to work and earn money for the chickens and the sausages and the wine that you consume with your good-time 'chin chin compagnia.' " And then she raised a glass but not to "chin chin," definitely not to toast to Ceci's good time, but to break it over his head.

My aunt shouted and shouted and she stopped being gentle and she stopped being nice. It was too much for my aunt, she had to keep guard over everything. She had to count the chickens and keep the sausages hidden, which was not such a great thing for sausages because sausages could go bad and mould when stored in the wrong spot. She hid them but Ceci didn't care. He found everything.

I remember once he even found the chocolate spread she had hidden in the attic for Nina. My aunt didn't buy the chocolate for Nina because she preferred Nina, she bought the chocolate because she had heard from another woman, whose daughter attended university, that chocolate stimulated the brain and it helped with studying. My aunt left nothing to chance. She bought the chocolate and hid it but Ceci found it. He found it and ran out the door and then called out to her as he waved the chocolate spread before he unwrapped it and ate it.

So now I still ask myself who hired Mr. Ficosecco. What to do with a Ficosecco and a Chica? Well, come to think of it, what do you do with a shrivelled-up dead fig, a cigarette butt or a dried weed? I would not pull them along with me even if they were trees. Dead things have dead roots. I would bury them and never remember. Not even in my mind's chamber would I keep them. Wait, maybe yes, maybe in a remote corner, yes. Maybe even in a prominent corner if they were to be useful. I would want to remember them as a warning. But a warning to me only.

My aunt never went to see Mr. Ficosecco. I don't blame her. I too didn't bother saying anything about Ficosecco to anyone. What chance did I have of being listened to when no one cared to pay attention to someone like Dr. Rafaelino when he said that milk is not to be tainted, that it was to be given to children white and pure?

Fungi

Heat up some real good olive oil
Throw in a few hot peppers
Some garlic
Add sliced fungi
When almost cooked splash with white wine
Add salt, pepper and fresh basil

Fungi

MAMMAROSA LISTENED to what I had to say. She paid careful attention. My Mammarosa was very old and very sharp. She didn't know how to read or how to write, yet she was very smart. Mr. Ficosecco had learned how to read and write so well that he was a teacher, but he was still stupid. Mammarosa was not stupid because she listened and paid attention to what I said.

I didn't have my own blackboard at home like Maria Pia, but we did have an extra-wide stone hearth in front of the fireplace of our home at 14 Via Monterosa. It was not Mammarosa or my aunt who built the fireplace of our house so fancy. My great-great-grandparents did that. I'll bet my great-great-grandparents had more money than Maria Pia's father, and they had never even heard of America.

You should have seen this hearth. It was wider and larger than the blackboard behind Mr. Ficosecco's desk. The house and the fireplace now belonged to my

Mammarosa, so I used the hearth as a blackboard to teach her the vowels and the whole alphabet. When she made a mistake, I didn't laugh, I just erased the black coal markings with a wet rag. And when my hands and face were black and soiled she didn't laugh either. She wiped them with a wet cloth. But when the lesson was over we both looked like the blacksmith, soiled and smeared with black coal, and we both laughed.

We washed with lots of water from a white enamel bowl. Mammarosa grabbed my hands in the water and wiggled my fingers. She especially wiggled my littlest finger when she said, "And this little pig said 'wee wee wee' all the way home."

When we stopped laughing I caught and held my Mammarosa's hands tightly under the water. "Again, again . . . again, Mammaro."

My Mammarosa was true. If she said she would wake me in the morning to take me somewhere, she did. Mammarosa wanted me to go mushroom picking with her. It was her idea that I go. She really did want me to go because she said with bread you could afford to make a mistake but with mushrooms you could not. "Picking mushrooms is a life-and-death thing," she said. And since fungi will always grow and people will always pick them and eat them, Mammarosa said I may as well learn all the rules early, because with mushrooms you just can't tell, you just don't know.

Mammarosa shook my sleeping body gently when the sun was barely peeking over the mountain. It would come up soon. You could tell by the pale radiance that inched up behind the mountain and made it glow. The forest where the mushrooms grew was not far, but mushroom picking took time, and the sun, pale now, would be bold and scorching come high noon.

Mammarosa made me zuppa before we left. She

moved slowly. She held the coffee grinder tightly between her legs and turned the handle. She ground the beans, fresh, a little handful at a time as needed.

I opened one eye. Mammarosa looked so small. The fireplace looked so grand. On the right side of the fireplace, almost attached, and part of the mantel, was a niche. The prettiest statuette of the daintiest Madonna used to live in the niche. The Madonna lived in it before someone gave my Papagiuseppe a Bible and he stopped going to mass because he and Don Antonio, the priest, all of a sudden couldn't agree. From that time on and even after Papagiuseppe died, the only thing that lived in the niche by the fireplace were a few rocks of salt and the salt pestle.

It was a handy place for the salt. Mammarosa always sat on her favourite chair to grind the beans and the salt rocks. It was a little chair, one fit for a child, with the woven rush seat all worn out. She sat in a child's chair, maybe that is why she looked so small.

I remember my aunt saying that Mammarosa was attached to the little Madonna at one time. She carried a picture of her, pretty, dainty, covered in a sky-blue mantle, with a crown of shining gold stars above her head. Mammarosa hid the picture of the Madonna in the deep pocket of her black dirndl for quite a while, my aunt said. When Mammarosa was tired or troubled, especially at night, she put her hand into the deep pocket of her black skirt and mumbled with her eyes closed. Just for a while, Mammarosa hid the Madonna, for just a little while. Now she was quite happy to just keep the salt in the niche. And when she was tired, mostly at night, Mammarosa covered her face with both her hands while her lips moved in silence.

When I looked at Mammarosa from the bed with both my eyes opened, that is just what she was doing. She had her face buried in her hands and she was mumbling and it was not even night. Maybe it had to do with our fungi expedition. Mushroom picking was serious, we might pick life but we could also embrace death.

Mammarosa and I didn't speak. Everyone in the house slept. I read her eyes. We didn't need to speak. When I finished my zuppa she pointed with her head toward the door. We left. The streets were silent too. The sound of our shoes on the cobblestones came back hollow from the house walls. You'd think eating mushrooms of any sort would be forbidden in San Giovanni, I said to Mammarosa as we walked along. But no, even after that incident last year when that whole family was buried, mother, father and children, all in one day, all of them dead from a bad batch of "cuculi," we still eat mushrooms! I searched Mammarosa's eyes for a reply. She never answered quickly. "Women die giving birth to children" was what she said while looking straight ahead as if she was careful not to lose her way, "and that has never stopped anyone from loving and making room for one more angel." And then she sighed.

Mammarosa taught me that mushroom picking is grave, as grave as life itself. It is an art, with its own rules and traditions, and she wanted me to know these rules and traditions well so that I would never, someday, when she no longer was around, rush and pick just any old fungus and place it in my basket without first putting it to the test. I could be picking death with my own hands!

When Mammarosa picked mushrooms she was very silent. She held each mushroom in her hand for a long time. She held it up against the sun and then she held it up close to her nose, and then very close up to her eyes for a long time. She checked every gill. She said it mattered where the little lines branched and how they branched. She checked if the gills joined the cap or if they joined the stem. She even pinched each of the caps, but gently, and then waited to inspect the colour of the bruise. Every one of the steps was important, not one of them was to be skipped or taken lightly. There were general rules to picking fungi which were good to know but were never meant to replace the proper handling and individual inspection of the crop.

The first rule of thumb had to do with the gills. Any mushroom with gills was not safe but there were exceptions. Second, all mushrooms that grew on trees were safe, but there were exceptions. And definitely a well-known rule, the third (even non-mushroom-pickers knew this one) was to avoid any fungi that cropped up near rusty tin cans or any metal. For this rule there were no exceptions. There was another important final rule, certainly not the least of them: you never embark on such serious expeditions alone. It is best to go with an old trusted friend, someone like Mammarosa, never with the young. I now understand why.

I do remember well that very first time I went mushroom picking with Mammarosa. There was a whole patch of porcini. I saw them in the distance, the brown little caps with the thick bulby stems. I would have shovelled the whole bunch of them right into my basket, got the whole thing over with and then run back home, I would have if Mammarosa hadn't grabbed my sleeve. "Not so fast," she said. Not one of them, I remember, made it into her apron until it passed every test and was examined against every rule and by every sense her body possessed.

And why not? I know now that impostors are potential killers. "This is how it is with men too," she said. "It takes a long time before you know if it is poison or life that flows through the heart of a man." Mammarosa said you have to finish eating a ton of salt with someone before you can say you know them. With the amount of eating and cooking we did I don't think I would ever get to know anyone really well. Why bother then, I said to myself, if fungi and men were indeed so vile?

Fungi are vile. When I first entered the place they dwelled I thought for sure they were vile. Suddenly I saw them as seducers who lured you into the forest. They lured the very sharpest of people, even Mammarosa. After watching and listening to Mammarosa it came to me that the fungi have a plan. They are clever. They have it all figured out. This is how they work: they wait until you are at the very edge of the forest and then they cast their spell. The forest too, the wind, the sun and the trees, the whole band of them lie in ambush and help orchestrate the snare. The birds hide, not timid but cowards, in the trees. They make not the slightest sound, not the flutter of a feather, not the faintest chirp. They are to blame, they are part of the snare or they would sing a song of danger, a warning to the innocent who are enticed into the forest.

I imagined in my simple child's mind that the vile fungi were laughing. They were laughing at us, the fools who approached the forest in search of them. I imagined the fungi, cunning, releasing their fragrance—the fragrance of life. The aroma of survival. The fungi release the aroma and entrust it to the wind, who blows it in the trees. The leaves of the trees dance in the sunlight to distract you, to haunt you, to make you fear with their shaking and their trembling. Soon, you too tremble and shake and then fret and rush to pick the mushrooms with greed.

When you eat them, the fungi immediately go to work from within. They grab you by the throat and choke you and you die. And then you lie in the earth and rot and the forest and the trees and the fungi will eat you. They will live and survive, while you have been seduced, while you have been trapped! This is how fools die. Over and over again this dreadful refrain haunted my mind in the fungi-full forest: "This is how the fools die, this is how the fools die."

It was my very first time. I wanted to rush home and couldn't understand why Mammarosa wanted to linger. She was wise. Why could she not see what I saw? Had she too been enchanted and lured? Was I now the wise? I remember wanting to cry on that very first trip in the forest in search of life or death. The sun's rays appeared as daggers in the tall pines. They were daggers that teased and flashed in the soft wind.

Picking mushrooms was a tradition that demanded respect but I lost mine that very first time. I remember pulling at Mammarosa's apron long after she touched her lips with her fingers, telling me to hush. I didn't hush. And she kept right on going with her silence and her testing. It was not that fungi were more important to Mammarosa than I was. Oh no, in fact when my Mammarosa called me, she never called me by my name. She called me Bene. Even when we didn't make precious bread because we had no grain, even then, when she called me and when I called her she answered, "Treasure, yes my bene." Mushrooms were not her treasure, I was her all. I was her bene. But picking them was important and I was to learn in silence, by listening and observing, not wasting energy with my imaginings. This is why my Mammarosa did not pay attention to the panic on my face. I knew all this but I still didn't hush. There was panic on my face and there was panic in my heart and I shouted loudly, loud enough to break any spell or enchantment. "Why?" I shouted. "Why then? Why?"

I will always ask why. If with mushrooms you just never know, if you just can't tell, why then why take the risk? If, after you have gone to all the trouble of following all the rules and respecting every tradition, you still might end up with a bad one, why? Why then why?

I never told anyone of this fight with my imagination in the forest. Not even my best friend Sara. Sara was my best friend because her mother Tata let me in her house to play with Sara. She let me in even if I was half devil. That's right, I was half devil.

Once there were twenty children playing in Lucrezia's house. Lucrezia was the new girl at school. It was Lucrezia's birthday and somehow I was in that twenty, although I can't remember being invited. When Lucrezia's mother saw me she looked surprised and smiled (as if I didn't see her spit on, under, and all over her fingers). Soon after that she said politely that there were too many children and that some would have to leave.

But I was the only "some." Me, the only one who helped Lucrezia up when she fell just a few days before her party. I cleaned the sand off the open wound on her knee with my skirt, my only skirt. Her mother knew that because I also helped Lucrezia walk home, but I still had to leave.

See, my Papagiuseppe stopped going to mass before any of us were born so I was not christened (everyone knew I was not christened). This meant I was not a Christian, which meant I was at least half devil. The other half, no one knew. Not a devil for sure, because on the outside I had no horns and I looked just like any other child.

I think Tata let me in to play with Sara because her husband, Gaetano, and my Mammarosa were first cousins, and devil or no devil, family is family, and duties are duties. Besides, she couldn't have thrown me out ten times a day. She would have run out of excuses for sure.

I had nothing to do with being half a devil. I didn't know any of the facts. I didn't know enough to judge if Don Antonio, the priest, or my Papagiuseppe was right. I didn't know who was right or who was wrong. I worked at it real hard in my mind once and I decided that Papagiuseppe was right. It was not because all of a sudden I had all the information, no, it was not that. It had nothing to do with facts, rather it was a feeling inside of me that whispered, as clear as the water that spewed out of San Giuseppe's fountain, that what Papagiuseppe believed was right. This is what I reasoned in my mind: when Piperella's daughter pulled my hair, my Mammarosa told me (a half devil) to just let it be. When I pulled her hair, or when someone did anything to upset any of Piperella's children, their mother (who was christened) told them to throw stones. She told them to bite and she laughed when they were angry and swore.

This observation alone was not enough though. It was not enough to convince me that my Papagiuseppe had been right to stop going to mass. I may have not thrown stones and kicked and lied in front of my Mammarosa, but inside I wanted to do all of those things too, and sometimes I did. Rather, what convinced me was a feeling. A feeling that I felt when in my head I heard the two women's voices. "Let it be," Mammarosa said. "Strike back," Piperella's wife said. When I heard Piperella's wife's voice and her words, "Strike back, strike back," it did not feel good. It did not feel right. The feeling was that of a raging tempest.

But when I heard Mammarosa's voice and her words, "Let it be, let it be," even though I didn't want to let it be, the feeling was different. There was no howling wind, no crashing waves. There was no tempest at all. In fact, there was a sweet silence and a stillness inside of me, as sweet as the fragrance that rose from the earth after a downpour, and as still as the air when the wind settled after it had unleashed one of its tantrums on our side of the mountain.

Sometimes I think these must be the angels that help you feel right and wrong. When you grow up you can't hear angels' voices anymore, but if you pay careful attention, you will feel them loud and clear inside of you, and if you listen they will guide you and you will always do good. (I must have heard Mammarosa say that.)

When I heard my Mammarosa's words, which were my Papagiuseppe's words, I felt good, and good is always right. So I concluded that my Papagiuseppe must have been right, and christened or not, I was no half devil. I was me, a whole me, and not a half of anything else.

Once Maria Pia and a few other girls she always played with started to be real nice to me. Maria Pia even asked me over to her house to play. Maria Pia's mother didn't even notice. She was busy talking to some men who were working at making their house bigger. An American picture-book of lights and grand chandeliers lay on the kitchen table. I think her father sent the book from America. It had to be from America because I did not see one word that I could read or understand, though the pictures were real nice. Maria Pia had been very friendly towards me and then one day she came right out with it: "If you come with me to Don Antonio and get christened I'll give you my globe. I will be your godmother and then we will be commari!"

Her globe? The one that moved around freely on the gold stand!? Oh, it was very hard. I had never held a globe, the whole world, in my hands before. Don Antonio started to smile at me like an angel after Maria Pia said that, every time he came up the stairs at school to teach religion class. I think he knew. I didn't know what to do.

What I did know now was what it must have felt like for that tree on the ravine, that naked tree that I had seen the day Mr. Ficosecco asked me to draw a picture of myself. Now, not only did it intrigue me, but now I understood it, because I too felt the earth I was standing on crumble and I too felt as if my roots were being ripped and exposed for everyone to see.

Then finally one day after I thought real hard, I shook my head at Maria Pia. No! I shook my head because like so many other trees I had seen from my window during a storm, if I buckled, I would snap and my roots would wither and die. I did not want to die. Naked, yes, but not die.

I really wanted that globe. I took the long way back home from school and I walked very slowly the day I said no to Maria Pia. All I needed was to arrive home late! I stopped and looked at my tree on the ravine. I held its branches, the ones that I could reach, and caressed them one at a time, slowly. Then as I looked closely, I saw that there were green and soft needles growing at the tip of the branches. Proud extensions of the old. It was new growth, soft, baby soft, not bristly at all. Suddenly I felt a burst of strength and I ran home and was not late at all. I no longer thought about the globe.

Sara walked with me the long way to school and back home when she could. This too is why she was my best friend. But best friend or no friend, I would never have told Sara of my trip to the forest and what I saw in my mind the day I went picking mushrooms with my Mammarosa for the first time.

If I told her, Sara would have laughed. I knew she would have laughed. Sara was such a know-it-all. She got it from her mother.

Tata knew everything and she feared nothing. She didn't fear Don Antonio, she didn't fear the politicians, she didn't fear men, she didn't fear the dark, the forest, life, and she didn't fear death. In fact it was Tata, Sara's mother, who was called to wash and dress every dead body in San Giovanni. She said she was called, but often I saw her there, just waiting. She dressed them all, those who died a good death and those who didn't. The murdered, the accidental and the suicides. Tata was always there to do her job. Like mother, like daughter.

Sara would have said I was a wimp. Sara would have slapped my shoulder until my body was flung backwards a mile and then she would have laughed. "You are crazy," she would have said, and then she would have pushed me some more and she would have laughed until she cried. Ah, who needs that!

Why tell anyone anything? There was nothing to laugh about because there was nothing funny about it. Sara may have laughed, but I know of someone who would not have. Teresa would have listened to me and then she may have even thought twice about going in the forest alone if she had heard of my experience on my first adventure fungi picking.

I heard about what happened to Teresa from the women who sat embroidering at the clearing in front of Piotta's door. It was a patio, sort of, that marked the spot on an indentation in Via San Francesco of Assisi. This indentation on the main street was Via Monterosa, my street, and Piotta's patio was where it began. Teresa was older than I, she was much older in fact, but I think she would have believed me and not laughed. Teresa was a good girl, the women said so themselves. She respected all the traditions and rules. I think she just didn't know that venturing alone mushroom picking was a rule not to be violated under any circumstances. I would have told Teresa not to wander in the forest and be lured. I would have told her that appearances are deceiving, that fungi are vile. I would have told her to be careful because it was all a trick. I should have told her. I would have told her, but I didn't know that Teresa was planning to go to the forest alone.

Poor Teresa, she never expected any of what was going to happen to her that day, the day Teresa strayed a little in search of truffles and porcini. In the forest she played with the sun-rays but I would have warned her they were daggers, not beams of light that flashed in the trees. "They will enchant you," I should have shouted after her. They did.

Teresa followed them to the brook. There she sat carefree on a soft clump of grass. She lifted the ends of her skirt above her knees. There was not a soul around. Her mother was not there to frown. Her feet teased the rushing waters in the stream. She had time, she thought. There were plenty of porcini. She could smell them in the air. Then the distinct sound of crushing pine needles slowly reached her ears. Feet, there was no doubt about it, heavy feet that crushed the forest floor. Teresa's heart skipped. She turned around to see but she was not scared. It was Nando. She knew Nando. Nando stood there smiling.

Nando was a perfect pick for her. How so many envied Teresa! Nando had passed all the tests. He was handsome and witty. Nando was next in line for a government job and his family had fertile lands. Nando was a good find and a good person too. Everyone thought so. He was young and a little cocky sometimes, but I heard the women say that even young restless roosters eventually settle down to their own corner of the coop, so that was no problem.

Teresa was enchanted. She was definitely enchanted. If she had not been under a spell her mind would have been clear enough to think and she would have asked herself what she was doing there in the forest alone with Nando. And then she might have also asked herself what Nando was doing there. Nando too knew the rules. But Teresa rushed. She didn't think at all. She smiled back at Nando.

He finished rolling his cigarette, and all the while he smiled. His cunning fingers rolled while his eyes longingly looked at hers. He struck a match. He held the fire cupped within his hands. He lit. Nando inhaled deeply, then let it out slowly, very slowly. It was so quiet and there was so much time. Slowly he moved towards her. Teresa knew Nando. He had declared his love for her. Well, not to her directly. His parents had spoken to her parents. The dowry had been settled. Now it was just a matter of setting a date for the engagement and then the real courting would begin.

Nando knew Teresa. They both knew the rules. Nando stepped closer. Had he no respect for rules? Teresa stood still. Her head could not think, as if she was intoxicated by some strange substance. I knew what it was. It was the fungi. They had released their luring substance. It was suspended in the air. She inhaled deeply. She floated. But he—had he no respect for Teresa's honour?

Aaah! wait a minute, maybe Nando was testing Teresa! A little testing was to be expected. The women said Teresa must have forgotten this very simple rule. If she had not been alone, enchanted in the forest, she would have frowned. She would have shot Nando point-blank with her eyes. She would have slapped him hard and then she would have turned around and walked slowly towards home, smiling. Hu, if she would have done this, if she would have only shot him a look and walked away, she would have passed the test. Yes, the test. Fungi are tested.

As a last precaution, when porcini are boiled, garlic is added to the water. If the garlic turns black the wise women of San Giovanni would tell you to throw out even the pot. If the garlic stays nice and white, the porcini are fit for life. The red mushrooms, on the other hand, are not boiled with garlic. That would not be enough. Red mushrooms are boiled for a long time with a few good pieces of charcoal, just in case. Women test fungi and men test women. How else was a man to know if his woman would be faithful to him for all his life, through thick and thin? How would he know if she would still honour him? Especially if she was beautiful. If the woman was beautiful then the man had to make extra sure because an old proverb said that of a beautiful woman you only have half, of a plain woman you have all.

Teresa was beautiful, there was no question about it. The women who embroidered and knitted around Piotta's patio said it over and over: "Teresa was beautiful, Teresa was beautiful." "But beautiful or not beautiful, any young woman with a little common sense and a little knowledge of rules and traditions would expect a little testing during her engagement." The women all nodded in agreement when Caterina stopped her knitting to say this.

Caterina continued on to tell of the time her fiancé, now her husband, put her to the test. She recounted her story with pride, her chest pushed out and her shoulders straight. She said he came to the house properly every night to court her. They gathered by the fire. Caterina said her mother sat on one side of her, and her brother, father and sister on the other. "There was a double wall of people between us," Caterina said. Her fiancé sat respectfully at the opposite end of the fireplace. The most she exchanged was a shy glance. "I was shy," Caterina said. "He was not. My face burned with shame when he looked at me too long." The women nodded when Caterina said she had burned with shame. It was a nod of respect, reverence, for Caterina's integrity and purity. "He should have been paying attention to what my parents were saying. It was our wedding plans that were being discussed. But no, he kept right on staring. I got up to place ashes over the hot coals. I was hot. The next day he came to test me. I think he came to test just how shy

I really was. He came to see if I really treasured my honour or if I simply feared my father." "Aha!" the women replied. And then they all at once put down their needles and leaned forward to listen carefully. "He wanted to know," Caterina continued, "he wanted to know if someday he could boast like his father."

His father boasted that he could send his wife into the middle of hell and the heat would not melt her. "So this is why the devil came to test me. He came to see if I could walk over the coals of hell someday and survive." Caterina looked as upset as if it had happened just yesterday. "He knew when to come and where to find me. But I was no fool. I was alone, but my mother and father were due in from the fields any time. I had done all my chores so I sat embroidering my sheets by the window. His face appeared at the iron bars and then he spoke real sweet. 'Make them pretty, you hear,' he said. 'Someday soon I'll be sleeping in them sheets.' "

"I felt mushy and warm," Caterina said. "For a moment he had me. I even stepped a little closer and looked directly into his eyes. He had me within reach now. With his hands he reached through the bars and grabbed me. He was strong as a bull, the son-of-a-bitch. I felt my body rise and leave the ground and my face was suddenly against the cold iron. I hung by the collar of my blouse. 'A kiss, just one kiss,' he said. A kiss? My blouse was in his grasp, but my hands were surely free. I reached, and right through the bars I mustered enough strength to give him the smack of his life. He caressed his face for a while, then he left. He smiled. I did not. I think my imprints were still on his cheeks when later that same evening he came and sat down politely by the fire. He smiled towards me often that evening and every evening after that. He expected that slap. The filthy devil! We had a whole lifetime to kiss."

Teresa too should have known it was a test. The women had no excuses for Teresa. She should have known that Nando had come to see if she would pass the test. Teresa blushed. She too was shy. Teresa even backed off some when Nando smiled and ran his finger ever so slowly along her beautiful profile. "I love you," Nando said to Teresa in the forest. This could not be a test. "I love you," he said.

Nando had come to tell her himself that he loved her. He had come to tell her himself?! Was that itself not a violation of a very important rule? He came to tell her himself! How inappropriate! A man to come and tell a woman on his own! What were parents for then?

Teresa was enchanted. There is no other explanation for her forgetfulness. She couldn't recall how she came to lie there on the soft leaves with Nando's arms across her breasts and his hands entangled in her silky tresses when voices, women's voices, brought Teresa back to her senses.

That very evening Teresa cut up onions, hot chili peppers and fresh plum tomatoes. She put them in the pan to fry, but there would be no evening meal. The garlic in the boiling porcini pot had turned black. "Nothing happened, nothing happened." Teresa swore that nothing had happened. But it was too late. The women who had washed linens further upstream said they saw Teresa and Nando. They were many and she was one. "Something happened," they said. "Niente e troppo poco." And because nothing was too little, the nothing soon became something and the something got bigger and bigger. Leave it to the women, it would get way bigger, just give them time, water and lots of dirty linen.

It was Nando's fault. He had violated her honour. He had not respected her and there was a rule for that too. Nando was to marry Teresa, that was the rule and that was the tradition. Teresa would not have a church wedding now of course, but there would still be a wedding. There would be a wedding as soon as Teresa and Nando's parents had the details worked out.

Poor Teresa, there was no agreement. There was no working out of details. It had been a test, nothing but a test. Teresa failed. Nando decided he would not marry a common whore. And, Nando argued, for whose caresses and under whose spell would she fall next? And Nando's parents agreed and so did the people to whom he spoke.

Teresa gathered her body in a corner of the room. "Nothing happened, nothing happened," she repeated while her head came crashing off the wall, over and over again, without mercy. Nando knew the truth. Nothing happened. She was not a common whore. "I love you," he had said. "Life of my life and heart of my heart," he had whispered to Teresa in the forest. What life? What heart? Nando didn't care about Teresa's life because he didn't have a heart. If he did, it was of steel, rotten, rusty-tin-can steel.

Nando didn't visit. Nando didn't send a message. His mother would have torn his heart (his rotten heart) right out of his chest (his rotten chest) with her bare hands if he dared go near Teresa. She was convinced Teresa was not the woman for her son, her only one, her Nando. Teresa remained in her corner for many days, crashing and crashing her head against the wall. Mourning her honour.

At the coffee bar on Via Roma, men moved over and made room for Nando when there was plenty of room already at the counter. They nodded, they almost bowed when Nando entered and said "buon giorno." After a while, in her corner, Teresa no longer spoke. She only hummed. She wailed a lament each time her head came crashing against the wall. Then finally her head could take it no more. It fell heavy and deep into her chest.

The bells of San Giovanni rang lethargic when Teresa was carried down Via San Francesco of Assisi. Tata, Sara's mother, dressed Teresa in white. She was laid to rest, gently, in a white box among white linens Teresa herself had embroidered. Her body was pale, covered in fresh white blossoms, branches from nearby blooming trees. She was carried to the edge of San Giovanni, past the bridge, over the Neto River. In the holy grounds, within the cypress-tree fence, she was laid to rest. Here Teresa was accepted. Teresa was not the first one. The women of Piotta's patio said plenty of fools were buried there. I thought within myself (I would never say this out loud), Too bad only Teresa had to pay! Why did he too not have to die? Who made the rules anyway?

Nina—not my sister Nina, another Nina—broke the rules. Nina lived next door to us. Nina was Barbara's daughter and everyone knew the prim and proper Barbara. Yet Barbara and Nina broke the rules. I saw them do it with my own eyes. Like I said, they lived next door. Nina, too, was engaged. The arrangements had all been worked out when her fiancé received a letter from Rome saying that his application to immigrate to Germany had been accepted. In the letter were his visa and passport. Everything was ready for the marriage but he had to go. Nina understood. A visa was hard to get. It couldn't be turned down when it arrived sealed and stamped, looking so official. Germany was not far. He would make money and come back real soon to marry Nina.

I remember the morning Nina's fiancé left for Germany. I was there to see it all. And they broke the rules as plain as day in the open and in full daylight. Nina placed a ring—what a ring!—on his finger as a final pledge of her love.

Barbara had money. She must have had lots of it

because at every occasion her son-to-be got a new piece of gold. Nina was not married to him, yet she wailed and she cried and Barbara needed the help of a few other women to peel her daughter's arms off his neck. "I can't live without you," she said. "Life of my life, heart of my heart," he cried. Nina kissed him and he kissed her and they both cried. Nina and Barbara must have thought they were in America and lived on Montrose Street instead of Via Monterosa, to have put on such a show. They broke the rules more than Teresa broke the rules. Teresa didn't throw herself on Nando. She was tricked. Nina was not.

Well, let me tell you, when the letters stopped coming and the months passed by, one after the other, and Nina did not hear even a word from her sweetheart in nearby Germany, she started to worry. Barbara started to worry too. His mother didn't worry. She simply kept a safe distance and became a little cool and then there was a nervous silence next door.

One day a returning emigrant (I could tell by the leather three-quarter-length jacket and the camera that hung from his shoulder—they all came back looking like that) came from Germany and for some reason thought he should pay a visit to Nina. "He spends a lot of time with a blonde," the man told her. "Her skin is as white as milk and her legs taller than a pine tree." And of course he would attract such a beauty! With all his chivalry, the knight in shining armour, with all his shining gold, with that ring on his finger!

Well, Nina didn't bash her head against the wall and Barbara didn't sit useless in a corner. In fact (though this I didn't see myself), Barbara and Nina set out alone, just the two of them, in the middle of the night, one dark night. They walked up, up to the top of the mountain and passed further up the basin. There, in a hut with a straw roof, lived a very ancient woman. Smoke came out of a hole in the hut in the dead of winter and in the dead of summer. The ancient woman let Nina and Barbara in and looked around before she closed the door. The smoke rose denser and thicker from the roof that night and soon it hovered over the hut like a dark cloud.

I saw Barbara whisper in a neighbour's ear. I heard her tell of dark chants and strange dances. I backed away real fast. I didn't want to know. God forbid, no, never, no.

Soon, a few weeks later or so, at about noon, shortly after the mailman delivered his pouch full of letters, there was a great commotion on the street. There were people rushing in and out of Nina's fiancé's house. Cries, loud cries came from there. The neighbours had wanted to help the woman who would have been Nina's mother-in-law, but there was nothing anyone could do. By the time they entered the house the poor woman's face was a mess. There was blood all over it and her hands were now entangled in her hair. She was pulling and crying and screaming and shouting "My son, my son," and no one could calm her down. Not even Tata. Tata was there of course, just in case it could have been worse. Her son, the letter read, had been in an accident at work. On the assembly line he left his finger and his gold ring.

Barbara prepared a bigger and better dowry for Nina and the bells rang happy and loud the day Nina was married. She was married by Don Antonio in the church to a very handsome man who had ten fingers and a ring.

Inside of me I felt a feeling, loud and clear, that Barbara and Nina should have let him keep the finger and the ring. I felt good when I heard this inside of me. It would be something my Papagiuseppe would say. My Mammarosa would say, "Let it be, let it be." No problem. But she never agreed with my Papagiuseppe when he said, "Let them have it, let them have it." My aunt tells me that Papagiuseppe said that often, and Mammarosa was always angry when he let people get what was not right for them to get.

Once, my Papagiuseppe came home barefoot. Mammarosa was very mad. He let a beggar have his boots just because the beggar asked. She was mad because the other pair of boots that he had at home were too tight and gave him blisters on the very foot, on the very side of his body that was paralysed. That's right, my Papagiuseppe was crippled. Giuseppe Marra, of the house of Colerusu, the bitter, the sad, the crippled one. That's what everyone said he was. But that wouldn't stop him, no amount of blisters or limping would ever stop him. He still would have given his boots to someone if they asked. This is why I think the feeling inside of me about Barbara and Nina and the finger and the ring came from a voice I had never heard with my ears but hear very loudly inside of me now.

The feeling was good, so for sure it was right. I didn't get a good feeling inside when I saw Barbara and Nina laugh. There was nothing to admire about their soliciting the help of that ancient hag. Nor when they laughed at her fiancé's mother, who walked around like a beast with her head down, her tail between her legs and her face all scarred for the longest time.

I did admire them, though, for not sitting in a corner like Teresa. I admired them for not bashing their heads against the wall. I admired them for giving the rules and traditions and those who made them up a loud "va fa n'culo." I admired them for giving those who pretended to know all about pane and vino an arm's length, never mind just the finger.

I did not share this feeling with anyone. I listened well to the women of Piotta's patio. I was there to listen and to learn about life, bread, wine and a lot more. I should have acquired a new fear, I should have been trembling. I should have acquired a new respect for life's rules and traditions after I listened to what the women had to say. After all, it was for the learning that my aunt let me sit with the women who embroidered and knitted on Piotta's patio. But I didn't. For saying "va fa n'culo" to Mr. Ficosecco I could have been sent to reform school or a convent. I don't know where I would be sent if I said "va fa n'culo" to the fear, trembling and respect I was supposed to acquire at Piotta's patio. When Piperella's children disobeyed, their mother bit them so hard she lifted their whole bodies off the ground with one of their limbs in her mouth. I wouldn't tell anyone what I felt.

The bells had cried for Teresa. I wanted to cry too. I wanted to cry out loud, Why? why, why even try? Why bother with the rituals and with the rules when the end of it could be death? I wanted to shout, Why could Nando be Nando and Teresa could not be Teresa? I wanted to say that this nonsense should be forbidden. Just like mushroom picking, it should be outlawed. I wanted to, but I never did. Not to my Mammarosa, not to my aunt, not even to Sara. Sara would have told her mother and her mother would have told my aunt, and my aunt had very good teeth.

I had tried to understand. I tried to pull and stretch these rules but they were not elastic. They were not at all like the roots of my tree on the ravine. They didn't make it on my imaginary trip with me around the world. They broke off. And when I looked for them beside me, I couldn't find them.

Basil

Basil leaves

Olive oil

Garlic

Pine nuts

Pecorino cheese

Salt and Pepper

Put the whole thing in a mortar

Pestle until ground

Basil

THE BELLS RANG AND RANG. They always rang. They rang for early mass, they rang for weddings, for funerals and for holy processions. They rang at sundown and they rang at noon, for the slightest of reasons the bells of San Giovanni rang. I heard that where there are bells there are whores. I don't remember from whom or where I first heard this but that doesn't matter. I heard people say it a lot anyway, as if it was a proverb in San Giovanni. I heard men call their wives whores, lousy whores actually, all the time.

"Hey you lousy whore, is dinner ready?" Piperella shouted to his wife every single day. There was not even a change of expression on the woman's face when she heard her husband call her a lousy whore as he started to kick chairs and pots or whatever came in his way. Smart woman, Piperella's wife! She didn't even say a word. It would have been useless, he was most likely drunk. She didn't worry because most of the time the children had eaten already and so had she, so he could kick and make all the noise he wanted. Her mother had told her what every mother in San Giovanni told her daughter before she got married: "Eat before your husband gets home, dear, don't wait for him. If, when he arrives, he is in a good mood, you will eat again; if not, you have already eaten."

And she listened. Piperella's wife could not read or write but she listened. I don't ever remember hearing Professor Ciano or Dr. Mauri saying something like that to their wives. Although maybe they did, inside their own homes, but I would never know.

The Cianos and the Mauris had a central heating system, a brand-new American invention, so their doors were kept shut most of the time. We all lived on the same street, Via Monterosa. The professore, the dottore, Piperella and a string of poor insignificant others like ourselves. The houses were arranged side by side in two neat rows. The south sun shined impartially on us all. Some of the neighbours probably wished it was not so, especially the professore and the dottore. They looked so annoyed when Piperella came home drunk and made a ruckus or when a few dozen of us children played under their window. The genteel doctor's wife stuck her head out and politely said, "Shhhhhhh." The professor's wife plainly told us, "Shoo, shoo," as if she was ordering flies off her face. She closed the windows and doors and told us to go away when the professor was attacked by a terrible headache or was in bed from sheer exhaustion.

I could tell when the professor had a headache because his wife wrapped his head tightly in a carefully folded kerchief. Then she called the doctor, not Dr. Rafaelino but another doctor, who also told us to clear the street. We did our best to make her happy. We did not know that we had just as much claim to Via

Monterosa as she did. All we knew was that we were the insignificant others who had few rights and little say.

There was little the professor's or the doctor's wife could do about the ruckus that Piperella made. He was so full of wine he would not hear anyway, even if they shouted "Be quiet" directly in his ear.

Things got better for us children after the professor's wife found out about her husband's little affair, his "double duty" the women called it, with the rouge lady who lived on top of Mancuso's store. No wonder he was always exhausted! After that she didn't bother us anymore if we were loud when the professor was sick. She even kept the window open when he was in bed.

We all lived together, side by side, and there was nothing anybody could do about it because property was passed on from father to son to daughter and so on, and that was that. It was a little like having a big nose or a pretty mouth, for generations it would be in the family like a landmark on a field. I had one single front tooth that refused to line up with the rest. We all had it, Nina, Ceci, Peppe, Julia and me. My brother and sister in America didn't have their permanent teeth in yet but I am sure the rebel tooth would show up in their mouths too. My father's father looked at our tooth and was proud. My Papagiuseppe, my mother's father, was still proud, although none of us had his deep blue eyes. Property was a little like my tooth.

It is also a little like a torch that burns immortal, in praise of those who came before. It is a pledge to those who have braved the past, an assurance that we will brave the future and they will live on. Some made that torch burn and shine bright. In the hand of others it barely flickered, it mostly smoked. In the Piperellas' hands, for example, the torch did not even smoke anymore, it was downright dead and cold.

They came from a wealthy lineage and his grandfather had given his son, Piperella's father, enough homes in San Giovanni for him and each of his children. But the Piperellas drank all their wealth away. All they had left now were these four walls across from us on Via Monterosa. They had lost their brightness and now they had become one of the dim insignificant others. If any of the insignificant others looked in someone's eyes like Dr. Rafaelino did to me when I had chronic conjunctivitis and said, "It is nothing, you will live," or if they said to someone, "It is serious, you will die," no one paid attention to them, because they had let their fire die. The light had gone from them. Who would pay attention to the directions of the blind? I think this is why Piperella drank a lot. No one paid attention or gave importance to anything he had to say anymore.

Everyone paid attention when Dr. Mauri, who lived next door, spoke. His torch blazed. The property his father left to him sparkled with newness. He had put in a marble floor and partitioned the house. Dr. Mauri's father was a simple man who had carried brightly the torch that belonged to his own father. He drank only one glass of wine, at noon. He saved his money and put his son through school.

Professor Ciano, of course, now used the fireplace only for atmosphere, since he had installed the latest American heating system. He even had a television, which I didn't get to see for a long time. The professor also bought a new car, a Fiat Topolino, and I was there to see it when he first drove it home. I was there, too, the day Don Antonio came to bless it and baptize it with holy water. (So now even the Topolino was Christian!) After the blessing the professor and his wife threw candies on the street as if it was their wedding day, but I didn't catch any. I couldn't, my aunt had snatched me in, so I just looked from the window while Sara stuffed her pockets with confetti. I watched the confetti crash on the cobblestones and on my steps, but I didn't get even one. My aunt said they were part of the same pagan show. They were Christian, the car was Christian, but the candies I wanted, the ones I drooled all over the window sill for, were pagan!

There was no doubt the professor's father would have been proud, too, just like Dr. Mauri's father. In these men's hands the torch sure shined. Mammarosa said that accumulating and renovating had nothing to do with carrying and passing on a shining torch. The women at Piotta's patio didn't agree. They said that's just how it was, pane pane e vino vino (bread is bread and wine is wine). "The world is a ladder, sometimes you go up and sometimes you come down." They said the more you shined the more you climbed and the further you climbed the more you shined.

Well, even I as a child knew that torch or no torch, ladder or no ladder, there were differences between certain people. The professor and the doctor for sure were different, and if there was a ladder, they sat on the top step. They even ate different from, say, Piperella, who came home with his hoe dangling from his shoulder every night from the fields already drunk, of course. "Hey, you lousy filthy whore. Where is that lousy whore?" he yelled, looking around. His wife stood there in front of him but he still asked, "Where is that lousy whore?" I don't think he could see. He bumped into passers-by and into merchants' carts. He sent biscotti, tomatoes and pasta flying. He'd tip his beret and politely nod a regret. He even tipped his beret to the wall when his face crashed into it. Piperella was polite. The one person he was not polite to was his wife. He shouted at her while he felt his way around. With one hand he secured his hoe and beret and with the other he reached for the railing of his staircase which came in and out of focus. He cussed and cursed, because when he grasped, there was nothing in his grip but a fistful of air. It was his wife who helped him find the railing but he still shouted, "Where is she, where is that lousy whore?"

I asked my aunt once if Piperella had ever held his wife's hand or if they had ever walked arm in arm like other couples did. She said no. "Not even when he first brought her here as a new bride? You saw them, didn't you? Did you ever see them kiss?" "No," my aunt replied. She shook her head while she said no and that meant a double no. She said that they would kiss when our doors, which were directly across from each other, kissed. And that would take a shaking, a trembling and a mighty earthquake. One as strong as the abbot Joachim had prophesied would come if his prescribed boundaries for San Giovanni were violated. And if that happened, we would all kiss each other one last good-bye kiss! I was going to ask my aunt a few other questions but then all of a sudden she got annoyed and started to shout, "So who cares! Why do you care and ask stupid questions like do they kiss, do they hold hands, do they do this, do they do that?" Fine then, but they must have kissed sometime, I thought.

I don't believe it anymore now, but then I believed this to be true (since Sara had told me), that women got pregnant because their husbands kissed them. Well, of course Piperella kissed his wife. Why did I even bother to ask my aunt? Every year Piperella's wife had a new baby! But this theory created a new problem, and more questions crowded my mind because now I couldn't explain why it was that Dr. Mauri kissed his wife at the door every evening when he came home and they did not have one baby, not even one! Maybe, I thought, this was a ladder and step question. The rich could kiss their wives and have no babies but the poor, if they as much as pecked their wives' cheeks, boom, another mouth to feed.

Mammarosa said that at birth and at death we were all equal. She said we all come naked, we all cry and we all arrive with fists clenched, ready for a good fight. She said when we leave, we all go away naked, in perfect silence, with our mouths shut and our hands unfolded. We leave empty. No exceptions, not even if you had a gold ladder all your own and you sat on the very top step.

She said we were all equal on one more thing: rich or poor, whore or not, we all had a stomach that made demands which, if they were not met, might just cause an early departure. So everyone ate to keep the stomach happy because, outside of a handful of people who ended their own lives even if their stomach was full, no one really wanted to depart earlier than necessary even if Don Antonio, and Bernardo too, talked and talked of nothing but a wonderful destination on the other side. There was one more thing absolutely everyone in San Giovanni had in common, ladder or no ladder. It was a strong sense of smell that favoured the basil plant.

Everyone had basil. All the important people had basil and all the insignificant others had basil. Well, there was one difference: important people had basil growing in pots all beautifully organized by size on their wrought-iron balconies. One pot of hanging red geraniums and one pot of luscious basil. Tons of red clay pots all neatly lined up. Others used odd clay pots or damaged kitchen containers to grow basil in.

We had only one, on our only one window sill. It was the old pot that had served us too long under the bed. This white enamel pot with a very nice handle had developed over the years several black spots. One day one black spot let the liquid out but my aunt would not throw the pot away. She said it would be perfect for a basil plant to grow in. She said the soil wouldn't leak and the water wouldn't sit, the water would drain through the hole and the basil roots wouldn't rot. So now we too had basil.

Basil, basil, basil, all summer long, basil. And with basil came tomatoes. Piperella's wife, the doctor's wife, Sara's mother and the professor's wife, no matter who and no matter where, they all canned tomatoes. Canning tomatoes was part of everyone's life. As much a part as sharing the nights with the person your parents chose. (At least in canning tomatoes a woman received instructions and practice. But that's another story.) The professor's wife, of course, had help when she canned her tomatoes, although she would fuss as if she was the one doing the work when in fact she simply went around harassing everyone.

There was no getting around canning tomatoes. It was a simple basic of life that I think started as a simple addiction to the basil plant. Until basil came around no one canned tomatoes. Tomatoes were just dried in the sun and were then brought to life with water in the winter. But preserving precious basil was a must. The basil lasted for such a short while in San Giovanni. No sooner would the chestnuts be picked off the ground than there was snow. Basil leaves are tender and delicate, and as with life, with basil one must be gentle. The real way to preserve and enjoy basil throughout the year was to plunge and hide the tender leaves between slices of fresh tomatoes in bottles. This is how it had been done for generations, after much trial and error.

Tomatoes were canned in bottles. All year long everyone eyed bottles. My aunt liked Millefiore liqueur but she did not buy it, because the bottle, although nice and tall, had a very skinny neck and that would not do. She bought Marsala on occasion because it came in a decent, sensible bottle. The glass was thick, the opening was right and the size was perfect. When she paid a visit and brought a bottle of Marsala to someone, which was the custom, she always said, "If you don't use the bottle, I will send one of the children to get it." I can't believe my aunt would say something like that. But she did, even when she knew better. Of course they used the bottle. They probably wanted the bottle more than the Marsala in it. Only Piperella liked the Marsala, or wine or vinegar or whatever, more than the bottle that contained it.

Canning tomatoes was part of life. It was simple and was meant to simplify life. At noon or in the evening, or when you were in a hurry, you could take a bottle of the tomatoes, pour it on sizzling garlic in hot oil, and by the time the pasta was cooked, your sauce was ready too. Simple, right?

Life was not simple. My aunt said it was not simple and she saw to it that it was not. I remember one year that we canned tomatoes (we didn't get to every year)—but this one season, our potato crop did so well that my aunt was able to buy a good fifteen crates of about twenty pounds each. My aunt was a mess. She pulled at her hair on several occasions during the day. First, she wasn't happy with the tomatoes. They were not quite ripe. Then, she was not happy because the ones that were ripe were mush. They had to be ripe and they had to be firm. My aunt slapped her face because nothing ever went right for her. The one year she could afford to can tomatoes, the crop was lousy, just plain no good. Although I should mention that no one else complained. Not even the professor's wife, and she was fussy.

We all had our chores around the big kitchen table in the middle of our one-room house. My aunt washed the tomatoes at the fountain by Mancuso's grocery store not far away, and then she piled them in a mound in the centre of the table, not ever without shaking her head in disgust. Julia and Peppe cut. Nina and I filled the bottles. Ceci was nowhere to be found. He was out somewhere, having fun. I was not. When I sent a handful of tomatoes back towards Julia or Peppe's direction because they had not cleared all the seeds properly, I was very careful not to let my aunt see me. She would start with the face-slapping again and that would delay the whole process and I wanted to get the hell out and play. I tried to be very careful in the way I stuffed the quartered and seeded little Romas in the bottles. I followed her instructions carefully. Anyway, I did what Nina did.

She was older and had done it many more times before. Nina filled the bottle halfway, she dropped in a few leaves of basil and pounded the bottle until the tomatoes and basil settled and were well packed. Then she filled the bottle all the way to the top with more tomatoes, more basil, a little more pounding, a little more settling and the job was done.

Well, mine were not packing so well. There were too many air pockets, my aunt said. So she pulled at her hair and slapped her face again. I ended up staying until the last bottle was corked, wrapped in rags and piled in with the others in the big copper pot.

While the pot boiled we cleaned up. By then it was dark already and time for bed. So much for playing. Oh, and time for bed did not mean time for rest. Every time I heard a *craaak* coming from the direction of the copper pot, I also heard my aunt swear. And I am not sure, because it was dark, but I think she pulled at her hair, again. Not so simple, huh?

But when that simple sauce cooked on the fire it would be worth it. The bells didn't have to ring and tell everyone it was noon. The aroma of basil and tomatoes, of garlic and hot olive oil, which wafted from house to house, from street to street, was loud enough. But the bells rang anyway. I saw the old women stop embroidering and knitting on my way from school. They left the chairs just as they were on Piotta's patio. They would be back. I would be there too, later in the afternoon. I skipped the last few steps of the staircase that led to our home. I counted out loud, "Thirteen, fourteen . . . and now I am in."

So was my aunt! She was in and she was sitting on a chair at the table in the middle of the room. She wasn't pulling her hair or anything. She was too exhausted for that. She had just carried a sack of potatoes in from the fields and the mailman had brought her a letter. It was a white envelope with red and blue edges. There was no money in the letter, I knew that much. Letters with money came registered in a brown envelope all messed up with red shellac and twine that connected the seals. She burned hot like the sun in the middle of the day and the middle of the day it was, which meant it was time to prepare yet one more lunch. She was sweaty, she was weary, and she said she was tired of living.

I wished I could have stayed at school. The school provided a marvellous hot lunch, free, and always at the end of every lunch a huge slice of fresh white bread loaded with jam or marmalade, to eat on the way home, also free! Every day I stared at those spectacular slabs of snow-white bread, dressed in thick colours of red, orange and blue. Once in a while Sara gave me a bite. She could eat at the school cafeteria even though their pantry was full and their bins were full too. They were full of grain and potatoes and apples and so many other things. They had so much that the place stunk. Sara's house always smelled of something rotten. Rotten potatoes, rotten figs, rotten onions, even rotten linens. I don't know why Sara's mother bothered to put rotten-smelling white balls in fine new linens.

If only I had a card, then I could have stayed at school for a free hot lunch like Sara and the other children. But no, my father was in America and that made me the daughter of an Americano and that meant I was rich, whether I was or not. If you were rich and lined up for a lunch card everyone looked at you funny because it was unfair.

I'll tell you what was unfair. It was unfair to think that people went to America to shovel the gold into sacks. It was unfair to think that every Americano was big, fat and wealthy like Maria Pia's father. Well, goodness, her father had been in America even before the war.

Mr. Ficosecco taught us a little history and he talked sometimes about the war. He said San Giovanni, in the very beginning, was a place of peace, not a place of war. San Giovanni was not even called San Giovanni at the very beginning when Joachim founded it. Mr. Ficosecco said that San Giovanni was called a "universitas" and peace-lovers came here to contemplate. In 1206 this place of peaceful contemplation was granted the status of "ius asyli"—the city of refuge—by King Frederic II. A perfect "asyli," a cradle, a basket, a pitch-covered basket. A refuge nestled along the slimy banks of a fertile river where bulrushes, willows and pitch-covered pines found their rightful place to grow along the heights of the rugged mountains that hid and made impregnable this city of refuge—San Giovanni.

There were no merchants, shoemakers, tinsmiths, blacksmiths, potters or goldsmiths before 1206. There were no grain or potato fields on San Giovanni's mountain until then. The mountain was just part of the sky, a heavenly cloud of green giant pines, until this "ius asyli" and refuge thing.

Then the refugees started to arrive because when someone is after your life, a cradle, hidden, has always been, since ages past, the place to lie.

In the year 1206 many came, more in 1492, and even more in 1497. They were tired and weary, yet they bent and kissed the ground. Strangers have come, some have gone, some have stayed. Rams' horns and blooming salvia decorate San Giovanni's underground walls. Strange silent remains from strangers who had come both from nearby villages and from far-away countries.

"Marranos, swines, from as far away as Spain," Mr. Ficosecco said. He said that many Christ-haters and heretics made their way to San Giovanni for refuge. He always looked at me when he said that. And every time I thought, What? Am I Spanish? Is my last name maybe Lopez or Iaquinta? There was in fact a Iaquinta in the class but, no, he looked at me. One of these days, when Ceci decides to slash Mr. Ficosecco's tires again, I might just go along.

Mr. Ficosecco said that San Giovanni had changed. He said we had started as a little place of peace and contemplation but then we grew and sent men out to war. He said this last war, though, had been all the Germans' fault. He said one fine day the Germans' brains failed them and they started to have delusions of being Romans so they wanted to conquer the world because that's what Romans had always done. He said our only problem was that we somehow believed they were Romans like us, for real, and we joined them when they set out for the conquest.

Right!

I saw some Germans. I saw them every summer, in fact. They camped right by the stream at the basin of the mountain. Not one of them was short and not one of them had dark eyes and dark hair like us Romans. Mr.

Ficosecco says the war happened a long time ago. On this he is right, because I cannot remember one thing about it. I was not even born but Mr. Ficosecco was, yet time and experience did nothing to sharpen his understanding.

He had a hard time putting two and two together because if the war was fought such a long time ago, and all this time Maria Pia's father was in America, didn't that mean he had a head start shovelling whatever into his sack, gold or horse shit? They both look the same when the sun shines in your eyes, anyway. If that's not unfair, I don't know what is. To think that as soon as someone's father sets foot on American soil there is no more need of a lunch card.

Horseshit!

My father wrote once and said that sometimes in America there were line-ups of grown men who used lunch cards. And you know what else was unfair? It was Maria Pia standing there, behind Mr. Ficosecco, helping him hand out the cards. She looked at every face and searched into every eye—eyes that did not want to be discovered, eyes that would rather look at the wooden platform than her brilliant smile. Every time, a few times a year, when Mr. Ficosecco said, "Those who want lunch cards please line up," I thought, This time I don't care. This time I am going to line up. But then I also thought about what Mr. Ficosecco would say: "No, not you. Your father is in America!"

He would have. When my aunt went to his office at the beginning of the school year so I could get free books like all the other children, Mr. Ficosecco said no. "Ask her father to send a few more dollars," he said. He thought he was so funny. There was nothing funny about asking Sara if I could use her books all the time. I had to wait until she finished her own work, and that took forever. Once, while I waited for Sara to finish, my aunt whispered to me that Sara was a donkey, a saddled and well-loaded donkey. She was a donkey and she got books.

My aunt didn't think Mr. Ficosecco was funny when he told her to ask my father for a few more dollars. My aunt wanted to say that children were children, they all had the same needs and things were not what they seemed. She wanted to say that nothing was simple, but she didn't. She decided not to waste her breath and I think she was smart not to. My aunt just said thank you and left. She didn't even look up at him. She was in a hurry to leave.

So I had not lined up for a lunch card again this time and now there was nothing in the pot. The pot was not even on the fire. My aunt was reading the letter from America and she was crying. "My dear sister . . . ," the letter read. But before that, on the very top, was a line of words separate from the letter: "All things work for good for those who fear God." These were the words that stood above the words in the letter. They were like a frame and the letter was the picture in that frame. "I try hard not to fear people but it is hard not to . . . senta e trema," the letter said.

My aunt cried a lot when she read this letter because my mother worked but my father did not.

This was not so bad, because when they both worked, the landlady looked after the baby, but one day the landlady didn't give the baby milk at all. My mother had run out of milk and the landlady wouldn't go to the corner store and buy it because she said it wasn't her job. When my mother and father came home that day, my sister had cried so hard that she lay limp in a corner of the sofa, sobbing without tears. This is why my mother said it was not so bad that my father stayed home, but it was not so good either, because he had to wash diapers. Not that he minded washing them, he just minded having to wash them in ice water in the middle of the winter because the landlady decided, for no reason (maybe to save money), to turn off the hot water. My father cried when he washed diapers because his hands turned red and then blue and then they were numb.

And then another day the landlady decided (maybe to save on the heat bill) to block the hot-air vents with newspapers. When my mother and father woke up in the morning they were shivering, and the baby's sweater that my father had hung to dry the night before was still wet, so my father wrapped my sister in a blanket. So what kind of America was this, I thought when I heard what my mother said in the letter. Was America real or was it only a dream, a mirage, a blinding trick the sunlight played on my mind?

I had told my friends that in America, Coca-Cola, milk and aranciata flowed from the taps, not plain water. I had told them that my mother and father ate from plates that were clear like glass and I had even said that in my mother's kitchen in America, the pots were made of glass. I had said that you could see the pasta swim and dance right through the pot and the glass did not break over the flame.

I don't know where in my imagination I dug up glass that did not break over a fire. My friends had said "ooooh ooooh ooooh" to everything I told them until the part about the glass pots. Then they turned away and said I was dreaming. They said glass broke with boiling water, imagine glass over a flame! "But it's true, it's true," I called out to them, trying to win back their attention. But it was no use.

Well, maybe it was not so true. Maybe my friends were right and I was dreaming. Of course, I must have been dreaming. How could I know anything about far-away America when I didn't even know my father, who was in America?

I didn't know my father. I didn't remember his face. I tried to place him over a tub washing and crying and maybe once in a while stopping to warm his hands with his breath. I saw his hands, I saw a grey mist that came out of his mouth, but I couldn't make out his face.

There is a picture of a man over our dresser by the bed. My aunt says it is my father but I don't believe her. No man dressed in such a fine wool coat, better than Maria Pia's father's, standing on such a shiny marble floor, would have had to leave for America or for anywhere.

Our floor did not shine, it had a matte finish. It was not of marble with a matte finish, it was of plain mattoni, terracotta, baked earth tiles.

The tiles would pop up once in a while because they were not cemented down. Once, when Ceci put a loose tile back in place, my aunt rushed in to inspect the job and with her big toe she lifted the tile right out of its spot. Ceci was mad and I think he was right. What did my aunt expect? Was she dreaming? Did she think Ceci was working with cement and marble? I wonder where she got the picture of that man standing on a shiny marble floor. That man was not my father.

I guess I knew my father like I knew the angels. I knew they were there and I knew he was there too, in America. It's just that I never heard his voice or saw him. My mother, too, I didn't remember her face, nor could I hear her voice, although I know she is there, in America. I couldn't think of her as an angel though, as I did my father. I saw angels the way Bernardo showed them to me.

Bernardo showed me winged beings, burning seraphs and gentle cherubim. He spoke of fighting angels and then once he said that an angel fought with a man and the man won. I think Bernardo doesn't have this story right. I think the angel let him win. The angel and the man were friends and if angels are so gentle as to speak with babies, they would be kind enough to let a friend win, just to make him feel good.

Bernardo spoke of soldier angels who fought in mighty battles and then he spoke of angels who kept guard with fiery swords over empty gardens. I could almost, almost, think of my mother as an angel, just like my father, because angels speak with babies and they watch over gardens, but it is the soldier and fighting part that stops me. I can't think of my mother as a soldier. Not even in my schoolbooks did I ever see a girl soldier. Although I am a girl and I could fight as good as any boy soldier.

I remember once Piperella's boy, the one who was born fat but now was a wimp, on top of my brother Peppe. I don't know how he got on top of my brother Peppe, who was born weak and thin but now was strong and fat. I saw him from far away, that wimp, pounding his fist on Peppe's chest. I ran so fast, and in no time I was on top of him and my teeth went right for his flesh. The wimp let out a scream, one howling yelp, and the fight was over.

So I can't explain why it is that I can't think of my mother as a soldier, if I, her daughter, am such a good fighter. I may have picked this idea up while loitering on Piotta's patio. I know I did. They said I was weak, not strong, because I had lost my hold on "decorum" the moment I ran determined to wrap my legs around a man's body. (A man! That wimp?) I will have to think this one over, sometime. For now I wanted to see my mother not as an angel but a little like God, because Bernardo once said that God gathers and protects his children like a hen gathers and protects her chicks under her wings.

A hen is definitely a mother. I don't remember my mother's face nor do I hear her voice but I do faintly, from time to time, feel the velvety softness of her wings. I could feel the softness of her wings just then when my aunt read her letter. My aunt said that my mother knelt beside the baby's dripping sweater and she cried. She cried to God and told him that it was not a big house she wanted. She did not want a better house than her landlady had. She said the landlady was talking about moving. It did not sound like it would be very soon, but when it did happen, they would have to move with her because it was hard to find a place to stay with a baby who still cried in the night. She just asked God for a little house, it didn't matter, as long as it was her own. And then she went as far as to ask God to give her a house before the landlady moved. It's not that she wanted to prove a point or anything, my mother thought she would just ask, my aunt said.

Well, this thing about the house was news to me. Life was not simple, all right. We had a house. We had a house here in San Giovanni. My father and my mother were not supposed to buy a house. They said they were going to America to make money and come back. Now, would they ever come back? And now, who would hear the end of it, even if it was not a real house yet, even if it was still just a prayer on my mother's lips? If the word got out about this house in America, it would no longer be a wish but a real mansion, with a peaked roof and green shutters and a courtyard and a dog. Just leave it to the women to decorate this simple piece of news.

And of course now I would never see a lunch card or a book or a pencil or anything. I even wondered if Mr. Ficosecco would make us pay a fee now just to attend school, since we were so rich! "Now people will think we are really rich," I said to my aunt. But she kept on weeping. I think I heard her mumble through the tears what she always said. That things were not always what they seemed, that there is no such thing as face value because people are people and not coins and not lira bills. And then she stopped crying and she clearly said that life was not simple. "It's not a pasta sauce, you know?" She didn't have to tell me that!

Mammarosa didn't make a fuss. But I think she did, inside. After all, my mother was her child and if she sent her roots deep in the soil of far-away America, would Mammarosa ever see her child's face again? Mammarosa was old and little, and getting littler all the time. Once, only one time, I remember she lost control and stomped her foot and shouted at my aunt, "I hold a lot in this stomach of mine. It is full and it isn't food it's full with!" I think there were storms that raged in Mammarosa's stomach. But she never showed it. She just sat in her child's chair by the fireplace. I saw her with one opened eye in the night while I was pretending to sleep. I saw the coals glow in the dark and I saw her there alone by the fire. Her face was inside her cupped hands and she mumbled for a very long time.

Mammarosa pretended not to pay much attention to my aunt that day at noon. She started to peel potatoes as soon as she arrived and in no time our one-room house was back to life again. Then Mammarosa said that if my mother and father had to buy a house, then they should. I didn't believe her! She said people went all the way around the world to feed their families, not because they wanted to, but because it was necessary. It was necessary because the body did not function if the stomach was not full.

Don Antonio, the priest, the high priest I should say, once preached on the subject of food and the stomach and survival. Don Antonio wore robes of many colours, black, purple, and once I even saw him draped in white lace, as if he was a bride. Other priests wore thick brown robes with hoods, even in the heat of summer. The others carried a wooden crucifix on a thick rope around their waist. Don Antonio's silver crucifix rested comfortably on his belly, hanging from a thick silver chain. Don Antonio said the mass in Latin, which was just fine, because even if no one spoke or understood Latin they still knew exactly when to rise, when to sit, when to kneel and when to say amen and go home.

One fine day Don Antonio decided to extend mass and preach. Don Antonio knew he had no say over who went to paradise and who went to hell. He knew that was St. Peter's job. It was St. Peter, Don Antonio said, who met you at the doors of paradise and looked over your report card and decided whether you were in or out. Don Antonio came to the realization one day that his job was to get those report cards as good-looking as possible, so that is why he started to say a little something not in Latin but in the language everyone understood after he said mass.

This came as a surprise the very first time. The faithful were about to leave when Don Antonio stretched out his arms and gestured for them to stop, sit and stay put, as if he were directing traffic. Like Professor Ciano's wife who followed (on foot) her husband in his Topolino until he drove past the blind corner at the descent of Via Monterosa. She was there every morning, with her arms frantically moving in every possible direction, telling people when to walk and when to stay put. Telling her husband when to stop and when to go. With one hand she motioned for children to stop and with the other she cautioned Piperella's donkey or the truck that came through the street once in a while selling plastic wares to advance and move up ahead and out of the way.

Everyone paid attention to Professor Ciano's wife, everyone except the plastic-wares man in his truck. I remember that he just turned up the music to drown her orders out.

The people in the church looked around. What was Don Antonio doing? Who was he motioning to? What was the meaning of this? There were many questions in their eyes but they were respectful and sat back in their seats a good while longer to hear what Don Antonio had to say. "The belly, the tripe. We labour for nothing but the tripe," Don Antonio said not in Latin but in the vernacular of the day. "We sweat, we steal, we cheat, we go to the ends of the world all to fill the belly, all of it for the lousy tripe. Is that all there is to life . . . the tripe the tripe the tripe!?" I had followed Sara down Via Monterosa, around the bend to Via San Francesco, all along the steep descent of Via Roma, all the way to the piazza, up to the church steps, I went after her and wasn't even out of breath—so what was wrong with going to the ends of the world?

It was St. John the Baptist's special day, the twenty-fourth day of June. St. John the Baptist was the patron of San Giovanni. The statue of St. John usually stayed in its own little house next to the electrical antenna at the very top of the mountain. Since he protected the whole town he had to be in this neutral spot. But on this day, his very special day, St. John had been carried all the way down the mountain slope and now he watched over all those who were present at mass in the church at the piazza. The church was full and then some more.

I did not go in. I couldn't. Not only was I not christened but it was at the doors of this very church, in this very piazza, that my Papagiuseppe and Don Antonio had their disagreement. I stayed outside the doors and craned my neck once in a while to see what Sara was up to. Everyone was wearing their Sunday best to please St.

John. It was no using calling on St. John when an earthquake struck the mountain or when the rains threatened to wash the slopes clean of every house and tree if you had not paid respect to St. John on his special day.

I saw Antonio (not Don Antonio the priest, he was in church saying mass, but another Antonio) approach the church. Antonio was a common peasant, well, maybe not so common. Most peasants spoke to you if you asked them a question. Not Antonio. Antonio didn't use his mouth often. He used his head instead. So he nodded his head for a yes, he shook his head sideways for no, and sometimes, if he didn't feel like using his head at all, he clacked his tongue against the roof of his mouth and that was a definite no. Oh, Antonio could speak, he just didn't want to most of the time. Maybe he didn't so he could save his energies for when he had something really important to say.

Antonio was on his way home. He had been at the butcher shop and carried a good kilo of tripe all neatly wrapped in thick brown paper. Tripe was cheap. I don't know why that was, because it took so long to clean the tripe. I remember having to soak it, scrub it, boil it and peel it. If I had a butcher shop I would give the tripe away for free, that's if I hadn't cleaned it. If I had cleaned it, I would sell it for the same price as steak.

Antonio looked surprised when he crossed the piazza and saw the crowds in church. I saw him peeking in too. He wanted to know what the crowding was about. He pushed the massive doors. They creaked. No, it wasn't a funeral and it wasn't a wedding. Oooooh, St. John's statue was on the altar. Antonio had forgotten it was the day of St. John the Baptist. How could he have forgotten!

Antonio hid the package in his jacket and entered the church. He walked all the way down the corner aisle in the middle of the service, nodding, bowing and politely waving at people he knew until he found a spot that he liked at the very front. Antonio didn't know when to sit or when to stand or when to say amen, even if he had been christened and confirmed. So Antonio looked around and did what everyone else was doing and said what everyone else was saying.

Antonio was glad he had entered the church. He was glad until Don Antonio spoiled it all when he started on his non-Latin part of the service. "The belly, the tripe, and the tripe and the belly . . ." Don Antonio would not let up about this tripe thing. He even started to shout special warnings to those who worshipped the belly, those who would do anything, who would even go to the ends of the world and spare no means just to satisfy the belly.

Personally I thought, If this damn tripe thing is so important, then for goodness' sake post it on the church door! Make it sort of like another commandment that would read something like this: "Thou shalt not eat nor worship tripe."

The package in Antonio's jacket started to slip and slide, as tripe would, because tripe is slippery. Antonio had looked forward to eating a meal that included meat, even if it was only tripe. But why was Don Antonio not pointing to those who ate steak? Why on St. John's day did he have it in for only those who ate tripe? Why does he only speak to me? Antonio thought. And how does he know that I have tripe?

That was a good question because Antonio had the tripe hidden in his jacket. Antonio decided that the priest must be a holy seer. Not only could he see what was in Antonio's jacket, but he also knew what was in his mind. In fact, thoughts of tripe had occupied Antonio's mind all through the service.

Antonio envisioned the tripe smothered in a red

"simple" sauce with lots of potatoes and garlic and tons of bay leaves, and these thoughts had even made him wish for the service to end real soon. He was feeling guilty. Maybe Don Antonio was right. Maybe he did worship the tripe. The poor peasant was not only convicted, but now he was also confused. Isn't tripe food, and isn't food life, and is there life without food?

I heard Don Antonio's sermon even from outside the doors and I too asked what could be so criminal about wanting a little food. What could be so wrong with working hard to get it? What was wrong with stopping by the butcher shop on a special day like this and buying a kilo of tripe?

Antonio was nervous, I could tell. He had to change the position of his hands constantly to keep the tripe from spilling all over the place. The service was getting long, his legs were tired and the tripe rebelled just as the priest shouted his accusation again: "The tripe the tripe everything for the tripe!" And that did Antonio in. Enough was enough. Antonio removed the package from the inside of his jacket and the tripe escaped. It plopped and spilled all over the marble floor. "The tripe, the tripe," Antonio mimicked. "Va fa n'culo, Don Anto. Take the damn tripe!" Antonio shouted as he looked one last time at his meal on the floor, without regret, and left.

Mammarosa said that Antonio should not have felt guilty. She said the poor man did not worship the tripe and Don Antonio, the high priest, should have minded his own business. She said he should eat his own food, mind his own belly and let others live. What did he know about survival, life and the belly? What did Don Antonio know about working, sweating and trekking around the world to fill a family's belly?

Don Antonio did not have a family. He did not have children. My mother had children, nine of them by now if two of them had not died while they still smiled and talked with angels because there was not enough brodo, not enough for my mother's breasts to fill with milk for the babies.

When my mother had children, after the real brodo was finished Mammarosa made my mother another kind of brodo. She merely brought water to a boil, added a pinch of salt, scrambled an egg, and then let it drop in the hot water a little at a time. She added a little olive oil, a few chunks of stale bread, and this she called egg brodo. My mother ate the brodo and then her breasts filled up with milk for the new baby.

My aunt said that when Peppe was born, the real brodo made from chicken finished very fast that year and Mammarosa had to make egg brodo. Ceci sat on the bed with my mother. The baby, Peppe, had my mother's milk and my mother had the egg brodo, and Ceci watched. Every time my mother had a spoonful she would give Ceci one too. Ceci was little, but he knew. "Should I go now, Mamma, should I go?" Ceci asked after each spoonful. And each time my mother answered, "No, no of course, bello, of course, no."

Ceci was little but he knew. He knew that Mamma needed a lot of egg-water brodo if he was to keep his baby brother Peppe. But Don Antonio, what did he know? Mammarosa said, "With all due respect, I think a woman could be a good thing for a priest."

More than once I saw the women at Piotta's patio put down their needles and pull their chairs over so they could whisper and I wouldn't hear. Well, I heard anyway. I heard them say, "It is a cruel, unnatural and a cowardly thing to do. I would rather die. Some people will do anything for the tripe. I would rather stay here and die than leave just to survive. I would rather eat onions and dry bread than leave my children and go halfway around the world in search of fortune to stuff the belly."

When the women whispered these words they looked so sad. They looked at me and shook their heads. And then they smoothed my hair. Oh shit, I thought they were going to cry! And I thought of doing or saying something that probably would bar me forever from sitting on Piotta's patio when, just in time, I heard a voice inside me that said "Let it be, let it be," and I did.

It was not my father and mother's fault if there was no bread here. We would have eaten onions and bread, but we did not make bread that often. My aunt says before my mother and father left for America we hardly ever made bread.

Once she saw Professor Ciano's little girl with a whole half-loaf of white, white bread. She was such a dainty thing, my aunt knew she would never finish the bread. So she sat there and watched Esterina peck at the loaf while she played. After a long while, the voice of children called out, "Esterina, Esterina." She stood up quickly and threw the bread on the dirt by the side of her steps as she went off to play. It had been worth the wait. My aunt collected the lovely loaf and cleaned the sand and dirt off of it carefully before she gave it to Nina.

Did the women on Piotta's patio, who claimed to know all about life and pane and vino, ever get up from their comfortable chairs in the sun to rescue a lovely loaf from the dirt?

No!

They would never leave to go anywhere. Not unless the whole of San Giovanni left at once, like a herd. Maybe then they would leave and follow. They were like Don Antonio, the shepherd who led them. Well, I did hear them say that they would rather die than leave, and this I thought was a fair and honest thing to say because the likes of them, I am sure, would never make it. These women surrounded by dainty doilies and pretty sweaters for sure would die if they ever attempted to be as brave as my mother and leave their familiar ground. Their roots were not elastic, unlike my tree on the ravine. If they stretched out, even just a little, they would break. The trunks would fall over, wither and die.

My mother, on the other hand, was strong and elastic, flexible just like my tree. She had been pulled, and she had been dragged halfway around the world, and she made it. I felt strong just then on Piotta's patio, knowing my mother was strong. But then when I got home from Piotta's patio I still wondered. "Mammaaaroooosa," I called reluctantly. "Yes, bene," she replied. "Would we do anything for the tripe? Do we worship the belly?"

Mammarosa said women who had time to loiter had no right to bread and wine. They had no right to speak. Mammarosa and my aunt knew what the women whispered. It was an old story they knew too well. There was no need for me to tell them all the details. They knew exactly what the women had said.

I thought for sure one day my aunt would explode. But she didn't, not today. She may have heard the same voice I heard, the one that said "Let it be, let it be." However, if ever someday my aunt decided not to pay attention to the voice that held her back, that gentle voice that whispers "Let it be," the women that sat on Piotta's patio would be sorry, because my aunt, when she does something, does it right or not at all. There was no half-ass anything with my aunt. "Hey, you whores," she would have shouted at them. And then she would have dragged a few heads of hair from one end of Via Monterosa to the other.

My Mammarosa did not agree with my aunt about letting me loiter with idle women. She said that good character, like a good sauce, was made at home, not at

Piotta's patio. At home, stirred by our own spoon in our own pot, sitting by our own fire. Around our own fire, in our own home, I heard my aunt say, "Don't jump, don't scuff your shoes, don't rip your clothes." She said if we ever took the time to squeeze the dollars that bought our shoes, our clothes, our food and our books, blood would come out of them. It was for the same (bloody) reason that she nagged, "Study, study, study." She said we had to because my mother and father walked in the deep snow so we could study.

At home, sitting around our fire, never did the thought that my mother was cruel occur to me. Actually, from time to time, I thought it was I who was cruel because not too long after she left (after I cried all that I could cry), days would go by and not even a thought of her crossed my mind. And later, more and more days went by before thoughts of her came to mind. Only when my aunt knelt with us by the bed did I remember.

In her letters my mother said she thought about me all the time. In February, while I picked violets along the brook on the mountain, I didn't think about her trudging in the snow. No, my mother was not cruel. The women at Piotta's patio didn't know what they were saying.

Mammarosa said Antonio the peasant had done right to throw the tripe in Don Antonio's face. And I wished now that I had a good kilo's worth of tripe. I would ask the butcher to cut it up in nice small pieces. I would not spill it on Piotta's patio, no, I would throw it in the women's faces. What did they or Don Antonio know?! Mammarosa said that Don Antonio for sure would never know. I am very sure that his stomach never growled. It was always so big. I wondered Doesn't his food ever get digested?

Biasi, the cripple, once told Don Antonio he was full of shit. Biasi was the only man in San Giovanni to go about in a wheelchair and he didn't like it at all. When Peppe, my brother, guided his limp legs and arms into his clothes and shaved him, Biasi cursed and cussed and swore. Peppe just laughed, and then soon, Biasi laughed too. Peppe took Biasi up and down the streets every day until the evening bells rang. Then he took Biasi's limp limbs out of the clothes and tucked him in bed under his plaid blanket.

Don Antonio met Biasi in the piazza once. There was a spring in Don Antonio's step that day, the crucifix bounced up and down off his belly and he laughed and smiled and played with the few hairs on Biasi's head. He poked at Biasi's belly and laughed when he discovered a thermos under the plaid blanket. "Hey, hey, what do we have here? Nice, real nice. It matches the plaid blanket. Take a look at the size of this thing." Don Antonio started a commotion and everyone was laughing. "You can stuff a lot of food in here!" Don Antonio liked to tease Biasi. Don Antonio would have gone on and on. He thought he was so funny. Biasi didn't think so. His hands could not poke or push very well but there was nothing the matter at all with his tongue. So Biasi started to cuss and curse and swear. Finally he shouted, "Va fa n'culo, Don Anto, I bet you just swallowed a good-size steak for dinner. This here thermos is full of nothing but beans. And you are full of nothing but shit!" Peppe was there when Biasi told the priest he was full of shit and he told us about it when he came home. Did we laugh! Ceci of course rolled on the floor. Don Antonio didn't know anything about the belly. Mammarosa was right.

There was an old man who lived at the end of Via Monterosa on our side of the street. He had a big belly. He was the only person I knew that had been to America and no one called him an Americano. Everyone called him zu' Michele because he was old. I called him zu'

Michele, Uncle Michele, because Mammarosa said that somehow somewhere back we were related.

Zu' Michele wore the same brown velvet jacket summer, winter and fall. It no longer shined like velvet, he had worn it for so long, and the buttons never met the buttonholes on account of his belly. His belly was so big that it squeezed his lungs out of their space, so he panted when he came up the incline.

You could hear zu' Michele before you saw him. He coughed, then he spit every time he coughed. And that was often. He even coughed and spit in his own house. His granddaughter Carletta cried when he spit, especially if her friends were over visiting. Zu' Michele's daughter Caterina tried to reason with him but he wouldn't listen to reason. "It's my house, and until I die I'll spit all I want and where I want." And that was that. And there was nothing anyone could say or do because it was indeed his house.

I went there because Caterina, his daughter, sometimes asked me to wash her linens at San Giuseppe's fountain. Sometimes she gave me a treat, sometimes she gave me a pat on my shoulder and said that I was very smart and very talented and that I cleaned the clothes so well with such little waste of soap! "Oooooooh—teh teh teh teh and with such little soap," she'd say. Ooooh is right! My ears hurt when she chanted her string of ooooh and teh teh teh. It was as bad as the sound of Maria Pia practising pizzicato on her discordant violin.

Really, I mostly went to zu' Michele's house for the warmth. The walls were thick and their doors were shut and there was always a big stack of logs for the fire. There was the smell of jams and bread and freshly thin-sliced mortadella, too. I didn't see the jams and bread, the provolone, the mortadella or the scented soaps, but I knew they were there, hidden somewhere in the cupboards and in the drawers. One more reason I went there was to spy on Carletta. That usually got me more than washing her mother Caterina's linens.

Once I snuck upstairs and what do you know?! There on the third-floor balcony was Carletta with my sister Nina in their underwear, pretending to be on the beach. And not only that, the two of them were shaving! They were shaving their legs and soon it looked like they would start on their armpits.

Nina and Carletta studied in the big city, not in San Giovanni, because even though San Giovanni started out as a "universitas," now it did not even have a real high school. Carletta had picked up a few things in magazines from America that she bought in the city. Things that could get her in trouble. I knew it because I had learned the rules. I had done my time on Piotta's patio. I knew about bread and I knew about wine.

Carletta had a friend who was a boy in the big city. I knew him too because he was from San Giovanni. In San Giovanni they pretended not to know each other but in the city they walked hand in hand and kissed in alleyways and even skipped classes to spend time together. In San Giovanni, I was their link. I brought the letters that Peppino trusted me with to give to Carletta. I remember Peppino. I remember him nervous, leaning against the stone wall of his house across from San Giuseppe's fountain, crossing and uncrossing his legs, puffing cloud after cloud of smoke until I showed up. He pinched my cheeks when he handed me the letters.

(I often thought next time he touched my face I would reach between his legs and pinch hard, but Sara said not to.)

When I handed Carletta a letter from Peppino she didn't pat me on the shoulder and say things like "Ooooh, you are smart" or "Ooooh, you are so pretty," like her mother did. No, no, Carletta did not say shit like that. She knew words were not enough to keep my words from leaking, so she gave me things. She gave me cake. She gave me a comb, or a ribbon, a pen or something she had suddenly decided not to wear, and I liked that.

Carletta was the best-dressed girl in San Giovanni. Zu' Michele had done what he had to do. He left alone, without his children, for the coal mines of Clarksburg, in West Virginia. "In the real America," he said to me. "Not Canada. Canada, where your parents are, is not the real America." Once in a while I covered his mouth with my hand, hoping he would not go on and on about Canada not being the real America. I whispered in his ear not to say that in front of everyone. I didn't want my friends to hear that my father had gone to the fake America!

In Clarksburg, zu' Michele had descended down the shafts into the black earth, and there with a pick and shovel he worked and worked. He worked for the house. He worked for the bread and the wood and the jam and the mortadella. And he had worked for his granddaughter Carletta's beautiful clothes.

Nina and Carletta strolled arm in arm down Via San Francesco and up Via Roma. Nina never looked as elegant as Carletta. When I saw them together I realized maybe zu' Michele was right—my father for sure had gone to the fake America.

Everyone complimented and admired Carletta. Nina didn't mind. She always told Carletta she was beautiful. And beautiful she was with her snow-white skin, her midnight eyes and her black flowing hair.

I don't ever remember telling Carletta that she was beautiful. I don't know why. I always meant to say it, but then when I saw her with her nose up and her hips going here and there, all dressed up in a new sweater or a new dress, I forgot about it. Instead, it never failed, I looked her over and then told her that I had seen her skirt or her sweater, or whatever it was that she was wearing, on so and so, on such and such a day.

Every single time I said that I had seen her clothes on someone else she cried. She pulled and plucked at her clothing and she cursed and she shouted, "Copycats, spiteful cats, I hope they die." She said they did it on purpose, just to ruin her life. Carletta would never again put that piece of clothing on, not in a small town like San Giovanni where she had to be original because she was Carletta. Carletta was stupid. Even her own grandfather, zu' Michele, called her stupid.

He liked Nina. Nina did well at school even though my aunt couldn't deliver gifts to the professors. Zu' Michele, on the other hand, was forever handing out money for the huge hams and big cheese rounds and the jugs of wine so that Carletta's professors would feel obliged to give her at least a passing mark. And they did. They took the hams and the cheese and the wine and gave her more than a passing mark, because it was not a crime for people to show gratitude. In fact it was polite. I think this is why the rich were polite and the poor were rude.

Mammarosa always said that if you want a door to be opened for you you have to knock with your feet, not because you want to damage the door, but your hands should be good and full, too full to reach for the handle and pound on the door. My aunt never knocked on Nina's professors' doors with her feet.

The day the gold medal was handed out it was not Nina who went up to receive it. Nina had much better grades than the girl who did, the daughter of one of the polite rich. I remember the professor shrugged his shoulder and tapped Nina on the back and smiled. He curved his body as if he wanted to make himself small, as if he wanted to hide, perhaps. But Nina didn't mind. She was just as proud as if it had been her name that was called, as if it had been she who climbed the wooden steps that led to the platform where the professor shook the winner's hand.

Zu' Michele always said that Nina would make it in life but he was worried about his granddaughter Carletta, because if his fortune ever ran out and they could no longer be polite, he did not think she would survive.

Zu' Michele knew about survival. He told me a lot about survival. When I saw him from far away coming up the incline on Via Monterosa, I ran towards him. I would grab him by the arm and then I would lead him to sit by the nearest step. That was usually the steps of Sara's house. No sooner would we be seated than a whole bunch of children, like a swarm of bees, buzzed in and took their place on the stone steps. "One more, one more, just one more story, zu' Michele," we all begged. He always had just one more story.

I followed zu' Michele on his battlefields in my mind.

"There were fires and the sky was black, there were men dead and there were cries." Zu' Michele said he did not like it on the battlefields. He did not want to stay and fight in that war. He said if he stayed, he would die, but if he found a way to leave, he might survive. He only told us, only the children, about his stories of survival. He would never tell the women of Piotta's patio his stories because they would not have understood. They would probably have said that they would have rather died than leave their station in life. So we had zu' Michele all to ourselves.

He told us that it had not been him who had sparked that great first world fight. It had not been him who had caused the war. He said it had been a man, only one man, who had killed a king's son, and the king wanted revenge. Zu' Michele said after a while he had seen enough fathers' sons dead for this one king's son, and that's why he did not want to stay on the fields of death any longer, because he too might die.

Zu' Michele was smart. He used what was in his head. Professor Ciano would probably say that there was not much in zu' Michele's head because he had not studied, he had only worked the earth and knew nothing more than planting and weeding and harvesting. Zu' Michele didn't worry. It's true, all that was in his head had to do with plants and fields so that's what he used.

Under the dark sky while men cried and died in the fields of death, zu' Michele spotted the plant of life. It was "vurra." He would know vurra from a mile away. His eyes sparkled at the sight. He almost cried. He waited for the silencing of the guns late into the night. Then he crawled among the greens and picked the thick stems under the white moonlight. The vurra's stems were full and soft. There would be enough milky sap for a bath if he wanted.

Zu' Michele spread the sap from the vurra all over his body and by morning he was burning and freezing with fever and his whole body was covered with red bumps. The doctor on the battlefield opened zu' Michele's eyes wide with his fingers. The doctor shook his head and looked very sad. Then he signed some papers and zu' Michele was sent home right away because it may have been contagious, and men had to die at their stations, not of fevers and red bumps.

Zu' Michele was sent home to die, but he survived. And when hunger and not war threatened his life again, zu' Michele left for the real America so he could buy jam and mortadella, and his family's bellies could be full and they could survive.

He left alone and he didn't care what anyone said.

When he came back, he fixed up his old house and bought his granddaughter the best clothes. They were all jealous. "Well, that's too bad," I said to zu' Michele once. Zu' Michele had survived on the dark fields of death and in the bowels of the black earth of the real America. Zu' Michele's belly always jiggled when he laughed and said, "I did what I had to do, so I survived."

Zu' Michele coughed and spit even when he told stories, so we sat in front of him, never on the sides. He said soon, one of these days, he was going to die. I looked at zu' Michele's face. I would not let him die. I would pull him and drag him along with me wherever I went and for as long as I lived. I knew he would make it because he was strong. He would live on. Zu' Michele would survive.

A brown envelope with a letter from America came after many more white envelopes with the red and blue edges. "Fear not, the waters will not overflow you." These were the words that were above the rest of the words and framed the letter. My aunt read the letter and cried. She said that my father and mother had saved a thousand dollars! My mother said the foreman at Canada Packers, at the end of Marion Street in St. Boniface, let my father clean the floors sometimes.

My father walked to Marion Street in deep snow and sometimes on ice. He got up at four in the morning to go from Alexander Avenue to Marion Street. One day, when he got there at Canada Packers, there was nothing for my father to do. My father kept on walking until he came to the railway yards. He wandered about there for a while and then he met a man. This man was a foreman at the yards and was looking for workers to fix the railways. My father said yes, of course he would go, and my mother too said of course. She didn't mind that he had to travel all the way to Vancouver, the other end of the country.

They had to do what they had to do!

My mother bundled the baby well and walked over to her friend Ina's house where the baby stayed during the day, because now they both worked. My aunt read in the letter that the manager at the Toronto Dominion Bank at Main and Higgins shook my father's hand and gave him a thousand dollars because my father had a thousand dollars of his own deposited at this bank. So now they had two thousand dollars and they bought a house.

So they bought the house!

My aunt said that someday soon, we too would be leaving for America. My father kept on writing in his letters that he was coming back but my aunt didn't believe him because my mother started to write in her letters that America was beautiful. She wrote that it was a great place for children to grow up. My father said no and my mother said yes. They now had the house and I had the feeling that soon one of them, hopefully not my mother, would win.

My mother said that it was not a little house at all. It had a big bathroom and nine other rooms if you counted the enclosed entrance, which was as big as any of them. It had a furnace in the basement with a stoker, and there was even a little shack at the southeast corner of the garden where my father and mother kept a wheelbarrow and tools. My mother loved the garden. They did not use all of the rooms of the house for themselves. My father said they didn't need so many rooms. My father didn't seem to think he needed much at all in America.

My mother said that sometimes my father would become cranky and out of the blue he said they didn't need milk. "Of course we need milk," my mother answered. But he still wouldn't buy it because he said maybe his other children on that day had not drunk milk. My mother wrote that when my father was in this mood he left in a hurry and did not sit for breakfast.

Each of the other five rooms in the house were occupied by some very nice people, my mother said, who paid her some money every month. My mother was collecting money without punching a time card and it was more than enough to make the payments to the bank every first of the month. In fact they had money left over, and they didn't have to pay anyone rent! My mother said it was a great big house and it was all their own.

My aunt cried. She turned the envelope over. It was true. The address at the top left-hand corner of the envelope was new. My aunt had never seen those numbers and words before. It read:

301 Fountain Street
Winnipeg, Manitoba
Canada

"That's right," my aunt said, "Canada." It didn't matter if it was in Canada, the fake America. But really, I mean, why couldn't life be simple? Because if life was simple then any place could be America.

Tomatoes

Wash, cut and seed tomatoes

Place in jars or bottles with tons of basil in between

Seal, wrap in rags, place in a big pot of water

Boil for an hour

Coca-Cola

AND WHY COULDN'T AMERICA "the real" be anywhere? Why did people have to travel halfway around the world to get to America? Why did it only have to be a pretty-coloured spot on the other side of the blue sea on Maria Pia's globe? I had seen Maria Pia's globe, the one her father sent her. The mountains were waves of different shades of brown, the sea of course was varying shades of blue, and America, on the other side, was green, all one shade of brilliant green.

Once Maria Pia's father sent her a postcard of America. She of course brought it to school. We all flocked around Maria Pia to marvel at the shiny colourful little square of paper. From over Maria Pia's shoulder I saw America the beautiful, the real. The sea was blue and tranquil. The houses by the docks were big and square and high. But higher than the buildings and wider than the sky was a woman draped in white. She held a book and a torch which shined so very bright. Above the flame above the shining sea, across the whole little paper that contained America from one end of the sky to the other, were these words: "The home of the brave and the land of the free!"

So there was more to America. It was more than a paradise, a promised land of bread, milk, honey, work and all that stuff. It was not the place for slaves and certainly not for cowards. Only the brave and the free lived in America. America could be anywhere children had plenty of bread and milk. But that would not happen in San Giovanni, not soon. Bread and milk and bread and honey and bread and wine were only words, nice thoughts that the peasants chanted at election time when they marched behind the motorcade of strangers that came around always close to voting day. I remember San Giovanni all decorated with colourful streamers and banners that read "Viva the Christian Democracy" close to voting day. Don Antonio handed out figurines of the Madonna, the mother of Christians, who would definitely vote Democracy, he said. But Tata told Don Antonio to "va fa n'culo" and marched in the front line shouting "Bread and work" with the rest of the men and women that too shouted for bread and work and wine and honey.

I don't know why it was that the well-dressed strangers in the convertible always won. There were so many peasants—I was there too—who cheered Tata. A whole marching crowd on whose faces was the reflection of the dark parched soil they worked. They marched briskly to keep up behind the motorcade but they never won.

The morning after the votes were cast I saw Count Berlingieri and the baron Lopez mount their horses and unleash the dogs, and off they went, shouting and trampling all over empty fields. Vast, fertile and green, fields that could have been sown, could have been harvested and made good the promise of bread and perhaps turned San Giovanni into America. But no, by noon the baron and the count, a whole band of them, returned laughing, trotting on their horses. I saw them. One little porcupine, only one, dangled from their side.

Not having bread and work and milk and wine and honey was not the only obstacle that prevented San Giovanni from becoming America. Bread and work and milk and honey would surely come someday soon, when enough people told Don Antonio and Berlingieri and Lopez to "va fa n'culo." The real hurdle was the brave and free part! San Giovanni could never become America because America was a land for the free. And free is not simple. You have to be brave to be free. You can't be scared to let others be free. Well, maybe someday we could have America right here in San Giovanni. Someday, maybe. But not for now. I for one was not making that happen quickly.

There was another man in San Giovanni. He too had a big belly. Actually he had a big everything. He was soft, round and very full. And when he walked he swayed a little. His name was Ghinghillo. Ghinghillo wore an all-season coat and pulled the belt real tight until it disappeared in the folds of his body. His face was smooth, a little tinged, like the colour of peaches in a bowl of milk.

Ghinghillo was a gentle man, as gentle as his castrato voice. It was so strange that so gentle a voice should come from so big a man. Castrato is what I heard people call Ghinghillo, and when they did, they didn't care if he was around. I remember that his face turned from peach to plum and he always shouted something high-pitched in defence. It came out like a squeal, a desperate squeal, like those of our pigs when Tata tied their legs and cut and sewed their flesh after, without mercy, she removed their balls.

Ghinghillo walked through the streets of San Giovanni a lot, because, although he did not have his own shop, he was the very best goldsmith there was. He went from house to house where he was called to restore lifeless gold. There was no one else the people of San Giovanni would rather trust with their gold, and yet, when Ghinghillo walked by, or when he sat in their homes, they had to try hard not to giggle.

I too giggled and teased Ghinghillo and said what the other children said, even if inside of me I sensed a bad feeling warning me. Inside of me, I felt this nagging that urged me to be brave and told me to be free. But I didn't have the courage to listen. I still shouted in chorus with the other children, "Ghinghillo, Ghinghillo cu lu culu piccirillu." Big fat-ass Ghinghillo is what we really meant. Even when in my heart I heard another chorus just as loud that said "God loves Ghinghillo, God loves Ghinghillo," I still didn't listen. And I felt miserable.

America, the land of the free and the land of the brave, could be anywhere a gentle voice could speak and be heard and be strong. I was not strong, and when I did nasty things like this, I felt miserable. And when I felt miserable, I tried to take my misery out on my sister Julia, who was younger and just a bit smaller. But I don't think I tried more than once or twice, because Julia, although younger, had a damn good set of teeth, and almost took a chunk right out of me.

I should have known better than to mess with Julia. Even Mr. Ficosecco didn't mess with Julia. She told Mr. Ficosecco to "va fa n'culo" many many times, especially when he said "not you" at the lunch card line-ups.

Once when my aunt went for an interview, Mr. Ficosecco told her that Julia was after his desk. Everywhere she went she had this compulsion to take over. He said she was a blazing fire. Julia never teased

Ghinghillo but she did call Don Antonio a fat slob. She called Don Antonio a fat slob because she was sure the idea that she was a half devil first came from him. (Julia was not christened either.) She called him a fat slob and she didn't run away. She walked slowly ahead, and from time to time Julia checked her shoulder to look in his face with disgust. She may as well have said, "Come and get me, come and get me."

She did the same thing to Bernardo. Bernardo came to lodge at our house on Via Monterosa before he moved permanently to San Giovanni and he loved to tease Julia. "Oh Julia, you are so pretty . . . but . . ." "But what?" Julia demanded. It was all over her face. She was about to explode. Bernardo laughed and laughed and continued with his game. "But Nina is prettier than you." Well, I remember Julia storming on the bed where he slept. She threw his covers and pillow all over the floor before she stomped and jumped on the mattress, determined to tear it apart, and shouted, "Go away from my house, pig! I don't ever want to see your pig face again!" Julia's voice could be heard all the way to San Giuseppe's fountain. There the women washing dirty linens quit their whispering and took notice. Don Antonio and Bernardo didn't mess much with Julia. She took a chunk out of me and they would have found a piece of them missing too if they ever took Julia on.

I think America could be anywhere the weak and "insignificant others" had a voice. Any place where your eyes were not "cat's eyes" if they by chance were blue. It would be anywhere a woman was not poisoned by a man when he said "I love you." America could be any spot on the earth where you could even have come from far-away Spain a long time ago and no one would look at you funny in history class. I think America would be anywhere people could stand up and be strong. Julia was strong. She was free when I was scared. If America was a little girl and not a place on a map Julia would be America. She would hold the torch real high and she would make it shine for ever and ever through all her generations.

America, land of the free and home of the brave. Land where fragile glass could brave the flame. Land of milk and Coca-Cola. (I know Cola-Cola comes from America. AMERICA—it is written in bold letters behind the sign that says "Coca-Cola" at the bar on Via Roma.) America, land of dreams and land of wonder. I wonder if in America, on Fountain Street, the street where my mother's beautiful house was, if there was indeed a fountain there. I thought if there was one it would be a real rival to San Giuseppe's fountain on Via San Francesco of Assisi, in San Giovanni. I imagined that in America, on my mother's street, the lips of the gargoyle that spit out the water were made of brass or even gold!

Oh dear, there I go again, I'm either dreaming or the sun is in my eyes.

A simple sauce

Heat up the best olive oil you can find
Toss in chopped onions, hot peppers and garlic
Throw in a jar of tomatoes
By the time the pasta water boils
and the pasta cooks, the sauce is ready

Horseshit

“HORSESHIT!” I SHOUTED while my aunt cried as she read another letter that had just arrived from America. “They shall mount up with wings as eagles, they shall run and not be weary.” These were the words that my aunt read first. They were written at the very top and stood tall above the rest of the words as if they were a crown on the rest of my mother’s letter. While I heard the rest of what my aunt was reading, I felt as if someone had slowly diverted the blinding sun-rays from my eyes, the glare was gone, and all of a sudden I could see things for what they really were. In a flash all of my imaginings and dreams of America someday being anywhere one wished it to be became just that—imaginings and dreams.

I should have listened to Mammarosa. She had told me a million times when I dreamed and imagined out loud in front of her, “Not so fast child, calm down, people are people and the world is a village, one big village.” She was right and what my aunt read proved it. San Giovanni had made it to America before America even thought of coming to San Giovanni. It was clear and I saw it clearly when my aunt read on. All that shined was not gold in America, not in the real, and not in the fake, and that is why I shouted "Horseshit!"

My aunt read that my father lost his job at the railway yards in America. He lost it and found it and lost it and found it, and then finally one day, he got so tired of this hide-and-seek game that he didn't wait for anyone to tell him to go anymore, he just quit on his own for good.

My father lost his job so often because he didn't like the rules. When the foremen came to work happy in the morning the whole gang would have a good day but it was not so when they arrived at the yards in a bad mood. These foremen must have had cars just like Professor Ciano and just like the professor they probably got up early in the morning to fill them with benzene. Yes, I could just see them all angry and fretful, like the professor at that ungodly hour, cursing and kicking the tires before they pumped them with air. And I suspect that once in a while these foremen got confused, because anger does funny things to people, and they pumped more than just their cars. I think at that early hour they got all mixed up and pumped themselves a little, too, and that of course meant that by the time they arrived at the yards, they needed to pick on one or two of the workers to release the pressure.

My father didn't quit each time because the foreman picked on him. Oh, no, my father was silent as he worked in his own corner. Usually the foreman hardly noticed that he was there. He worked with his head down but he saw everything. My father saw everything and he boiled. My mother was not happy when my father boiled because she watched the sauce boil and she watched the pasta water boil and she knew that boiling was a consuming thing. If you were not careful, she said, there would be nothing left at all. My father knew that she was right but he didn't even try to contain his boiling.

This one time my father was looking down, waiting for a railway tie to budge under his pick, when from the corner of his eye he saw one of the foremen give a man (who my father didn't know, but who worked further down the line) a good shouting. My father lifted his head because the shouting had become pushing, and the pushing had become shoving. It became louder and harder until soon that worker silently buckled on the gravel by the rail line. Well, whatever it was that boiled deep within my father boiled over. He threw his pick a few yards away and in no time his hands were at the foreman's collar. He lifted him off the ground and then the foreman too ended up on the gravel.

My mother said it was just as well that my father quit. She said there was no hope of him ever getting anywhere on the railway ladder. If he was lucky, he would move from gang to gang until he had quit from every single one or been fired from them all, and then he would be left sitting someday at the very bottom with nothing but his pick and shovel.

My mother once told my father to bring the foreman a bottle of whisky because some foremen on the railway liked whisky. I imagined this foreman to have an extra-large red nose with pinpricks and black dots all over it because Piperella had an extra-large red nose with pinpricks and black dots all over it and he liked whisky. My mother had made the suggestion to bring a little gift, like a bottle of whisky, to the foreman because not so long ago Ina's husband, who always brought whisky to his foreman, got a better job and brought home a little more money. But no, my father said no whisky. My mother said it was just as good that he quit.

I am glad my father didn't bring whisky to the foreman. My father was silent and looked down when he went about his work, but he saw everything. He could see deep and he could see wide and far into the day. Much wider and much farther than I now saw America in my mind, and I tried hard to see everything, while my aunt read the letter. My father saw that if he started bringing whisky and things like that to people, just because they sat higher on the ladder, he might end up like Carletta.

Just then, as I was thinking and imagining being in America at the railyards, balancing myself one foot carefully in front of the other along the tracks, I no longer heard my aunt's voice reading. So I tugged at her skirt. She shook me off. I tugged at her skirt again and she stomped her foot and it looked as if she was going to slap her own face but instead she turned around and said, "Is there ever going to be a moment of peace and solitude for me? Ever?" She brought the letter close up to her face and repeated over and over, "A u to mo beeel . . . auto mobil . . . automobile! Automobile!" as if she couldn't read.

My father had bought an automobile! I couldn't believe it. Even my aunt couldn't believe it. That's why I couldn't hear her. She had been reading the lines over and over to herself to make sure that she was not imagining it but that it was really true. "Oh my! Oh oooooh! A car, you mean a car like the Cianos'? Is it a Topolino? Is it a Fiat Topolino? Oh why couldn't it be, why couldn't America be here?"

My mother said it was not a new car and it wasn't really a car. It was a car with the back as spacious as a truck, but it was not a truck because it was not high enough. It was long and low like a car, the colour of latte macchiato, with panels of fake wood on the sides. And it coughed up a whole cloud of black dirty smoke because my father had to keep the gas pedal down a little before he started this car, this truck. No, I guess it was not like Professor Ciano's car, but my aunt said quite proudly that from the sounds of it, it had to be bigger, much bigger and better than the professor's car, because my father packed a whole bunch of crates full of fruit and vegetables in the back of that car.

The very first morning of the very first day that my father filled the back of his car with fruits and vegetables, my mother said in the letter, it was cold, very cold. The wind had howled all night. It played and passed its time shaping and reshaping the peaks on the hills of snow. Now the peaks were on the left and then they were on the right of that street in Winnipeg, between Elgin and Alexander, known better as Fruit Row.

Morning had not yet broken when my father stood puzzling before crates and crates of fruits and vegetables piled high, almost to the ceiling, against the walls inside Rogers Wholesale.

My father's hands were on his little bundle of dollars deep in his pants pocket. One second he was ready and confident, the next he didn't know. My father shook inside and he shivered. Really, he did shiver even though he was warmly dressed and out of the cold. He finally decided and took the dollars out of his pocket to pay for the fruits and vegetables he had chosen before piling them on a cart. The man at Rogers Wholesale on Fruit Row was very happy. He patted my father on the back when he took the money and he even helped load the car with the grapes, bananas, oranges, broccoli, tomatoes and so many other things.

It was late in the night when my father came home from his very first day peddling fruit. My mother was stirring a simple sauce with a long wooden spoon when the door opened, bringing in the howling frigid wind. A whirl of powdery fine snow settled itself quickly in a corner. My mother could tell, so she didn't bother to ask, and my father didn't say because he knew that she could tell.

One by one he carried the wooden crates of the delicate cargo into the entrance room that was as big as any of the other rooms in my mother's beautiful house at 301 Fountain Street. My father sat quietly at the table while the icicles that had clung to his moustache and eyebrows melted and ran down his cheeks. He didn't look up much, nor did he speak. How could he, his lips were quivering so. Still my mother didn't ask and my father didn't say.

She too sat there, quiet at the table, and just imagined. She imagined my father's constant knocks on strangers' doors and every one of them shaking their heads to say no, no, they didn't want any. My father had tried to return the goods to Rogers but Rogers too had obviously said no.

My mother lay quiet on the bed in the darkness of that cold first night. She covered her face with her hands and mumbled.

In the morning, while my father loaded the car again with the grapes and the bananas and the broccoli and the lettuce, my mother didn't speak. She was still mumbling. The snow that had settled in the corner of the entrance the night before had melted, her feet stood in the puddle. The women of Piotta's patio would have said it was a good omen but my mother didn't notice. She didn't move. She still mumbled and she kept on mumbling while he left to try peddling his fruits again in far-away parts of the city.

My mother said that he went to Windsor Park. I don't know where Windsor Park is and I don't think the other fruit peddlers in Winnipeg knew about it either because they never went there. But my father did on that second day. He was shy and he was shaking when he knocked on the first door. The woman who answered the door did not speak English very well, neither did my father, but they both could say broccoli. "Broccoli? Broccoli?" the woman said, surprised. "Yeah, broccoli, broccoli!" my father replied. Broccoli at her door!

The woman, who my mother said was from Greece, bought broccoli and bought grapes and tomatoes and lettuce. And then she called her friends who lived down the street and those friends of hers sent my father to more houses down another street not far away. My father came home early that second day because he had nothing more to sell.

My father now worked not just the Windsor Park route but he went down the streets of Fort Rouge as well. There Mrs. Palmisani knew exactly when he passed by and alerted everyone on her street. Well, she tried. She stuck her head out the door, even in the middle of winter, and shouted just like the fish lady on the streets of San Giovanni. "The fruits, the vegetables, Teresi', Cateri', he's here," she shouted in the direction of her friends' houses. Even when she knew that her friends, Teresina and Caterina, down the street from her at 681 Mulvey were indoors with their windows and doors shut and couldn't possibly hear her, she still shouted "Teresi', Cateri'."

My father worked hard and he lived by his own rules. This was no horseshit and it was no news to me. This was my father just as I imagined him. He had gone halfway around the world, and just like my tree, although dragged and pulled, he stood strong, with his roots in place.

Mammarosa said it was easier to live by someone else's rules because these were visible. They were clear-cut, set and given by visible people to whom you were accountable and usually accompanied by some visible reward. These live in the mind.

Not so with the invisible rules, she said. They are set by your conscience and hidden in your heart. They too can be clear-cut but there is no visible authority and certainly no visible reward. The invisible rules have a tough time surviving, she said, because while the mind shouts, the voice of the heart is gentle, as gentle as the voice of angels. I think this is why she often pressed her fingers over my lips and insisted I develop a sharp sense of hearing, inside.

My father knew how hard it was to follow these invisible rules but he didn't mind because he was silent and went about quietly so his hearing was very sharp. He was able to pick up the faintest and gentlest whisper. Late one evening when my father came home from peddling fruit all over the city, he sat at the table as usual, and while the pasta cooked on the stove, he counted his money. My mother said in her letter that he had found a strange- looking bill in his pocket that night. There was an eagle with great wings spread out majestically. He had never seen one like it before. It read "fifty dollars" and the word "America" was at the very top and bottom too. My father put the fifty-American-dollar bill aside and counted and recounted the rest of his money.

The pasta was ready and it was very dark and late but my father insisted that he had to go out. My mother said she understood. She just covered the pots and waved before she shut the door. It was only after he left that she shook her head and slammed the cupboard doors. I don't think she slapped her face like my aunt, because although my aunt and my mother were sisters, they were not alike. Mammarosa whispered this to me once when my aunt was having a bad face-slapping kind of a day.

My father knew exactly where he was going. There was only one place that American fifty-dollar bill could have come from. He had gone there earlier that very same night when it was just beginning to be dark, when the sky was a deep blue, almost black, lit by the half moon and the first flickering stars. The Santinis' lights at 630 Langside had been dimmed to keep the mosquitoes from seeing their exposed arms and legs. The Santinis were full of life. Every living part of them moved when they spoke and my father remembered they had all spoken at once. "Ei, compari, whariugonnadu, that's America for you, even the insects want blood." "True, compari, but here at least we get bread in exchange for what pours off of our brows." On and on they went as my father came to their door.

Mr. and Mrs. Santini and the guests made such a commotion when they saw my father on their stairs. "Come, come . . . you don't want espresso? No espresso? How about a glass, just a little glass, of wine?" They all talked at once. "Where is a glass, Carmela, give me a glass," Mr. Santini shouted at his wife. He wasn't angry with his wife. Oh never, he just wanted my father to know that he really was serious about that glass of wine.

But my father wouldn't stay and sip wine, not because he didn't want to. Oh no, there was nothing he enjoyed more than a good argument over politics and America, but it was late, it was his last stop and he was tired. So he just weighed the fruit and said "Two dollars." My father had simply said that the grand total for the fruit and vegetables came to two dollars and all of a sudden, all at once, they swarmed towards him, dollar bills flying out of everywhere: pockets, hands, sleeves and even from between breasts. They were pushing, all of them, as if to win a race, to get the money into his hands first.

It was the Santinis' guest, an uncle from the real America, who won the race and put money in my father's hand first. "Here," he said triumphant and out of breath, "two dollars." He had put the money in my father's hands and he closed my father's fingers tightly around the crisp bill while pushing all the other contenders out of the way.

My father didn't know what to do because he knew this man was a guest, and guests, as a rule, never pay. He knew this man was a guest because when my father first entered the porch Mr. Santini proudly motioned my father to enter and said, "Come, come on in, this is my uncle, he's here visiting from America."

The guest had insisted on the money, and my father, in the middle of the commotion, had slipped the bill in his pocket in a hurry because he knew there would never have been an end to whose money to take and it was getting late. Yes, Mr. Santini's guest was the man. It was his money and this was the place.

It was pitch-black when my father arrived at the Santinis' house on Langside Street for the second time in the same evening. The lights were completely turned off and the porch was silent now except for the relentless sound of crickets. A breeze rustled through the lilac bushes. Their fragrance rose hot in the air. The smell of espresso, wine and cigarette butts still lingered. A cat, frightened, leaped and rattled the cups on the table. The stairs creaked loudly under my father's boots, much louder than they had earlier in the night. And for a moment, while he waited there in the empty porch, he didn't know if he had done the right thing coming here, intruding, so late into the night. But he stayed.

He stayed because, though gentle and faint, he heard well the voices that reminded him of his hidden, invisible rules. My father knew the morning would bring yet another day to load and unload and knock on doors and he needed to sleep. There would have been no sleep with that strange money in his pocket.

My father knocked and waited patiently and quietly. A short stout woman came to the door. It was Mrs. Santini in her nightgown. She took the money and shook her head smiling while she held his hands warmly for a long while in hers and then my father left.

It was late and he should have been tired but all of a sudden he was strong. He felt so strong he could have leaped, perhaps even flown over and beyond the moon that unveiled the immense prairie's night sky.

Chestnuts

Take an old frying pan

With a hammer and nail punch holes
all over the bottom

Prepare the chestnuts by cutting a little slit into each of
them (or they will burst in your face)

Place them in the pan and over the fire

When roasted (while still on fire)
drench with brandy

Peel the charred skin off and eat

Chestnuts

I ASKED MAMMAROSA about the meaning of the words above the words that were in my mother's new letter: "They shall mount up on wings as eagles and they shall run and not grow weary."

I could ask my Mammarosa questions and hound her with a million whos and whys and she never tired and she never fussed. She always had time.

Mammarosa pulled her favourite little child chair by the fireplace, close to mine. "Sometimes while we walk on our life's journey, we encounter dangers, terrible dangers, big mountains. Unaware, your very next step could be the edge of a ravine, or the earth on the escarpment might crumble under your very feet. Or all of a sudden the mountain could become too steep and impossible to climb and it is then that you discover who and why you really are." Mammarosa was about to say much more but her head bounced up and down on her chest and her eyes were very tired. So I too closed my eyes.

I remember once my aunt, Ceci, Peppe and I lingered for a little too long at the vineyard. Even as the clouds above the mountains crowded into each other to form the wildest, darkest beasts ever to inhabit the sky, we still lingered. There were so many chestnuts scattered all over the road and we wanted to collect all of them into our sacks. The chestnuts had not fallen there willingly. The wind had shaken the trees and most of them fell still wrapped in their porcupine-needle skins. There were many and they were prickly. It took us a long time before we started on our way back home to San Giovanni.

It was late in the evening already when we came to the place on our journey where we—my aunt, Ceci, Peppe and I—came face to face with a mountain, a real mountain! It was the mountain that faced San Giovanni on the other side of the Neto River. We saw it in the distance, but before we even set foot on it, we were caught in the middle of a storm, a raging war among those dark beasts above it in the sky. The eagles perched high on the pines looked down and stirred nervously as if to warn us when we approached the mountain. "Danger, danger," it seemed they said as they flew overhead.

We all walked close together, hand in hand, my aunt, Ceci, Peppe and I. We had become one body, feeling our way through the sudden deep darkness. The wind hissed and howled and fought with the trees on the slope at the summit and on the descent. The trees bent and bowed to the earth, and some of them, no matter how much they bowed, snapped before my very eyes.

By the time we reached the summit the rain pelted our heads and bodies. The sky was black. The earth dissolved as we walked down the descent. It shook and trembled under our feet. Whole pieces of it broke off the mountain and rolled down towards the engorged Neto River below.

As a rule, we should have run. Back on the streets of San Giovanni, when the rain took me by surprise I did run. I ran and ran until I was safely home. But on this mountain, we dared not take a single step in a hurry. The blackness was too thick. We heard the waters rushing below but there was no way to tell how far up the banks the river had overflowed. One wrong step and we could have been just like any of the fallen branches or the loose rocks that tumbled down the slope and were carried away by the raging waters.

We did not run. To run across the newly formed ravines and escarpments, which were hidden by the darkness, was a sure way to die. So we waited, patiently; even when we felt like running we waited for the lightning to strike across the sky and illumine our path to the bridge below, if indeed it was still there over the Neto River, before we stepped forward. We waited patiently, but we did not sit and do nothing, oh no. To wait patiently is not the same as sitting and doing nothing.

I heard Mammarosa's words which warned, "To sit and do nothing is certain death, as certain as running carelessly across the ravines." So we stood, we always stood while we waited. We never sat. We felt our way around gently and then stepped forward but only when the lightning lit the path. I remember I was very frightened of the lightning, as much as I was of the sound of the rushing waters below. I closed my eyes at first and let Peppe drag me along. I hid my face under his arm as my feet shuffled beside his, until slowly, one eye at a time, I befriended the lights that ripped the sky. Together, one body, hand in hand, we made it across the bridge over the waters that roared below.

The eagles flew even in the middle of the storm. They flew as the rain poured and the thunder roared. I saw them when the lightning struck. They flew overhead, back and forth across the sky, as if they wanted us to follow them to safety on the other side. But we didn't have wings like the eagles, so we descended the mountain carefully and fearfully. We did not fly high above it at all, like the eagles did.

When we arrived home that night Mammarosa said it didn't matter. She said that we all—Ceci, Peppe and I too—were eagles. She said we were eagles, even if we really didn't fly. She said we were eagles from the time we were little, when we not only couldn't fly, when we hardly even walked.

Figs

Open figs in half

Place a walnut piece in each half

Join back together

Bake until golden brown

Figs

AS SOON AS WE WERE OLD enough and steady enough on our feet we walked to Mammarosa's vineyards, all of us, Nina, Ceci, Peppe, Julia and I. The vineyards and the house on Via Monterosa were the torch that Mammarosa's father and mother entrusted to her. It was her job to keep that torch flaming bright and she did. Once, for no reason at all that I could see, a woman passing through Via Monterosa smiled at Mammarosa and said, "Don't shake your hips in such a fury, Maro'." Yes, my Mammarosa was in a hurry sweeping the steps and her hips were moving a little, but you should have seen this woman's hips! She walked with a big basket of fresh bread balanced on her head with no help from her hands at all. But her hips shook in more than a fury, they swayed to the right and they swayed to the left, like a boat in troubled waters they swayed. "Don't fret and don't hurry. When the hips shake in such a fury, the balls get damaged." The woman went on and on, and then she laughed and Mammarosa put her broom down and laughed too.

I saw Mammarosa change her skirt when we arrived at the vineyard once. She didn't say "Go out and play now," like she said to Ceci and Peppe, just to get them out of the room. So I was there when she took off her good skirt to put on the one she wore for working among the vines. I looked and there were no balls that I could see. She may have had them hidden inside maybe, because after my Papagiuseppe died, and even after my father left for America and there were no men left in the house, her vineyard still blossomed. She pruned it, she tilled it, she harvested the fruit and it flourished just like the ones tended by Paolino and Sciurillu next door, and they were men, and they for sure had balls.

Mammarosa's vineyards were far, past a whole different set of mountains, over the Neto River bridge, beyond the cypress fence around the holy grounds where my Papagiuseppe rested. This was a long way from San Giovanni, but when you got there, and stood in front of the house at the vineyard, what a sight you would see!

Far above the hills, if you stretched your neck (if you could), you would see a patch of blue, and that was not the sky, it was the sea. Never on the hills of Macchia di Fava would you ever see a patch of white. Not even in the harshest winter did the snow ever dot the green hills. There it was, always the blue of both the sky and the sea that marked the horizon at the vineyard.

Peppe complained and sometimes cried when he walked to the vineyard. Mammarosa picked him up and carried him and promised him lots of grapes and figs and raisins and peaches and blackberries which grew at the vineyard. The promise made him smile and walk until he got tired one more time and then Mammarosa had to remind him of grapes and figs and blackberries again.

When I was old enough to walk to the vineyard, I too got tired and complained, and then it was Peppe that carried me a little ways and promised me grapes, figs and blackberries. But when we left the main road and started our descent towards the valley that was Macchia di Fava, I never complained, not once.

There was a cold, lively spring right off the main road at the very start of that fragrant valley. The spring was capped by an emerald slippery rock and the sun shone on the water that gushed all around the rock, making it shimmer. The water ran along our side of the valley down to Mammarosa's vineyard and beyond, between the hills, and then finally it became part of that blue spot on the horizon that was the sea. A warm breeze swept through the trees along the descent and teased my nostrils with the delicious fragrance of Mammarosa and Peppe's promise. Time no longer mattered when we walked down the descent and no one asked, "When will we be there, are we there yet?"

I ran to catch the sun-rays when they played hide-and-seek through ferns and tall grasses along the way, and in no time I had walked to the little house at the vineyard, no, I had raced there, and I felt as swift and light as a butterfly. In San Giovanni butterflies did not stop to kiss the flowers. At the vineyard, though, right in front of our little door, they came in swarms dense as clouds to chase a single bumblebee from their tree.

At the vineyard, when wild fennel was blond and the sun baked it hot, when the figs cracked open and the bees drank their tears, then the grapes were ripe. I helped Mammarosa bake cluster after cluster of ripe grapes until they shrivelled up and smelled sweet. I helped her bake the figs, the white and the black too. We baked them in the brick oven next to the little door of the house at the vineyard.

Sometimes we split the figs open and stuffed the purple halves with walnuts which Peppe and Ceci had gathered from the side of the road. Mammarosa was very careful with the figs she baked because in winter when we woke at night and cried, she would reach and give us a handful of figs from a basket on the dresser by the bed. After the figs had cooled and set, we carried them gently in sacks, on foot, all the way back to San Giovanni.

Once, while we climbed up the valley with the figs dangling from our backs, Paolino passed alongside us with his two donkeys. He too was heading back to San Giovanni. Paolino said "buon giorno" to Mammarosa with his eyes down, fixed on the stones and rubble on the road, when suddenly he jumped back. A snake had just crossed his path! He looked frightened for a brief moment and then he laughed. It was a harmless black snake that wound its body around pebbles and stones across our path. So we all laughed.

It was when he lifted his head to laugh that Paolino saw the bunch of us—Mammarosa, Nina, Ceci, Peppe and I—all loaded and weighed down with figs, sacks of figs. Well, all except me, I only carried a basket because I was just a child. Paolino insisted. Although his donkeys were loaded, he still pulled at Mammarosa's heavy sack and dumped it on one of his donkeys' backs.

I told Mammarosa I didn't understand why Paolino, who was walking in the middle of his two donkeys, decided to load our heavy sack of figs on the donkey who was already carrying the bigger load. I needed to know why, so I tugged at Mammarosa's skirt. She pulled my body close to her side, whispering, "Paolino knows his donkeys and he knows on which to put the load," and then she pressed her fingers against my lips.

I did not like Paolino. Paolino was unfair to the donkeys and Mammarosa was unfair to me because I had to keep silent just when I wanted to keep on talking. So I frowned, even pouted, the whole trip back to San Giovanni. So unfair! It was so unfair.

Mammarosa told me that once, a long time ago, before my mother and father went to America—in 1943, in fact, she said it was, during the time of that terrible world fight—a big storm hit San Giovanni. Don Antonio and the other priests carried St. John's statue down the mountain and set him up on the altar of the church in the piazza and said a special mass for the storm to stop. But the winds and the rains did not obey. Mammarosa said she waited. She waited and waited and she prayed. She prayed that the angry wind would not blow the black clouds in the direction of the vineyards.

When the rain subsided she set out to see if the storm had visited Macchia di Fava. Sure enough, when she got to the vineyards it was very clear that the wind and the rain had been there. The fig trees had had such a shaking and a quaking she was surprised their roots were not naked and exposed. Not one fig was left on the branches of the trees. They had fallen, all of them, to the ground. She was able to save no more than a handful. She picked them carefully, like brands out of a fire, gently laid them in a basket and carried them to the little house. The rest of the figs just lay there already rotting on the ground.

"Unfair," I shouted at Mammarosa after she told me this story. I was all mixed up and confused. I frowned and pouted. And this time she did not press her fingers against my lips, she let me talk.

I talked and talked and reminded her that once when I had complained about walking the endless miles to the vineyard she had frowned at me. She said I should have been thrilled at the very thought of going to the vineyard because vineyards were special. So special that even God had a vineyard. She said the fig trees were special among all other trees because fig trees gave and gave. Even their leaves they gave for us to eat.

I reminded her of something else. She had said that in his vineyard, God loved the fig tree the best, although He cared for the grapes too, because God loves everything and everybody. "Do you remember?" I asked. "Do you remember?" "Yes, I remember."

"Well, then, why? Why? I can't understand! If the fig tree was so good and was loved the best, why did God close His eyes when the wind and the rain tore through the vineyard and ripped the figs off the trees?" The vines and the grapes had been shaken too but it was the fig tree that had taken the real beating during that terrible storm in the year of that terrible war.

I told Mammarosa that Don Antonio in religion class said only the bad get punished. And then I asked why and why and a million more whys. So many that if Mammarosa had been at all like my aunt, by now she would have turned around and slapped my face after she slapped her own.

Why? I asked.

Why is my father not here?

Why does he not visit like Maria Pia's father?

Why is Biasi in a wheelchair?

Why is Mr. Ficosecco in charge of the lunch cards?

Why can't I have books?

Why did Teresa and not Nando die?

Why do we grow old and die?

Why? Why? Why? I asked Mammarosa.

But she walked ahead calmly without saying a word. Even while I tugged at her skirt she kept her tranquil pace. Not once did she say "quiet," and all the more I shouted "Unfair!" and asked why.

Why can't I be beautiful?

Why can't my hair be like Maria Pia's?

Why? Were the figs bad? Am I bad?

"Oh, no, no!" Mammarosa finally replied as she pulled me close by her side. "You are not bad and the figs were not bad either. God knows the fig tree and He knows you." Mammarosa said I was good and the figs were good too, even on the ground where they fell, they were good. "What is judged as worthless can sometimes turn out to be something very good and very beautiful," she said.

On Mr. Spadafora's counter I had seen tons of worthless, ugly and broken things. But every piece he turned into something beautiful. I saw Mr. Spadafora do it like magic, right before my very eyes. I remember watching Mr. Spadafora from outside the window of his goldsmith shop on Via Roma not too far from San Giovanni's little railway station.

I went there often, pressing my face right against the glass of his window so I could watch him work more closely. He pumped the fire, not a big one like the one at the blacksmith's shop, but a fire just the same.

With a sweep of his hand, Mr. Spadafora cleared the counter of old bracelets, bent earrings, old teeth and other broken pieces that no one, if they saw them lying on the street, would guess to be gold, and he threw them in the fire. But Mr. Spadafora knew.

I watched him as he melted the worthless lot and I saw it bubble over the flame. I watched him as he poured and cooled, and heated and beat, and heated and cooled the shiny liquid over and over again, until before my very eyes he held a beautiful flower with petals and leaves. Once I even saw him put red and green and blue stones on the petals of a flower that he made.

Mammarosa had a gold flower. Her Mammateresa gave it to her when she was just a child. It had a pin attached to it and she wore it to keep her head-covering in place.

Once I asked old Mr. Spadafora (not his son because his son always motioned me to go away when I peeked through the window of his shop) why gold cost so much money, and why they had to put it in the fire and beat it so much.

Old Mr. Spadafora sat on a chair by the door of his shop to take a little sun. He wore a jacket even in the summer, although I don't think his shaking was because he was cold. Mammarosa said that he was just plain old. He didn't mind when children stopped by and sat on the stone pavement by his chair to ask him why.

When I asked the question old Mr. Spadafora laughed and his whole belly shook. After he finished laughing he put his hand gently on my head and said that one had to go through a lot of dirt to find a little gold. "Lots of dirt looks like gold. But no one would waste time putting dirt through the fire and beating it because you can heat it and beat it all you want. Dirt is dirt and it will never be gold. Only gold is worth the fire and only gold is worth the hammer. Only gold."

Mammarosa could make nice things too. I remember that once she turned a useless dead branch which had fallen off a fig tree during that same terrible storm of 1943 into a little wooden horse for Ceci and Peppe with nothing but the tiny folding knife in her pocket.

She could fix and she could make things. She could even make fire. Yes, I remember, Mammarosa could indeed make fire. She didn't make fire just for the fun of it, oh no. The maids that answered the doors of the doctors' beautiful homes in San Giovanni knew exactly what Mammarosa carried hidden in her apron. They pulled her quickly in the vestibule before they gave her money.

Making fire was a secret so Nina, Ceci, Peppe, Julia

and I took turns making sure the guard, who patrolled the vineyards and the forests in the area, was not in sight when she climbed up the ladder to reach into the high storage tanks to get the special shiny pot with the long thin spouts from where the fire would come out.

Mammarosa used the worthless and crushed remains of grapes that lay in a stinking pile in the corner of the little house at the vineyard to make fire. Fire for the learned, for the healing of wounds and the soothing of sores. She made it from the lifeless dried bunches. To look at them you would never know that once they had been luscious clusters of plump juicy grapes at all. But she did not think they were useless. A little at a time she put them in the special pot, added a little wine and then boiled it long after we had all fallen asleep.

Once I struggled and fought with my sticky eyelids that wanted to stay shut—but I won! I did not fall asleep so I heard the dead remains of the crushed grapes roll and tumble in the wine. I heard them hiss and scream inside the pot as it boiled and boiled on the flames in the fireplace. And then just as my eyelids were about to close, and my head to fall heavy on Mammarosa's lap, I saw her reach and catch the first few falling drops from the spout into a spoon.

What came out did not look at all like what was inside the pot. It did not look like wine and it certainly did not look at all like dry leftover grape peels. It was clear like the rain and shimmered like the water that gushed from the spring at the top of our mountain. And when Mammarosa placed the spoonful of it over the fire it burst into a high-reaching flame with the sound of the wind at its tail. She stepped back and pushed me back too.

Mammarosa could fix and make things just like Mr. Spadafora, she could even make fire, but she couldn't fix the dead fig mess that lay all over the vineyard the day of that terrible storm.

And I told her that but she said it didn't matter because there was nothing to fix. Even those dead crushed and rotting figs that had fallen during the storm of 1943 were not worthless, because right where they had fallen they would bake and shrivel in the hot sun and then they would turn to dust, fine and white dust, like the ashes in the hearth of our fireplace. And although it did not happen suddenly, although it would take a long while, even then, when they were still visible on the ground, the rotting figs were already at work.

They were valuable and they had work to do. The ashes would climb up the roots of the weakened tree and nourish it. And then someday, when their work was done and the tree had gained its strength, they would appear on the branches of those same beaten trees as fragrant blossoms that turned into figs. Champion figs to pick, Mammarosa said.

And there were! Although it was not until the spring of five years later, after the storm, when the real champions began to appear on our fig trees, the ones that Nina, Ceci, Peppe, Julia and I ate now were indeed the best. "Strange, isn't it," Mammarosa said, "that out of death should come life." I think she wanted me to smile, but I didn't. I frowned. Mammarosa asked me if I thought she too was worthless because soon, she said, she would lie down like the figs after the storm, die and turn to ashes. "No, no, you must never die and turn to ashes."

Although, when I looked at the hands that held mine, I saw that they were already shrivelled. There was nothing but a veil of transparent skin covering her blue veins and protruding bones. No, no, I would not let Mammarosa shrivel and turn to ashes. I would hide her from the storm in a very special chamber in my mind and there she would live forever. I would keep the keys of this secret chamber safely hidden, entangled among the hair-like roots of my very special tree on the ravine. Only those who took the long way to school and stopped to caress a lonely naked tree would find the keys to this special secret chamber.

Biscotti

Equal weight of flour and honey
An orange squeezed
An orange peel
Vanilla
Amaretto liqueur
A pinch of baking soda
A little baking powder
One egg and lots of almonds
Mix it all in a bowl
Shape into two loaves (they will be
a little sticky and that's okay)
Bake until golden
Remove from oven
Slice into long wedges
Return them to the oven to be
twice (bis)
baked (cotti)

Biscotti

MAMMAROSA WAS PROUD of her vineyard but most of all she was proud of her figs. She was proud of all of us but most of all she was proud of Peppe.

Peppe came home all sweating and out of breath one day. My aunt was about to shout at him, "Don't waste precious energy running, you need to grow . . . ," and she would have gone on about food and money and sweat and ice and snow and all that stuff but after Peppe emptied his pocket on the table she stopped short and stood there with her mouth open and nothing to say. There on the old table among the dry rounds of bread we called biscotti (no, not at all the same as the twice-baked, sweet, crumbly things that Carletta and Sara ate; those were made with oil, butter, sugar and honey that all cost tons of money) Peppe had laid a shiny smooth leather wallet bulging with bills, lots of bills for tons of oil, butter and sugar and honey.

We stood around silent while my aunt counted the

bills. Three times. And each time she ended the count with the same number. Thirty-three. Thirty-three thousand. At the end of every count her hands flew in every direction as she said, "Quiet, be quiet," and we had not said even one word.

I saw her stop for a brief instant to take a deep quiet breath while she looked at us all gathered around our meal of stale bread at the table. Then she quickly grabbed Peppe's hand and the wallet with the money and darted out towards Bernardo's house. She didn't need Bernardo to tell her whose wallet it was because there were papers with the man's name all over it. But my aunt still thought first to go to Bernardo.

Maybe she thought Bernardo was like Don Antonio, who had the power to make everything holy by sprinkling water on it, even lira bills. It's true! When Dr. Mauri had enough bills in his special wallet at home so he could count up to a million, he threw a big party and Don Antonio was there as a special guest for the special purpose of sprinkling water over the wallet. It turned out that Bernardo (although he never sprinkled the money with special water) did know the man whose wallet Peppe had found and told my aunt precisely where to go.

The gentleman lived in a new elegant palazzo, just before the elementary school at the bottom of the hill, not far from Lucrezia's house. I played on that street almost every day. I had seen the tall forbidding structure with its marble threshold and the gold button on the side of the door for visitors to press if they wanted to enter. I had never seen anyone come out of that door. Their doors were shut like Professor Ciano's and Dr. Mauri's. They must have that new American heating system. I can't imagine a palazzo like that without it. I can't imagine people with that kind of money not having it. They had geraniums, red, white and pink, climbing up the iron balconies, because in America people have flowers everywhere. These were Americans and they had never been out of San Giovanni.

I squeezed myself between Peppe and my aunt when they went in, so there I was, inside the palace too. I don't know for how long my mouth stayed open. There was endless marble on the floor, on the stairs, and halfway up the walls. And gold trim everywhere. Gold and sparkling stones. The lightbulbs shined through crystal shapes. They didn't just hang from a black wire in the middle of the room like ours did. And there were lots and lots of lights that danced and sparkled when the breeze touched them as we entered. Not like our one lightbulb that cast scary shadows on the walls when it blinked off and on by itself for no reason.

The man was very nice and he offered my aunt and Peppe espresso and his wife gave me biscotti, sweet crumbly biscotti. She passed them around and each time I ate and ate and each time there was room in my stomach for just one more of this kind of biscotti.

Lucrezia's mother (the same woman who spit and spat on account of me, unchristened, being in her house) saw my aunt, Peppe and I, the whole bunch of us devils, go in the beautiful palazzo (much more beautiful than hers) and we stayed. I stayed and looked and looked, and no one said go, like at Lucrezia's house or at the Cianos' house the night I finally got to see the television.

Yes, I must tell you that finally I did get to see what a television was really like. I don't know how, but one evening the Cianos' had a change of heart and let a whole bunch of us children come in and watch television.

I got in, but didn't stay long. I saw the black box with the glass face in a special room all of its own. It towered high on a metal stand. Hidden under a special embroidered cotton cover, full and flowing, like that of a veil on a bride. Professor Ciano lifted the cover off gently and slowly. No, he didn't kiss the television, he switched on a button and adjusted a dial.

Everyone sat motionless, in awe, with their mouths open and their eyes fixed on the television. Except me. The sounds, and the sights, and the people, and everything in that box were so real that it was impossible for me to stay motionless. I had tried to sit still and be polite like the rest. I even put my hands under my thighs but I couldn't stay glued to the chair for very long.

So I got up quietly, and on all fours, under chairs and on the floor, I crawled until I was under and then behind the television. I was not restless because I was bored, oh no, I loved Popeye. I had seen Popeye stickers on the Galbani chocolate-spread bars. In fact, Sara and I played with a big Popeye balloon that we punched and punched and it always came back up for more. Mancuso gave Sara the balloon because she had bought so many Galbani chocolate bars and kept all the stickers.

What made me anxious about the television was the unexplainable question in my mind of how people became so small and how it was that they were able to enter and fit in that tiny box. How was it that men and women kissed and moved and talked during *Carosello*, all in that little box? I would be happy to sit and be quiet and fix my eyes just like the rest as soon as I had discovered how that happened. That's why I was behind and under the television in Professor Ciano's house in that dark room with all the lights out while everyone gathered and sat politely to watch.

Something inside of me warned me that I was up to no good when I first left my chair, headed for that spot in the corner where the back of the television was exposed. I should have listened. Every time I tried to answer these kinds of questions that troubled my mind, I always got in trouble.

I got in trouble the last time a package from my mother in America arrived. Under the tea and the chocolate squares, the sugar and the cocoa, was a doll. Two dolls actually, one for me and one for Julia. After I delivered equal packages (my aunt was careful they all had to be equal) to the neighbours, which contained three bags of tea, one square of chocolate, a cupful of sugar and a cupful of cocoa, I played with my doll.

The doll actually cried! I would have gladly played with the doll like everybody else but I couldn't. Not until I found out what made my doll cry. She was fine when she was on her tummy but when I lifted her up she cried. I thought maybe she didn't like me. I made my doll cry and cry and then, even before I had given her a name, my mind got troubled with unanswered questions about crying dolls and I just wanted to know why.

So when no one was looking, when it was just me and Julia in the house and we played making our dolls cry, I got up quietly and went through all of my aunt's drawers until I found her pair of scissors hidden under a pile of letters in white envelopes with blue and red ridges.

Julia watched me cut. First across my doll's ankles and then across her wrists and then across her tummy. "Don't worry," I said to Julia, who was clutching her doll tightly against her chest. "I will get a new doll and then I will use the cut-outs for shoes and gloves and pants."

While I said this, my fingers found a little round can with holes in it. I discovered then that my doll was not unhappy, she was not crying at all, it was this little box that was making all the noise.

I turned to Julia and asked her if she too wanted to see what made her doll cry. She looked at me funny with wide-open eyes and swung her doll hard right on my face, mostly across my eyes, and for a moment I thought it was night and someone had turned off the lights.

I remember that the lights were off and the room was dark at the Cianos'. They were until the professor spotted me under and behind the television. Soon there was a rustling of chairs and shuffling of feet and someone turned the light switch on. All of a sudden the attention was on me, on the floor on all fours, with my dress all dirty and my hair all over the place, full of lint fluffs.

There was a commotion!

Professor Ciano slapped his bald spot and then he asked his wife for a handkerchief to wrap his head in. She got up as if to get the handkerchief, I thought, but instead she turned towards me, stiffly, with her lips tightly pursed. She grabbed my hand and led me swiftly to the door. I didn't say anything and my friends didn't either. I think they were all glad to watch television without me there.

Now, the woman at this gentleman's house, where Peppe, my aunt and I went, didn't show me the door. She let me look around and she stroked my cheeks with hands that felt like silk and I touched anything I wanted. I was very careful though. I brushed over the stones and golden trims with my fingers, not my whole hand.

The gentleman that lived in this house was glad we came and he too didn't mind if I looked and touched. He built palazzi and hired men to do the work and at the end of each week he paid them with money, except for this week, because his wallet had gone missing.

My aunt counted the money in the wallet that Peppe found in the man's presence and then she handed the bundle and the wallet to him across the table. "Thirty-three thousand," my aunt said.

"Thirty-three thousand," the man replied and smiled.

He took the money and gave Peppe three thousand of it. Then he shook Peppe's hand. Peppe was just a young boy. (He could have bought lots of sweet biscotti.) But Mammarosa said that Peppe was big.

Wine

Crush grapes until the peels are dry
Place the juice in a barrel or jugs
Let it boil and boil and boil
When the boiling stops, seal carefully
Several times a year filter the wine over and over gently until the "mother" (at the bottom) has totally disappeared

Wine

MAMMAROSA SAID THAT WE WERE BIG even when we looked so small, that we were eagles even if we didn't fly at all. She said this to all of us—Nina, Ceci, Peppe, Julia and even me. But there was one thing she didn't say to everyone. There was one thing she said and meant only for Nina, Julia and me. (And my sister in Canada too, of course.)

She would never say it to our faces. Oh no, she couldn't possibly look into our eyes and say, "You are barrels of wine and we have to get rid of you right away before you will turn to useless vinegar." No, never would she say it. But once or twice I did see Mammarosa nod in agreement with some of the old and wise women when they said, "Oh, please, God forbid. Not a daughter! Daughters are wine barrels to be rid of as soon as possible because wine can turn to vinegar and men drink wine, not vinegar."

My aunt and Mammarosa made wine. My aunt

rushed around when we made wine and Mammarosa called out to her and every one of us, "Be careful and do it right, you hear? Remember the cat that rushes has blind kittens." But we still hurried with the basketfuls of grapes. And sure enough, when we hurried, the grapes slipped on the ground and then it took twice as long to do the job and twice as long before we could climb onto the "parmiento" and start stomping the plump clusters with our bare feet. And that was the fun part of making wine!

Mammarosa didn't rush. She didn't rush to make it, she didn't rush to sell it, and that is why I can't understand this rushing to get rid of daughters and get rid of wine stuff coming from her.

I know where she got this idea! I am quite sure she got it while loitering on Piotta's patio with the women when she was just a little girl. While they sat on Piotta's patio, women spoke of wine and vinegar all the time, forgetting that they too were daughters.

I heard Maria Francesca (she was always at Piotta's patio) say that she was only sixteen when her father said yes to the man who became her husband. She had never seen this man before but her father insisted. "It's not as if you bring a profit into this house like your brothers. You don't work and it's expensive to keep you in school with all the books and clothes and things you need. Now is a good time for you to go. He is a good man and you will marry him." And that was that.

Then he pinched the butt of his cigarette between his fingers and sucked on it real hard. A whole cloud of smoke came out of his mouth. Even while he lifted his glass and sipped his wine the smoke still spewed out of his mouth, filling the room, and Maria Francesca's eyes started to water. Her mother just stood there nodding, agreeing with the devil, with nothing of her own to say.

Maria Francesca said that she was only seventeen when she delivered her first child. "When the labour got rough the midwife called the doctor," she recalled. But when Maria Francesca saw Dr. Rafaelino in his white overcoat, approaching the bed with his bulging little leather case, she closed her legs in the middle of a strong contraction and screamed.

Dr. Rafaelino understood. He went in the other room and from there gave the midwife instructions. "She is just a frightened little girl," he said when the midwife apologized. What he should have said was that she was wine, and not vinegar, and it would not have hurt if she had stayed a little longer with her mother where she belonged.

Once Mammarosa sent me to get a bottle of wine from the downstairs cellar and I remember her saying I should be careful and not shake it. When I gave her the bottle she pointed to the dark murky area at the bottom and said, "This is the mother."

Mammarosa said that wine, whether in barrels or in bottles, always rested on its mother, and that wine was not good until it had totally "shed and deposited, or acquired," whatever it was that it needed to "shed and deposit." It was a give and get between the mother and the wine. Wine was not wine until this exchange was truly and fully done. It was complicated, this mother and wine idea, so to make sure I understood I said to Mammarosa, "Oh, you mean that taking wine from its mother before it's time would be like making a baby come out and cutting the cord before it was fully grown and could breathe on its own?" "Yes, wine is just like people," she said.

The "mother" at the bottom of the wine bottle was patient and never rushed, but not some mothers in San Giovanni. Maria Francesca's mother had rushed. She had married her daughter off in a hurry to the man her husband chose. And because the dowry was not ready (on account of the terrible rush), they agreed with the groom and his parents that some of it would follow at a later time.

It never did and Maria Francesca's husband never let her forget it. Neither did her mother-in-law, who had a list of the missing linens and things and money. Maria Francesca's husband started to drink, because that was what he saw his father do, and when he did, he told his wife the same old story. "Your parents unloaded you on me, they sent you away with nothing but a few rags. But don't worry! I have big shoulders! I'm a good donkey. I can do it. I can lug you!" He kept on and on while he ripped the sheets off the bed in a fury and flung them across the room.

Maria Francesca let him speak. She kept silent and looked after her children while he raged. Maria Francesca had learned to be silent a long time ago. The very first week she was married she learned that silence was a safe island, a perfect place to retreat.

Maria Francesca said she was actually happy those very first days. She looked forward to going to the fields and being close to him. She carved a whole loaf of bread and filled it with fried red and green peppers, tomatoes, garlic and basil, tons of basil. Maria Francesca followed him to the fields that day on foot. She couldn't ride the donkey because her husband had loaded him with tons of things and the poor beast was having a hell of a time himself climbing the steep slopes.

In the fields, Maria Francesca spread the lunch on a tablecloth on the grass and called out to her husband when the sun was high in the sky. "I poured the wine and then sat on his lap while I lovingly handed him the glass with a big smile," she said.

She sat on his lap? I thought. Did I hear this right? Aie, even I knew better. And where had Maria Francesca been!? In America, maybe?

She said she didn't think. She just followed this warm longing to hold him and caress the rough weathered skin of his tired face and perhaps even kiss his forehead. It was the first of those very first, special days. She tried to love him, to shower him with kisses and caresses as if he was her very own, as if he had come from within her, as if he was part of herself. She tried to embrace him and hold him tightly to her breasts but he would not be held.

Instead, within her arms she gathered fire, a blazing devouring flame. He burned hot. "You women are all the same, whores, whores is all you are!" Maria Francesca's husband grabbed the glass and removed his knee from under her, shoving her to the ground.

That's when she first kept silent.

"I was so lonely and there was such emptiness around me. Actually a fullness, I should say, because I had and wanted to give so much but there was no one to give it to."

No one until that first child, a daughter, was born when she was only seventeen. The child soaked up her love, she cooed, she smiled, and even cried when her mother wasn't near. When Maria Francesca's husband came home she did not go near him. She waited in silence for the wine to dull his senses as the last words of the old-rag story faded on his lips: "Nothing but a few rags, they gave you." She never replied. She just kept silent.

And when Dr. Rafaelino shook his finger towards her husband and said "No wine," again she kept silent. Maria Francesca didn't say a word when her husband replied that he didn't even make wine.

And he didn't. He didn't care about making wine. He didn't care if it was red or white or rosé or what fragrance it aroused in his mouth. In fact, once Maria Francesca had a jug of vinegar in the cupboard that she was going to use to preserve a good bushel of green tomatoes she had picked in the fields. But as soon as he saw the wine jug he demanded it. Maria Francesca forgot to keep silent and tried to reason with him, but he pushed her out of the way and drank the whole jug that very night.

"Your liver is showing bad signs," Dr. Rafaelino said as he moved his hands across his chest. "Bad signs," he repeated when he pried his eyes open to take a deep and long look. He heard Dr. Rafaelino and grunted but he never listened and Maria Francesca kept silent. She kept him happy and poured him a few extra glasses, even when he was not asking. And he drank them every time, until his liver refused to pump any more of the stuff, just like Dr. Rafaelino had warned.

The night her husband died, Maria Francesca couldn't force one single tear out of her eyes. In fact soon after she pinched his eyelids shut, while his body was still warm on the bed, she went to the cupboard and pulled out a sausage, and for the first time she even poured herself a good glass of wine. Maria Francesca and her sister, who was there with her, ate and drank, and then they put on the show. They rushed out of the house, as was expected, howling and crying and tearing at their faces. I was not surprised to hear what Maria Francesca said. On the other hand, what is a woman to do?

Someone should put a stop to this big wine sale, I remember saying to the women on Piotta's patio. But they looked at me funny. "Not so." They insisted that when wine is kept too long it turns to vinegar and that is irreversible. You are stuck with it for good. "And I say that when you disturb the wine and remove it from its 'mother' too soon you have no wine at all," I shouted. And then I ran because I saw one of the older women put down her embroidering and shuffle her chair, threatening to get up. She stared at me with her chin dragging on the patio. "Azzo, even the chicks want a say in the coop!"

Men would tell you that wine is a delicate thing to make. I don't know what could be so delicate about crushing something until it is unrecognizable! But anyway, they said you had to work with it while it was young and still boiled if you held hopes of transforming it into something you could call your very own creation. It had to be young and boiling because it was not easy to attain a delicate rosé colour or a deep clear red if it had sat too long somewhere. It was not easy to evoke the fragrance of the forest floor or the aroma of wild berries after wine had finished boiling, they said.

Once I sipped wine from an elegant crystal glass at a wedding. I was not invited to the wedding but Barbara next door brought me along so I could play with her daughter's little boy while they ate and danced. I was not at the vineyard and yet it was those berries that grew among the thorns and climbed as if to escape over the stone wall that I smelled and tasted when the wine touched my lips that day at the wedding.

It was a delicate thing making wine, men said. Everything mattered. Each little detail gave a different twist to the fragrance, the bubble and the taste of the wine. I heard grown men argue over how to filter wine, and when the wine had shed, and when it was time to separate it completely from its mother. They argued where best to keep the wine—glass bottles, big jugs, small jugs, wooden barrels, in a cold or in a warm spot. They argued, disagreed and shouted because men took pride in their skills to make wine.

Men did not argue though over this one fundamental belief about making wine: nothing, absolutely nothing, was to be done without first observing the sky. It was the cycle of the moon that determined the fate of the wine. No one argued over this point, no one except Mammarosa, who turned up her nose at this important rule. She said that when you walked you had to be careful and watch your step and if you spent time gazing and staring at the sky for directions you could end up down some ravine without ever knowing how it was that you got there.

Some time ago in the middle of the crowd at the market, I saw Maria Francesca gesturing and shouting at her mother, who was walking further ahead. Maria Francesca was angry and was shouting loudly above the crowd, "Disgraziata, wait up, disgraziata." I heard Maria Francesca call her mother "disgraziata" with my own ears! If my aunt ever caught me saying "disgraziata" she would pull my hair as hard as if I had failed a subject at school.

Once I called Ceci "disgraziato" and my aunt heard me but since she thought it was my first time she decided just to give me a warning. "Never, never!" She shook her finger so close to my face I was soon wishing she had pulled my hair instead, because eyes, unlike hair, don't grow back. "When you call someone "disgraziato" you are wishing that their mother and father had never lived," my aunt explained.

Oh really? Then why was Maria Francesca calling her mother "disgraziata"?

I asked Mammarosa this question. She said we are not wine whose fate is determined by the moon in the sky and by those who crush and filter and drink until the barrel is dry. Mammarosa said that Maria Francesca had come to a stop. She had come to the foot of an insurmountable mountain and she was just sitting there doing nothing but looking at the moon. And if soon she wouldn't budge, she would die, and the birds of the fields would pluck her eyes out.

I thought Maria Francesca was really frightened and lonely inside even if she didn't look like it and shouted so much. But Mammarosa was right. Maria Francesca was doing nothing.

I promised myself that someday when I would be alone with Maria Francesca at Piotta's patio I would tell her that all she had to do was to go about quietly. And when she sold a sack of grain or potatoes she wouldn't have to buy linens for her daughter just because it was the rule, if she didn't want to. Maybe if one by one we all did that, maybe someday soon, we would grow wings, and no longer would daughters be called wine, but eagles. Eagles are not frightened at the sight of peaks and mountains. They do not gaze at the sky, they have wings and they fly.

I am sure glad Mammarosa didn't shout much, nor did she rush. Except once, yes, only once do I remember that she fretted and almost rushed. It was after we made the new wine. After we went through all the hard work of carrying basket after basket of grapes into the little house. After we stomped all over them with our bare feet, and after we drank the sweet juice that flowed into the vats. Only a few weeks after, Mammarosa fretted and announced that we had to find a buyer for the wine, quickly.

She said we had to because she detected something strange and she didn't want it to be too late because that could cost us a lot. (When wine gave signs of turning to vinegar you had to start adding boiled concoctions of sugar and figs and pears and honey to correct it and keep it sellable.) Mammarosa thought about it for a long time and then decided that she would let the mother that the wine sat on worry about it. And you know what? The wine never turned to vinegar. In fact, it was the very best ever. Mammarosa was glad she didn't rush.

She never went around rushing like the other women. But I do remember her nodding in agreement with women who turned up their noses at wine and daughters and said that they both had to be rushed out of the house before they became vinegar. And I was upset. The very remembrance of that made me upset. Many thoughts came rushing to my mind. I thought hard and while I thought I remembered many things. I remembered words that my aunt had said. She had said that Mammarosa was especially happy whenever the midwife shouted, "It's a boy!"

And I also remembered her saying that when Ceci was born my father went up and down Via Monterosa handing out little glasses of Millefiori liqueur from a big tray. He carried it smiling and shouting thanks for the million congratulations from neighbours and passers-by. And I was upset. I couldn't believe that my father even bought that expensive useless liqueur, knowing that in the end we wouldn't even be able to use the bottle.

I asked my aunt why everyone made such a fuss when Ceci was born and she was very polite. She said that it had nothing to do with girl or boy but it was a celebration of a double gift of life since the birth had been so difficult and my mother's life had been at risk. Somehow I felt that she was not telling the whole truth about Mammarosa's and my father's extra joy when the boys were born. But I did not argue with her, because at least she had been polite.

Tata was not. She had no boys and she didn't care that her daughter Sara was around when she proudly recounted a million times how she had told the midwife to "va fa n'culo" when the poor woman announced that it was a girl she had brought into the world. And you know what? That may be why Sara hissed "va fa n'culo' to Tata, a million times, behind her back. I heard her!

I remembered my aunt saying that when I was born, Caterina, Carletta's mother, came down our steps shouting in her annoying discordant violin voice, "Who cares if it is a girl when they are this beautiful?" Sure, thanks. I was pretty good wine. I could be sold off real quick with no added expenses of sugar and figs and whatever other tricks people did to keep wine sellable.

Anyway, I wasn't there when Ceci was born and I can't remember being there when I was born either, so I really can't say. But this I can say for sure: Peppe and Ceci could trample through the vines with their little wooden horse, no problem. Mammarosa pretended to shout at them but she never did anything. Nina and Julia and I were not even allowed on the horse.

But then I thought other thoughts, and I remembered Nina and Julia and me on Mammarosa's knee. She bounced us up and down in the quiet dark evenings by the fireplace at the vineyard while the crickets sang and the boys galloped on their horse around the house and she hummed. She hummed and sang softly in our ears, "When I cannot walk you will hold me up and when I cannot sleep you will lie with me, you, only you. When to the river I can no longer go, you, only you, will capture the sun that makes the water shimmer and bring it to my bedside to shine on me, you, only you."

In Nina's, Julia's and my ears. Not ever in Ceci or Peppe's because Mammarosa was no fool. She knew that someday sons like Ceci and Peppe married and their wives, although they would still call her mother, and she would call them daughters, would not lie next to her.

They did not know how. They had not nestled against Mammarosa's breasts and they had not rested on

Mammarosa's lap when they first arrived, when their light first shined, when they still spoke with angels.

This was our song. And the words were not those of a woman who wanted to get rid of her daughters. No, she wanted us there, near her, until the very end. And that is why I could not understand this nonsense of nodding in agreement with women who really knew nothing about wine and vinegar.

Anyway, after all this thinking and remembering I looked around and I did not need to remember nor think any longer because right in front of me was the real evidence that we were to stay for a very long time. Mammarosa didn't look worried about us turning to vinegar at all because there were no bottling preparations for us in sight. When my aunt sold a bag of potatoes she bought us a book. When Tata sold a bag of grain she bought Sara linens because Tata saw that Sara was blooming and a flower is at its best when in bloom. We were in bloom too and my aunt made no plans and struck no friendships with women who had eligible young sons, like Sara's mother did.

One time my aunt even whispered that Tata and Sara could keep all their pretty linens and Mammarosa agreed. She said she would rather our brains were full of grey matter than white cotton. If my aunt and Mammarosa really thought we were wine about to turn to vinegar they would not have stressed this grey matter stuff. They would have done the sensible thing, which was to respect tradition and rules and collect cotton and linen like all the other mothers did for their daughters. But they didn't!

For a moment before I pondered and took the time to sort through all the thoughts and memories I felt sad and lonely. I felt the dimming of the lights inside of me, and for a very brief instant I thought Mammarosa was like the gold on the streets of America. It did not shine at all. For a fraction of a second I even entertained the thought of shouting "Horseshit," right to her face. But I didn't because her song rushed out of a special chamber of my mind to rescue Mammarosa, my aunt and me.

There was one thing I still wanted to tell her, though, and it almost slipped off my tongue. I wanted to tell her that if she ever was going to be worried about wine going bad she should keep her eyes on Ceci. He had already turned to vinegar. I am glad I didn't say that because I might have hurt her feelings if I did. You see, she really wanted Ceci to change, and he would someday, I am sure, if there was indeed such a thing as turning vinegar back to wine.

Vinegar

Take a bottle of good wine
Abandon it
Don't care for it
Don't seal it
Don't filter it
In no time at all you will have vinegar

Vinegar

ONCE WHEN MAMMAROSA'S WINE threatened to turn to vinegar she just let it be. She didn't shake it and she didn't stir it and it worked, that wine was the best ever. But not my aunt. She tried to reform Ceci and she tried everything. She tried patience, she tried understanding and even prayer. The last time, when by some fluke Ceci happened to be present at the midweek church service, my aunt even pushed him towards the front, where some very pious men earnestly prayed on his behalf. There were people on every bench wiping their eyes and Nina was sobbing out loud.

I saw it all. You see, it didn't matter if I opened my eyes once in a while during prayer, and no one minded if I looked around because I was still a child. Ceci was standing in the middle of these very fine people, fidgeting. One of the older and more fervent men had his hands wrapped tightly around Ceci's head. It looked as if he were squeezing Ceci's brain. (My aunt always said that

Ceci had a hard head. Maybe this man was trying to do her a favour by softening Ceci's brain a little.) I saw Ceci open and close his eyes to look around, inspecting every corner, door, window and wall. You'd think he was planning a quick escape route.

To tell you the truth, I think that if he wasn't so definitely sure that my aunt would have reduced his thick, hard skull to a pulp with the two-ton hymnal she held in her hands, he would have laughed and roared and thrown himself on the floor of the little church, just like he did at home. And then he would have escaped.

The next day when my aunt saw that Ceci was still the same, she threw up her hands and said that she had had enough of patience, understanding and prayer. She lost it. And she had good reasons to. After all her efforts, even prayer, Ceci was getting worse.

Lately he had started to show up a little unstable at night. What I mean is that his legs were a little weak and they had a hard time deciding which direction to take. They certainly didn't follow a very straight line. One night there was Ceci at the door, limp, held up by two members of his "good fellows company," two bosom buddies of his. One was Geraldo and the other was Nicola. Ceci had a smile on his face but the smile didn't stay long. It was erased by an upset stomach, which decided just then at the door, in front of my aunt, to send all the wine that Ceci had drunk back up.

"Aha and sick too, I see," my aunt said. And then right where he was, on the threshold of our house at 14 Via Monterosa, Ceci fell. He did not fall because his friends no longer wanted to hold him up by the arms. He fell because my aunt decided she'd had enough of putting up with nonsense, enough of patience and enough of good manners.

That was the very evening that her approach for a

solution to a problem called "Ceci" changed. My aunt lifted a nice sturdy chair off the floor and she let it come hard and heavy on his head.

Ceci's friends saw the chair coming and that's why they let go of Ceci's arms and ran. They were young and they were strong but they were no match for my aunt's fury.

My aunt was in a rage and to make matters worse the last sausage count had revealed a few missing links. Sausages were not made once a week or once a month, They were made only once a year, in the dead of winter, and even then you prayed for colder drier weather on the days you made sausages.

The making of sausages, women would tell you, was just as delicate as the making of wine. They were never made in summer because first you had to raise the pig, you know! And pigs were bought in summer.

Lately, every summer we bought at least two pigs. It was thanks to the contents of schellac-sealed letters from America that now there were pigs in the enclosure under our stairs. In fact these schellac-sealed letters arrived more frequently now since my father had met a man whose name was Max Olin at Rogers Wholesale on Fruit Row where he still bought the fruit and vegetables to peddle on the streets of Winnipeg.

Max Olin summoned my father with a wiggle of his index finger into the cold room in Rogers' building. There among boxes of green onions and red peppers he whispered, "I have a deal for you." My father liked the deal. So my mother no longer worked in the clothing factory but in her own grocery store on the first floor of Max Olin's building at the corner of Lydia and Notre Dame.

Max Olin was there almost every day at the beginning, just to help. It was not easy, my mother said in a letter, those very first days. But when she brought in pastas and plum tomatoes and Parmesan cheese and fresh meats she was so busy that she no longer worked alone.

My father soon had to give up a few of his routes. He even sold the car and bought a real truck to deliver groceries to the many new customers' homes.

My mother didn't write as often now, but when she did, the letters always came in brown schellacked envelopes. And this is why every summer lately we bought at least two pigs. My aunt opened the envelopes right where the postman happened to hand them to her, on the stairs, on the street, even in Mancuso's grocery store. She opened the letters and she didn't care if anyone was jealous or nosy because she said she had worked so hard on the land that the skin on her face had acquired the tinge of the soil she tilled. She said she'd had enough of people shaking their heads and saying, "Oh you poor creature, oh you poor thing."

My aunt had money but now decided that she would buy nothing. Ever since my father stopped writing love letters to his homeland my aunt had suspected that they would not be back. But when the letters arrived about the children, the house, the car, and now the store and the truck, she knew, beyond the shadow of a doubt, that they would not be back. And she was not going to buy one thing because America was a long ways off and the less baggage one carried the better it was.

When I say she bought nothing, I mean nothing. When everyone else cooked on a gas stove, we still had to light the fireplace in the heat of the summer to boil the pasta water. The only thing she bought was a clock because one morning Piperella's mother was so annoyed hearing the same question—What time is it, what time is it?"—that she told my aunt it was time to get a clock. So she did.

My aunt and I walked down Via Roma, past Lallo's shoe store and past Lallo's brother's butcher shop. Not too much further down from there was a goldsmith shop. The goldsmith smiled for a little while until my aunt started to turn up her nose at everything he brought out for her to see. He brought out the best, he brought out the worst. He showed her clocks gilded in gold and those dipped in plastics. On his counter he laid out the imports and the home-made but she was not happy. Then she finally came out with it: "I want the best clock for the cheapest price." The goldsmith's face burned red-hot and he didn't smile when we left his shop.

On the way home my aunt still wondered if she should have bought a clock at all. "That goldsmith was a crook," she said at home when she put the clock on the dresser by the bed. She should have offered less, she was convinced of it, because it just didn't look like the best-quality clock and now it was too late. Outside of the clock she bought nothing else. Except, of course, for the pigs.

My aunt was not so happy the day she bought the pigs at the fair. As usual she was a real mess. Julia and I went to the fair with her. We went up the slope to the basin of the mountain by the spring. There next to the electrical antenna and the house where St. John's statue lived, the merchants had set up their little corrals for donkeys and horses and pigs. Julia and I went up the mountain because my aunt had promised to buy us each a pig. What she really meant was that she was going to buy two pigs and we were each responsible for one.

We saw the squealing bunch playing from far away. "Look for the ones with long bodies," my aunt said. She was convinced that a piglet with a long body would become a pig with lean meat. Next, she said to look closely at the tail and the snout, but I am not sure for what reason now.

My aunt pointed out two little pigs to the merchant, and when she was finished telling him how sickly they looked, and how she would be lucky if they survived the summer, she offered her best price.

I thought the poor man was trying to take off and fly away because his arms went up and down in frantic desperation.

"Get serious, signora, at this rate I may as well pack up and go home." He turned around and kicked the first piglet in his way, which happened to be the one with the curly tail and the long body that my aunt had eyed. So my aunt shouted back that she should have a further discount since this was one of the piglets she had planned to buy and now for sure his hip was bruised and that meant that the "prosciutto" might not turn out right.

Truly she did buy Julia and me a pig each, but we didn't leave right after she paid as the man had hoped we would. My aunt stood there for a long time counting and recounting her change as the merchant massaged his face with his hands over and over again. It was a good thing that my aunt didn't change her mind about the pigs or say something because I think he would have slapped his face just like she did when she was exasperated.

Finally when my aunt decided that her change was correct, we left. I remember quickly looking back, for what I don't know, and I saw the merchant take a very deep and long breath which he let out very slowly as we descended the mountain and headed back to San Giovanni.

Julia and I made a home for the little pigs in the enclosure under our steps. We tried very hard to keep the pigs' house clean, but the pigs didn't care. They were very smart though, because they knew when the pail I carried was full of slop, and they knew when it was empty. They were always so hungry that they never waited until I had poured their food into the nice new troughs that Sara's father had made for my aunt out of the trunk of a chestnut tree.

The pigs didn't care what they ate. They shoved and pushed. They didn't care if it was the peel and not the watermelon or if it was the bran and not the flour that I mixed in the slop.

They didn't care what they ate and they didn't care where they ate it. When I carried their food, they stayed close by me and tried to get their snouts into the pail, so it always ended up on the floor. After a good scrap with Julia over which pig was the villain, we decided to work together and solve the problem before my aunt got involved.

She would have given us a good lecture about showing gratefulness for a pigsty that finally housed pigs, and snow and blood and sweat and tears, and then, of course, she would have slapped her face if we would have as much as blinked while she spoke.

So the next time I emptied the pail in the trough while Julia distracted the pigs with a stick. Soon the little pigsty was clean and tidy like a real house and the pigs ate out of their trough just like people eat out of bowls and my aunt was very happy.

There was one thing my aunt was not happy about. She wanted the pigs to rest and sleep because while they rested and slept the slop in their bodies turned to flesh. But she forgot that these were our pigs and they were our pets so they followed us everywhere.

I don't think they would have followed us to the slaughterhouse, though, if they knew that is where we were taking them on that cold January day. But we called them and they came, even to the slaughterhouse they came.

To make sure the pigs would keep on following us,

my aunt bought a bag of dried broadbeans, and every step or two she would drop one and they came. The pigs followed my aunt, Julia and me down the road lined with sweet broadbeans, all the way to the slaughterhouse on Via Santa Lucia. They grunted and played all the way there. They were happy. If only the pigs knew!

Ceci knew. My aunt had told him a million times, "The devil is luring you, Ceci. The broadbeans taste good but you will find yourself in the slaughterhouse. The devil himself is taking you there."

The pigs were safely in the enclosed area within the slaughterhouse when my aunt ran out of broadbeans. They were weighed and shoved in another area where a squealing bunch had already been marked and numbered. Julia's pig and my pig were both marked and numbered too.

When the pigs realized where they were, they tried to escape. They shoved and pushed and squealed, but it was too late.

"Someday, someday it will be clear to you but it will be too late, Ceci. Too late to do anything. It will be impossible. You will reach to bite your elbow with your mouth but it will be impossible," my aunt said to Ceci when she was still trying to reason with him.

A man entered the enclosure and my pig squealed real loud. In the man's hand was a thick iron stick with a hook on its end. How delicate and pink my little pig's snout was on the day I got him! Now it was black with dirt and bright red with blood.

The man pulled on the hook but my pig refused to go. The blood rushed out of his snout but he didn't care. He planted his hoofs on the concrete floor and would not go. Finally after a mighty struggle I saw his hoofs dragging on the floor and soon there was nothing left but a trail of blood as far as my eyes could see beyond the open door. If only my pig had known what was at the end of the sweet broadbean road.

My pig now was in another area of the slaughterhouse. His legs were tied and his breathing was heavy. Two men yanked him with ease over a black iron grill. He was tied side by side with a whole row of defeated pigs. None of them struggled any longer, not even my pig. I remember I heard them grunt from time to time as their whole body shook. When the grill was full the knife was ready. One cut and it was all over.

The owners of the pigs stood nearby with a bucket under the grill to catch the blood. My aunt was not there. We did not make blood jam. She had warned us never to accept blood jam.

When the man came over to my pig I was there watching over the railing. I saw him plunge the knife over and over into his throat. My pig struggled with renewed strength. He kicked and shook in one last effort to untie himself, and then he died.

The butcher laughed, "He must have been a pet pig. Pet pigs struggle when they die." When he said that I cried. My aunt had cried with me the morning my kitten died but now she was too busy signing papers and paying dues. I was sure at that very moment she was reserving herself a seat in the veterinary's office in the slaughterhouse because this was the most important part. With a stroke of the pen he had the power to say who ate pig and who didn't. I cried and stayed there with my pig until the very end. A woman I did not know placed her bucket under my pig. She looked my way scornfully. What? I thought. It's not my fault.

Papagiuseppe said no blood jam and so did my Mammarosa and so did my aunt. We were not above it, we just didn't eat it. Well, I must confess a deep dark secret that has been inside of me for a very long time. My aunt doesn't know, but once (only once) I must have been so hungry that I didn't notice immediately that the spread on the huge white slice of bread Tata gave me was too dark to be strawberry jam and too smooth to be cherry. I took one bite, and then I took two, and then when I was almost finished, I decided to pay attention to the loud voice (a squeal) inside of me that shouted, "Blood jam, blood jam," and I threw the rest of the bread away.

The vet at the slaughterhouse took a little slice of flesh and looked at it very closely through some special glasses and then he told my aunt that we could eat our pigs. Men wearing bloody white coats carried the halved carcasses of our pigs over their shoulders to our house. My aunt had moved the linen chests to the middle of the room and covered them with a wide sheet of wood so the men could slam the carcasses on it, which they did with a loud thud. This was a festive and glad event because if my aunt managed wisely (and Ceci didn't steal too much) we would have meat for the whole year.

Before those thick brown envelopes started to come so frequently from America we ate meat only once a week. Every Sunday morning my aunt gave me five hundred liras and I was to go to Lallo's brother's butcher shop on Via Roma and buy chicken. And I did until the day I discovered that not so far from the butcher shop, children's storybooks were being featured in the bookstore's window. So every Sunday, when I was about to enter the butcher shop, I thought of the colourful pictures, and the shiny covers, and of magic mirrors and princes' kisses and wolves and foxes that spoke and I never made it straight to the butcher shop. First I went to the bookstore. After the bookstore started to display those wonderful books my aunt started to complain, "We used to get enough chicken for all of us with five hundred liras."

Then one Sunday I noticed that there was no chicken

on Mammarosa or my aunt's pasta. There was just plain sauce on it and a thread or two of meat that had fallen off a bone. So I stopped buying storybooks, which was very good for me anyway since I was starting to get really harassed from within for lying to my aunt on Sundays about Maria Pia being so nice for lending me storybooks.

Well, now we had a lot of meat, but it was also a lot of work.

There were guts to be cleaned, tripe to be scrubbed, hams to be salted and headcheese to be simmered. Then most important of all there were the sausages to be made.

Needless to say my aunt was a mess that day. Nina put the meat, ready for stuffing, in the grinder. Peppe turned the crank. Julia pricked the sausages to let the air out and I held the casings in place.

At first I pouted, because what I really wanted to do was squish the meat and knead it and mix in the salt, the chilies and the red pepper sauce, which was the real fun part of making sausages. But then after Julia got carried away and pricked a little too hard and the meat gushed out of the casings I didn't mind my boring chore.

My aunt watched as it all happened, the casing ripping, and the meat plopping on the wooden plank, but she couldn't do anything. Oh, she shouted and swore, but she couldn't slap her face. She couldn't slap her face because her hands were in and out of the sausage meat, squishing and mixing, so she stomped her feet and bit her arms instead.

We made sausages and we made soppressata too. Soppressata was a different-looking kind of sausage. It was made from a leaner mix of meat and my aunt worked whole black peppercorns in it instead of red pepper sauce. The soppressate were stuffed in the wider casings that had pockets hidden on either side of the line that defined the casings' middle. You would never know that these large casings had pockets until the meat rushed through and stuffed them. To me they looked like balls.

Once Maria Pia brought a book to school which her father had sent from America. It was a science book and it had a lot of pictures. One day in the schoolyard I saw a whole bunch of girls gathered around Maria Pia's book and they were laughing. When I looked over their shoulders I saw that they were laughing at the picture of a naked man on the page of the American science book. Big deal, I thought, was this all there was to balls? They looked just like the two bubbles at the bottom end of a soppressata. Had they never made soppressata?

Ceci hardly ever made sausages and soppressata. I wonder where Ceci was while we were having so much fun! Playing balls maybe?

He finally showed up when the sausages and the soppressate were already hung. My aunt hung them from the beams on the ceiling, as close as possible to the fireplace. Mammarosa made the fire and she kept it going for days on end, not for the fire but for the smoke which rose and cured the sausages.

While the sausages cured, most people prayed for few visitors, because you couldn't entertain visitors with only a glass of wine while so many sausages danced in the clouds of smoke overhead. Another reason visitors were not a good idea during the curing process was that among the visitors there might just be a jealous someone with an evil eye. And the evil eye was far worse than sharing a few sausages with visitors, because if someone came and eyed your sausages with evil intentions, the whole lot would mould and rot.

My aunt said she did not mind sharing her sausages because she knew what it was like to stare and swallow empty. She also said she did not believe in the evil eye but I didn't know what to believe. She rushed that whole smoke-curing process above the fireplace and gave herself and no one else rest until she had the sausages safely hidden. She counted them over and over and shouted, "Quiet, quiet, I said," when we weren't saying a word. We just stood there counting silently in our heads with her. She counted them and hid them, but I knew where. Every time she took one she counted them again.

At night, when we gathered around the hearth, my aunt took out a sausage for us to roast on the fire. She divided it in five equal parts, one for Nina, one for Ceci, one for Julia, one for me and always a little bigger piece for Peppe so she wouldn't have to hear him cry. We never complained because we didn't like to hear Peppe cry either. She never cut a piece for herself or for Mammarosa. They ate the bread on which the dripping from our pieces fell.

My aunt kept watch over the sausages because she knew that Ceci also kept watch. Ceci, she said, didn't care if there would be enough sausages to last until the end of the winter. She said that all he cared about was his "good fellows company." And how many times she had warned him to watch out for sweet broadbeans on the journey because the end of the broadbean road was the slaughterhouse. She had told him a million times, "Ceci, when the devil sweet-talks you, don't trust his words, he is after your soul. He will take it, sweetly, with a bottle of wine, a song and a guitar."

But Ceci didn't care and that is why my aunt kept watch. My aunt kept watch for any possible clues that would indicate when and where and how Ceci would strike. Around the time of the Carnevale my aunt got real serious with her sausage count and she kept extra watch.

I remember the Carnevale. Harlequins and Pulcinellas and Zorros roamed the streets of San Giovanni laughing and doing things grown people normally weren't allowed to do, because now they were hidden under a little black mask. Ceci and his "good fellows company" would not settle for just dressing up like Harlequin or Pulcinella. Ceci had to do it big. He wanted to impress everyone in town—and he did. He planned a whole procession of people in masquerade. It was a big and long procession of a wedding party on its way to church and Ceci himself was the bride. He walked arm in arm with the groom, and he looked great in the white organza dress that Nicola, the groom, had stolen from his mother's drawers. Ceci looked beautiful, even with his black thick body hair peeking through the white lace. And of course, being the bride, he carried the bouquet.

The bouquet was a white enamel bedpan full of a fragrant clear verdicchio wine, all the way up to the rim, and in it floated a couple of links of freshly smoked sausage. The mock procession of masquerades stole the hearts of the folks in San Giovanni as it made its way down Via San Francesco of Assisi, under Piotta's patio, on the way to the church.

The balconies were full of people laughing, cheering and throwing paper streamers like they did during the last election when the big fat man who promised bread and work for everyone drove through in Professor Ciano's Topolino. They cheered and Ceci looked up and waved at them. He didn't lose his balance once on the high-heeled shoes because his hand was locked firmly in the groom's arm.

The procession made many stops along the way and Ceci pointed to the bedpan, his bouquet, at each stop. He pointed and he waited and everyone knew this bride's desire. With nothing but the movement of their chins or a simple hand gesture men summoned their wives from balconies and windows and the women knew precisely what their husbands' gestures meant. I even saw Professor Ciano's wife come out and drop a good link of sausage in the sack that the groom carried for the purpose of collecting such valuables as soppressate and sausages (not that they would ever turn down a good bottle of wine). The groom accepted the gifts with a grateful smile. The sack looked pretty full.

My aunt watched the whole procession go by from the window. She knew that the sausages in the sack came from people along the street. What she wasn't sure of was the origin of those plump links that floated in the wine in Ceci's bouquet. My aunt knew Ceci, and she knew her sausages too, and they sure looked familiar. She would have said something if it wasn't for the problem of the sausage count. You see, to complicate matters, at that very moment she couldn't remember. She wasn't sure if it was fifty-two or fifty-four sausages that she had counted earlier that morning.

My aunt stepped up the security after the Carnevale because even if Ceci and his company had collected a sackful of sausages, there were so many boys that she knew they wouldn't last long. She knew, and yet there was nothing she could do. She could not do much unless she caught Ceci red-handed with a lovely link in his hands.

She swore that if she did indeed with her very eyes see him take a sausage, she would break as many chairs as were necessary to split his skull wide open. Ceci heard her threats. She had spoken them loud enough for him to hear. "I will catch him—whoever he is. Someday I will for sure catch him with his hands in the jar and then we will see." My aunt looked straight at Ceci when she said those words and of course Ceci laughed. He laughed and laughed for as long as he could and then he took off real quickly because my aunt had just put her hands around the back of a good solid chair and had started to rattle it.

Being caught red-handed sounded like a promising way to have a little extra fun to Ceci. So he waited, until the day my aunt was idling outside on the porch in the hot summer sun. She pushed a broom here and there because she wouldn't want any of the neighbours to think she was relaxing a little while humming a hymn in her own very special way.

Once I told my aunt that she should sing louder in church because her voice was more beautiful than any of the others but she didn't believe me so she hummed quietly. My aunt loved trills. She rewrote the melodies of songs in her mind to include her trills. Trills and more trills. Her whole head quivered and she swayed. Only at times like these did she seem enraptured and at peace.

While my aunt was enraptured, the devil transported Ceci, out of nowhere, to the bottom of our steps on Via Monterosa, right in front of the downstairs cellar door. I saw Ceci sneak quietly into the door. He didn't see me but I saw him. He carried a good-sized square of brown paper, the kind Lallo's brother used for wrapping our Sunday chicken. He was headed for the cellar where my aunt kept the sausages and I remember a feeling of panic. Soon there would be trouble.

Ceci opened the door a sliver and slipped his body in very slowly. The door creaked a little but my aunt didn't hear. She was as if absent, lost in her singing.

I climbed quietly and slowly halfway up the stairs and sat pretending to play by the little window that looked smack into the whole downstairs. If only the stack of firewood wasn't in the way and if only the metal bars didn't prevent me from stretching my neck I would have seen exactly what he was up to. So I squeezed and turned and squeezed and turned, until my head came through the metal grill squares and I could see Ceci.

I couldn't see too much of him but I could see his face. He looked flat, as if someone had pushed his head in, and his body, scrunched like an accordion, had disappeared like in the comic books.

I looked a little closer to see Ceci better. Yes, he was flat and scrunched, in fact he was squatted on the floor with his feet wide apart planted on that brown paper. Suddenly his eyes met mine. He would have said something, I could tell by his angry look, but he didn't, because he couldn't. He was pushing hard, his face red, his eyes on fire and bulging out, as if he was trying to do something on the floor, on that paper, and was out of time and in a hurry.

He tried to motion me with his head to move it, get out of the window. But that wasn't easy, you know; I had to twist my head in a million directions before I found the right angle to remove it from inside the iron grill bars.

But I did move and very fast, as the foul smell from the downstairs floor where Ceci was squatted started to rise. I did not want Ceci to be angry with me so I quietly moved up a few steps above the window to breathe fresh air. There I played quietly while my aunt sang and Ceci finished his awful business.

My aunt looked so peaceful, her whole face turned up towards the sky while she sang. But the peace was short-lived. It was abruptly disrupted by the sound of a door violently being slammed shut.

It was Ceci. He rushed from the downstairs with a package so nicely wrapped you would think he had been to Lallo's brother, the butcher. Ceci looked straight into my aunt's face, gave her a big smile that turned into a laugh and then he ran.

"The sausages, the soppressate," my aunt cried. Now she had caught him red-handed. Finally she had him! She had seen him with her own eyes. My aunt threw the broom and rushed down the stairs, skipping them two by two. In no time she was on the street.

Well, a miracle! A timely miracle! Not so far away, down the street, who do you think appeared? It was Luigi, Mancuso's son. He had closed the grocery store and was doddling home for lunch, perhaps even a quiet afternoon nap. Luigi heard my aunt's desperate cry: "The sausages, the sausages! Luigi, catch him. Catch him, Luigi!"

Ceci did not expect this. He did not want Luigi to catch him. He wanted my aunt to catch him, after he had her running for a little while, of course. Ceci looked to the left, he looked to the right, but it was no use. He was sandwiched. On the far end was my aunt and on the other, very close, was Luigi. Ceci surrendered. He handed the package to Luigi, jumped over the containing wall of Piotta's patio and in a flash was on the main road, free and laughing.

Luigi looked puzzled as he felt the warm soft package that had just been handed to him. My aunt was yelling, "That pigheaded devil! One by one he is finishing the sausages off. He doesn't work, he doesn't sweat. When people don't sweat they don't care." She was shaking, all out of breath.

Meanwhile there was a foul odour coming from the package in Luigi's hands. Luigi was not paying much attention to what my aunt was saying, not because he didn't believe her. Oh no, Luigi knew Ceci well. And he was not being rude either, because Luigi always lent a helping hand willingly when he could. But Luigi was not paying attention because he was busy thinking now how to solve a problem of his own.

The package in his hands had him worried. It was soft so indeed there could be a sausage in it, but it was also warm! And now it stunk. And the more he handled it, the more it stunk. In a split second Luigi had to decide. To thrust it, to keep it, or to hand it over to my aunt. He threw it. I saw it.

I saw it fly high and smash right against the parapet that contained Piotta's patio. It landed all over the place where the women sat to speak of bread and wine.

We all laughed that night when my aunt retold the story. Even my aunt laughed, although she would never admit that she did. She tried hard not to. She swore and slapped her face and bit her arm all at once but I could tell that inside she was having just as good a time as the rest of us because her eyes were not so blue. I saw her lips desperately trying to stay together to suppress that hidden laugh. And laughter came through over and over again in the streets of San Giovanni when the story of the counterfeit sausages started to circulate.

One day when the laughter subsided I saw my aunt pick up pen and paper and I had to rethink about whether she had been laughing at all that day. She was writing about Ceci and she was writing to my father in America. This was a threat she had uttered many times but I thought she never would carry it out, unless of course she was tired and really wanted us to go. My aunt had taken enough. I knew deep within my gut that this was going to be one expensive sausage. This was going to cost too much. Ceci never paid for anything, but I thought this time he would. And we would all have to pay along with him.

Once I paid for candies for the whole bunch of us children on Via Monterosa. I gave candies to everyone. Maria Pia's father was in San Giovanni on one of his visits from America that same day I paid for the candies. I had seen Maria Pia sitting on her father's knee for a very long time, and then just before she stepped down, when she had had enough of kisses and caresses, he put his hand in his pocket and out came not coins, but paper lira bills. He gave them to Maria Pia. The night before I had seen my aunt with lira bills. I saw her lift the papers in the right-hand corner of the bottom dresser drawer, then I saw her reach with her hands deep between her breasts and withdraw a little roll of paper money which she hid in that drawer.

Mancuso was happy to sell me mints and jellies and chocolate-covered cherries, which I ate with my friends all evening long. They shoved and pushed to be close to me.

My aunt's face was already red and swollen when I came in the door that night. From the steps outside I heard her shouting, "Someone took the money, who took the money?" She was slapping her face, pleading, "Who took the money, who took the money?" Who took the money?

Who else would take the money, I thought I should say to my aunt. Who steals the chickens and the eggs and the sausages and the wine? Who? Who? And then as if my aunt read my mind she started to look in Ceci's direction every time she asked where the money was.

Ceci swore, "I didn't take it, I didn't take the money." For a moment I thought she was going to believe him but then Ceci started to laugh. He laughed and laughed and he threw himself laughing on the floor but he didn't stay there long because my aunt was heading towards him. He ran fast, out onto the street.

I did not think about any of this happening when I reached with my hands into that bottom drawer and took the money. I had not wanted to spend all the money. I didn't want to spend any of it at first. All I wanted to do was have it in my hands. I should have listened to the gentle voice that first spoke to me from within when my hands were not even on the handle of the drawer.

"No, no," the voice gently whispered.

Of course no, I was not going to take it, I just wanted to hold it, to have it in my hands for just a little. So I took the money and held it in my hands and then I put it in my pocket, even while the voice kept on saying louder, "No, no, no."

I went to Mancuso's grocery store because once I had the money in my hands, I decided that I would only buy one chocolate-covered cherry, just for me, and then put the rest of the money back. But every child on the street, it seemed, knew that I had money and followed me as I entered the store.

They were all smiles and they wanted to play with me. They all shouted, "Me, me, me." You'd think I was Don Antonio handing out Madonna figurines when I pointed to mints and chocolates and jelly beans on Mancuso's counter. I tried to plug my ears with my hands but they shouted, "Me, me, me."

They were loud. I could no longer hear even one gentle "No, no, no" whisper in my ear, they were so loud. So I bought everyone a treat and Mancuso hardly gave me any change back, there were so many.

So when Ceci ran outside the night my aunt wanted to know who stole the money, I ran too, and my aunt followed after me. She was about to run after Ceci but she saw children everywhere with handfuls of candies surrounding me, as if all of a sudden I was Maria Pia. So she stopped.

I remember when my sad eyes met my aunt's blue eyes. I called for the sky to stretch itself out like a mantle and cover me. I called for darkness to come and quickly hide me, but there was no answer. I was convinced that I was not, and had never been, an eagle. And I had never flown and neither would I ever fly.

I had wanted the sky to fall and cover me but all I got

was the back of my aunt's skirt. I hung onto it tightly. She walked fast as I was dragged along. She tried to make me face Mancuso, who was shrugging his shoulders behind the counter of his store, but I stayed buried in the cloth when she told him, "So much money and she was just a child, just a child." Why had my aunt not worn her big dirndl that day? So much shame, so little cloth.

Mammarosa said it didn't matter. I was still an eagle and yes, I would fly, she said while she dried the tears that fell hot from my eyes. Mammarosa said it didn't matter because sometimes even eagles stumbled and fell, especially young ones. They fluttered and fell often, in fact, when they first started to fly, she said. She said if they sat and cried and doubted who they were, or the strength of their wings, they would never get up and fly again, or grow to be as majestic as God meant them to be. "You will flutter and you will fall many times yet," she said, "and each time, you will cry. But you must never sit for too long on the ground, because you are an eagle. And you were meant to fly."

I wanted to tell my aunt to give Ceci one last chance. Maybe he would stop fluttering and falling. Maybe he would finally take off and fly, but she wouldn't have listened. I could tell. I was quite sure she would not have paid attention to anything I had to say because as soon as she heard my footsteps coming towards her she stretched out her left hand to stop me from getting closer while she kept on writing with her right. She never turned her head to look in my direction. She was serious about writing that letter. Finally she was carrying out her threat and we would all have to pay dearly.

Cheese

Before you attempt to make anything out of milk,
find the stomach of a nursing baby goat
(one that absolutely has not ingested grass)

Fill the stomach with goat's milk

Hang it and let it dry

Crumble the dry contents

Dissolve them in water

Keep this solution in a cool place

Put a pot of milk on the fire and allow
it to become tepid

Remove from the fire

Add one or two tablespoons of the goat's-stomach
solution and let it rest for a few hours

You will see that the milk will start to gel

Return the pot of milk to the fire

Start heating it up while with your hands you squeeze
and collect the cheese (the heat will cause the cheese to
harden and make it easier to collect)

Put the cheese in a small round basket and set aside in
a fresh airy spot to cure

Devils and Angels

MY MOTHER SAID NO. It would cost us all dearly, too dearly, she said, if she let my father have his way. Our future was at stake and that indeed would have been too much! I understood, I followed my mother's reasoning and believed the words my aunt read in the letter. What I couldn't understand or believe was that my father had said yes and my mother had really answered no. I had never heard of anyone doing that before. Doing it and getting away with it that is, not in San Giovanni anyway.

"One God, one man," Tata had told Sara ever since she was old enough to understand that God alone made the world and man alone ruled it. The few times Piperella's wife tried to argue or dared disagree with that drunk of a man she washed and cooked for, whenever she did, whenever she said no to him, she paid for it, dearly. Too dearly from what I saw. The last time she opened her mouth for a breath of freedom and uttered nothing more than those two little letters, the letter N and the letter O, her eyes were black for days. Then they turned blue, then purple and then yellow, and her lips, oh her lips were thick and plump, but only on one side.

I had always wanted thick lips because Maria Pia had thick lips. Once I fell and my lips swelled, and although I could not speak or eat comfortably, I didn't cry. In fact I was happy. I got up, walked to school and held my chin up high. I remember that I gathered my new thick lips to form a good pout so everyone would notice. I didn't want anyone to miss seeing my new plump mouth, almost as plump, it felt, as Maria Pia's. Until on the way home from school I saw my reflection in Mancuso's storefront window and realized that I looked just like Piperella's wife after she had said no.

Oh and yes, every time she did say no, the women on Piotta's patio looked at her and shook their heads. "She should have known better," they said. Only whores had the boldness to break that rule. This is why whores paraded up and down city streets at night, bold as if they had balls, as if they owned the sidewalks.

I was glad my mother was not here in San Giovanni, now that she had become so bold, bold enough to say no. The women on Piotta's patio always shook their heads when they called my mother "cruel" for going to America. Now they would not only shake their heads but gasp, and for sure add "whore." I could just see them all intent on their sewing in the cool of the evening saying their Hail Marys together, gasping and looking at me with their pitiful eyes, saying "whore whore, cruel whore" of my mother if they had heard. Even my aunt gasped when she read this defiance in the letter.

Nine years before, when my father wrote in one of his letters from America that my mother should join him for just a little while, she silently packed her trunk and left. She had not said yes and she had not said no. She said nothing and left. I still remember the day my mother left even if I was not quite the age of four. I remember a fraction of that morning, a wink of it in fact.

I was sleeping peacefully at the foot of the bed when the muffled sounds of tears and laments woke me. It was not morning yet. Our one lightbulb was lit, casting mocking, dancing shadows on the ceiling and walls. And then I saw the door open. In the dim light of dawn I watched as a blur of bodies moved across the room and out of the door. One of them was my mother's. It had to be hers, my mother's, the dark shadow that stretched high and wide across the wall. It was of her arms which fluttered like giant wings, like those of a great bird who was desperately trying to fly but was too wounded. Yes, now I know that it was my mother's. Hers was the shadow being pulled, dragged by force over the threshold that morning.

I remember that in silence she struggled and fought. She cried and cried, without making a sound she cried. I know she cried because a stream of tears on her face captured the light and glistened in the dark. Yes, silently in the dark, like a thief who had tiptoed in, she was sneaking out. She was leaving undecided, as if she had left behind what she came for.

It is the shadow of this woman, struggling to stay, yet ready to leave, her feet planted on the floor, refusing to budge in the middle of the door, that I still see in my mind every morning before dawn breaks. I did not understand that morning why or whose shadow walked away. Yet I too cried. "Mamma, Mamma, where is Mamma?" And I do remember that it was not my mother but my aunt who rushed to my side. "Sleep, sleep," she whispered, "Mamma is gone." I think now that I should have cried more, a lot more, that morning, but I closed my eyes and rested my head on the pillow just like my aunt said and fell asleep. “Sleep, sleep,” my aunt said and I slept.

It happened such a long time ago. I am not trapped by the spell of my aunt’s words now. I don’t close my eyes and sleep any longer just because she says “sleep, sleep,” and she still does! Even when she knows I won’t listen she still tries. She says sleep, she says go, she says come, she says get and she says do. I don’t know if this is good or bad but what I do know is that sometimes I just don’t want to.

For example, when my aunt asks me to drain the pasta, she stands over me the whole time and tells me not to let the hot water go to waste down the drain. Sometimes I listen and save the water for her in a pot in the sink. But sometimes, even after I have said yes, I don’t. I don’t because I think to myself that it is pointless to save the slimy pasta water when for the last five years I have not had to fetch water in the clay pots or the barrel at the fountain in front of Mancuso’s store because water has been running out of the taps into the stone sink right inside our own home!

My aunt says yes and I say no. She shouts, “Someday, someday I am going to have you in my hands.” All the while she pulls at her fingers as if she is going to rip them out of their sockets. That’s when I usually run for the outdoors. She follows after me to the door and yells that my face is as hard as a sidewalk. I always promise myself that if it is slimy pasta water she wants, then that’s what I will give her. But the next time she asks me to drain the pasta I will most likely let the water down the drain. I just know I will and I really don’t know why.

It must be part of growing up, this yes and no thing between my aunt and me. In fact I think I have grown. The clothes my mother made for me before she left no longer fit. My aunt says my mother worked wonders with her hands, her fingers in fact. They can transform things. Things like an old blanket into a warm coat or a worn sheet into a pretty dress. But that is all. That is all the magic they were able to do.

In 1950 when the potato crop failed my mother's hands were not able to do anything. And in that same year when my baby sister cried in my mother's arms and turned her face back and forth across my mother's chest in search of milk she found nothing. With her hands, my mother massaged and worked her breasts all the way from the shoulders down, but her hands failed their magic. Not a drop of milk, not even a trickle of moisture flowed from my mother's breasts.

There was plenty of moisture on the pavement of the piazza where my father's lumber lay stockpiled for months and months, though. It rained and rained and the lumber rotted and no one bought it, not even for firewood was my father able to sell it. And there was nothing my mother's hands could do. But that night, when the doctor looked into the baby's eyes and said, "Nothing, nothing, there is nothing left to do," my mother's hands knew just what to do. All night long her fingers worked, they did not stop, no, not once. And before the baby had gasped three times and died, there on the bed lay the finest princess gown.

Professor Ciano's wife reached over the white-lined box where the baby lay, and with her fingers caressed every ruffle. She traced every stitch of embroidering and pinched each of the blue velvet bows on the pure-white gown. Even the ones that were attached to the little white satin shoes that were really only cardboard, pretty lace-covered cardboard. She nodded several times. She was impressed. Out of a ballroom gown that no one wanted, abandoned at the bottom of an American Aid box, my mother's hands, her fingers, had worked magic.

My mother's magic covered my body too for a long time after she left, but for a while it has not been able to contain me. It has lost its spell, it seems. I have grown. None of the clothes my mother made me fit. I couldn't even call them clothes anymore.

My aunt let Julia wear them out because she is younger and smaller. Then she used them to fill the cracks in the walls and the fissures of the windows and doors to stop the wind from rushing in when the cold winters settled on San Giovanni's mountain. After that she mopped the floor with them. And now there are only shreds of them that I see tied around the inside and outside of the cement pipe connected to our toilet right where the pipe meets the wall.

Once, on the way home from the vineyard, I was intent on dreaming and imagining so the time and the miles would fly by quickly. While I was thinking what to do with the green undulating fields of wheat that we came upon, Mammarosa came to a sudden stop. "Careful, careful where you step," she whispered as she pointed to a peach tree close by on the field. "That long piece of rag hanging there from that branch on the tree, do you see it, do you see? It is not a rag at all." It was a snake skin, a viper's, she said, who had grown out of his garment. "And snakes, or any animal for that matter, in their new clothes are dangerous," she warned. I wanted to remind Mammarosa that I, for one, had grown out of my clothes and it didn't make me dangerous, did it?

But I didn't because I was not about to listen to a long list of dangerous things I may have done in the last little while ever since my clothes started to fit snug, especially since they became tight across the chest area. It was not that I did not value my Mammarosa's advice, oh no, it's just that my aunt had already told me a million times and in a million ways all about the dangers that come with growing up. Her warnings about these dangers ranked just as high as her warnings of the importance of a good education.

For the longest time I had to listen to my aunt chant day and night, "Study, study, study." And now she had added new lines to her song: "Think, think, think. Careful, careful, careful." Not to mention whole verses like "Tell me who you hang out with and I'll tell you who you are." And of course her very favourite: "When choosing friends go up a step." I can't understand why anyone should want to sit with someone just because they are on the top step of the ladder.

I should tell my aunt to pay attention when Bernardo speaks (she always tells me to) because once Bernardo said (and he was very serious because his face was all red) that it is best to take a lowly seat. I think he was right because if the ladder ever tips, it is the people at the top that will fall the hardest. But my aunt wouldn't listen because she never stops talking. It is as if a switch to a hidden phonograph inside of her body is automatically turned on by my presence anywhere in her vicinity. And then I have to listen to the same song over and over again because her phonograph, it seems, can only play one record.

Just last week I did something that I don't think I will do again because it is one thing to listen to this tedious song of my aunt's alone and it is another thing to have it sung in front of your friends. As soon as I walked into the door, I knew. You'd think my aunt had overnight graduated from medical school the way she examined the new friend I brought home. She looked her up and down and all around. And although she didn't look quite close enough into her eyes as a doctor would, she pronounced words that only doctors dared to. "Nothing, nothing, there is nothing left to do." (My aunt started talking and shaking her head at me before my friend had stepped out of the door to go home.) She said it would benefit nothing to give advice to a pigheaded stubborn donkey like myself. And then the music started: "Who is her mother? Who is her father? What do they do? Why did they move to San Giovanni and from where? Her skirt is too tight, her limbs move too freely when she walks about, her chest is too far forward, how old is she? Too forward, too forward, too old, too old," she chanted. "Too old to be your friend," she said as she pointed to her chest. (As if it should somehow be my friend's fault that I didn't measure the same in that area yet.)

She was not too old, I wanted to say, we were exactly the same age and in the same grade, in fact. But I didn't. I didn't say yes and I didn't say no. I just stood there in silence. Yet my aunt was angry and I didn't know why. Although now that I think about it, the rolling of my eyeballs and the strange contortions of my lips may have had something to do with it. She pushed the broom very hard across the floor she was sweeping. But I didn't complain, I kept on keeping silent. After all, that broom could have been sweeping hard across my head instead of the floor. "To wash a donkey's head is a waste of time," she went on and on, still shaking her head. "It is a waste of time, soap and water. You'll see, you'll see," she said.

But I had already seen. I had seen and heard it all. I had memorized every danger that I should beware of as I was growing up. I had already heard her say that this was a time when I could be dangerous, when I could do harm—to myself mostly. It was the time at the intersection of my life, when I would come upon the sweet and pleasant road that leads to the slaughterhouse. And like the pigs we led there, I wouldn't know that I was walking on it until it was too late if I did not listen, think and be careful.

I thought and I listened all right and I promised

myself I would be careful because this growing-up thing was indeed dangerous. So dangerous, in fact, that I was starting to think it threatened my very existence.

It all started with my aunt not letting me play with boys. Then I couldn't wander away from our street. Then I had to be in the house by eight and that meant I had to sit and stare at the fire for the rest of the evening. And then lastly this new thing, when she started to inspect and examine anyone that I even said hello to. And next—I don't know what!

I remember my aunt on her calm days trying to reason with me, saying quite gently then, "Stand alone, stand tall, stand true and stand still." But I didn't want to. I wanted to be together with others who too were changing and growing out of their clothes. I didn't like to be alone, at least not all the time. I was too short to stand tall, and as for being true—I tried, I searched into the deepest chamber of my heart but I heard too many voices there and could not decide what was true.

My aunt wanted me to stand still. "Don't fly about like a senseless butterfly. Don't chase the wind. Stay put with your feet planted on the ground." But I didn't want to. I had seen waters that stayed put, waters that just sat there in their spot, and was not impressed. Too quickly they became murky and in no time the bottom was not visible, and sometimes a foul smell, especially during the heat of summer, rose from these still waters.

I liked my lonely stream at the basin of the mountain, close to the ravine, where my tree stood tall. It ran and ran. It was so clear and true you could see the tiniest pebble at its bottom even when the sun threatened to hide behind the mountain, when the evening bells rang. When I sat there alone with my thoughts, even my sad thoughts, I heard different music flow from the water that hit the rocks.

I had heard my aunt's woeful song and music over and over again. This is why I did not engage Mammarosa in a conversation or disagree with her about whether the snake, who had grown out of its clothes, was dangerous or not. I walked on carefully beside her and dreamed and imagined. And as I did, the fields of wheat became a deep green sea whose rolling waves the wind transported gently across the valley between the mountains that surrounded San Giovanni. I imagined plunging my body into these green waters in the valley. I imagined treading among the green waves of this new sea. I pulled away from Mammarosa's tight hold and ran towards the waves of the rolling sea, but when I came to the first patch of wheat, I saw nothing but green tender plants that had shot up bravely through the cracks of the earth in the valley. Close up it was not at all what I imagined.

I thought I saw another green wave coming towards me so I ran to meet it to throw myself in, hoping that it would hold me like the real waters of a blue sea. But when I got there I saw that it too was just a patch of tender green blades of wheat. Each blade stood alone making the smooth sea. The togetherness was a mirage.

I turned to see where Mammarosa was. She stood by the side of the road smiling, shaking her head, waiting for me. I don't know why but I think she had plunged into a deep green sea just like this one herself once. I ran to Mammarosa and walked quietly by her side. Mammarosa said that if a blade of wheat did not grow when it was time to, it had little chance of doing much growing later, because the weeds that grew around it would choke it. They would get thick and tall and block off the sun. Plants that could not tell time rotted and died. And if, perchance, any survived, they brought no fruit at all. I had seen the wheat fields grow and I had watched green tender plants slowly turn to full-grown sheaths, swollen thick with wheat kernels. And by June these fields no longer looked like a mere body of green water rocked by the wind, but a luscious sea of real gold. When Mammarosa's little plot of green changed to gold she was happy. She said that some changes were good, very good in fact. But changes must take place when it is time, she said, not too early and never too late.

At the vineyard Mammarosa watched carefully over the young fig trees. At the right time she tied them to a branch, a straight one of course, so the young tree might grow strong, tall and straight. Mammarosa said that it was no use trying to straighten a crooked old tree, that is why timing was so important. "Once you are, you are who you are," she said. "Time is of no value after you are who you are. It does nothing. The crooked trunk just gets thicker with time and the branches just extend further, crooked and more crooked, further with time, that's all."

Like old Giovanni, Mammarosa said, who had no regard for women. Not when he was alive, not when he was dead did he show any. Since he was a young man, old Giovanni, down the street, had had no regard for women. His mother should have tied him to a tree, a nice straight branch of a big tree, but those are hard to find, Mammarosa said. She told me that one has to look very hard and be careful and ask all kinds of questions. (I think she meant the kind of questions my aunt asks every time I bring a friend home.) Even after he married and had a woman all his own, Giovanni didn't change. He still whistled and ran his eyes from the top of a woman's head to the bottom of her feet, regardless of how many times he was told to "va fa n'culo." She said that women had even turned to spit on him, but in reply he laughed with delight and blew kisses in their direction. When old Giovanni was really old he still had not changed, not even a bit.

I remember, not too long ago, while Nina and Carletta were walking arm in arm on Via Monterosa, Giovanni was coming out of his house, actually he was shuffling out. I saw him try to steady himself on the back of a chair that he dragged along, to a spot on the western wall to soak up the last warm rays of the setting sun which restored his old bones and warmed up his cold body. Even though he was bent and trembled all over, when Giovanni saw Nina and Carletta walking and laughing and swaying to the left and to the right it seemed for a second his strength would return. He sighed in sheer delight. He tried to steady himself and straighten his crooked old bones, but by the time he looked up again, and turned around to follow and search Nina and Carletta up and down with his eyes, they had already turned the corner.

The night old Giovanni lay dying men gathered around his bed to say good-bye. Giovanni lay motionless, sleeping it seemed, in the middle of a big bed. For days already he had hardly said a word. The men quietly recalled the good, the sad and the happy days they spent together. And then, of course, as it is with conversations among the men of San Giovanni, the subject changed to women. So the voices got louder and louder and there was laughter and then more laughter followed and because everyone was talking above everyone else it was hard to make out what anyone was really saying at all except for the word "women, women, women" that came across loud and clear. "Women!?" echoed a faint voice. Though feeble, the sound startled the men. They turned. The voice was coming from the middle of the huge bed. Giovanni opened his eyes. He stuttered as he spoke but the words came out clear. "Women? Did you say women? Count me in. Keep me present, you hear?" Old Giovanni sighed for the last time and died.

Mammarosa said that it would take a miracle before an old crooked tree would go straight because she said there is a time for everything, even changes. I wanted to tell Mammarosa to keep in mind that we were not really trees and that we can choose to change anytime we want to. I wanted to say, "Remember, Mammarosa, do you remember the swarms of butterflies in front of our little house at the vineyard every summer?" I remembered because I spent hours watching them before they looked like butterflies. One by one, when they chose to be free, they gathered courage, and from inside their white constricting walls they pushed and struggled, until they emerged fluttering, proud and free. No longer a worm but a beautiful butterfly.

My mother had changed. I could tell from the letters my aunt read. She was not the same and yet she was old, older than some of the trees in our vineyard. It all began when my father's grocery store at Lydia and Notre Dame in Winnipeg started to do well. My mother looked around and told my father that it was time for all of us to be together. She told him that we were going to join them in America, because America, my mother was convinced, was the place to be.

My mother told my father!

She told him no and she told him yes. She told him whatever she thought to tell him. I remember when that letter arrived. I was going to interrupt my aunt while she read it and say, "What's wrong with Mamma, talking like that! Does she think she is in America?" And then I remembered. Of course, Mamma was in America! And just then a quick flash of Maria Pia's postcard, the one her father sent her, the one with that woman and that inscription, "The land of the free and the home of the brave," crossed my mind.

My mother looked around and said yes and my

father looked around and said no. He said he didn't want to stay in America. He said that he had done what he came to do. He had more than the little money he had come to collect, a lot more, enough to make a little America right in San Giovanni. So my father decided to sell the store. My mother started to push and kick and fuss. This is when she started to change and for the first time she behaved not like herself at all and shouted, "No. Never, no, no, no."

It was Friday night. The bells had rung at Goldberg's and Freeds and Peerless and Raber's and at the rest of the other factories that surrounded my mother's store. The women who worked there gladly laid aside their sewing and turned the machines off. They rushed into the store all at once, Mother said. Mrs. William, Mrs. Banning, Mrs. Pritchard, Mrs. Langside and many more. These were not their real names, of course, these were the names of the streets the women lived on and that is how my father kept track of what boxes and bags to deliver to who and where.

Friday nights were very good nights. The back door was full of emptied banana and apple boxes, now loaded with cans, bottles, lettuce, green onions and broccoli brimming from paper bags. And of course brown paper packages of wrapped fresh sausages, mortadella and provolone. There were tons of boxes, addresses marked with thick black ink, 630 Langside, 540 Pritchard, ready to be loaded in my father's truck and delivered.

That night my father was nowhere to be found and my mother was nervous, standing by the butcher block at the back door in the middle of this mess. Once in a while she shouted towards the cash register at the front of the store, "Pack the fruit on top, don't squish the bread, please." These were all things my father was supposed to look after but he was obviously somewhere else, doing something he thought was more important.

Finally he walked in when the customers were no longer having to squeeze against the walls of canned goods and brush against the noisy refrigerators to get through with their shopping carts. But there were still plenty of people everywhere and a line-up at the check-out counter when he arrived.

My father walked in but he was not alone. He had brought a fine-looking man along and was showing him around the store. My mother was just walking out of the refrigerator room with a whole hind of beef on her shoulder when my father walked in the store with that strange man, who quickly made himself at home and looked up and down and touched things and opened doors as if he owned the place. My father walked through the crowd smiling and greeting people, looking so happy and proud. And my mother stood there a while, swallowed by the white cold mist that gushed out of the refrigerator room, petrified, with that carcass, limp and moulded to her shoulder.

My father was determined to sell the store. My mother was determined to keep it. She was tired of keeping silent. She was tired of gulping tears and standing there saying neither yes nor no. If her hands had been free and if she had been at home instead of at the store she would have slapped the kitchen table good and hard to make her point. She would have taken her wooden spoon, even if it was in the potful of sauce, she would have smashed the stove with it, but she wasn't, so she just slammed the beef hind extra good and extra hard on the butcher block while she gave an extra-big smile to the good women around her because they too were tired. She knew.

They had worked all day in the humming of a thousand machines and now they stood in line for their rewards, a good cut of meat. Nothing to be taken for granted considering they all came from places like San Giovanni where they probably had passed by the butcher shop a million times, and swallowed empty a million times too.

They were tired. These women were tired indeed because the reward was not the end of the day. There was another full shift ahead—of cooking and cleaning while their men summoned espressos from the sofa. It would be late into the night before they dropped half-dead on their real reward—the bed. Yes, they were tired and my mother knew it so she didn't start anything with my father just then. She went right on smiling while she sliced and chopped hard across the beef's ribs.

But she cried and cried when she was alone in the refrigerator room. She went in there often that Friday evening, making unnecessary trips for things she didn't really need. There among the hanging carcasses, in the middle of death, she dried her tears and mumbled silently.

That very night, at home, after she put my sister and brother to bed, after my father came in from cleaning the walk, my mother shouted for the first time with all her might: "No." My mother told my father that this time she was not budging. She said it was not right to throw everything they had worked for out the window, and with it our future. She told him he had to go alone, if he wanted to, and see for himself. Test first, to see if indeed it was a wise and good thing to take America and bring it to San Giovanni.

My mother said in the letter that she was tired. She said every day she wrestled, and it was not with flesh and blood that she wrestled. I think she meant devils. I had heard that line before from Bernardo many times as he stood bent over the little wooden pulpit on Sunday nights. "We wrestle with devils, with devils," he hissed, standing on his toes trying hard to stretch his thick body over the pulpit and across to me. I always thought it was my ears, only mine, that he wanted to approach so he could tell me long-kept secrets about fighting devils. But I fell asleep across the first row of benches before he could.

The women on Piotta's patio always called their husbands devils. I remember Mr. Ficosecco in grammar class once read a story. " 'Buon giorno dear,' said the father. 'Buon giorno, amore,' replied the mother," Mr. Ficosecco read, and as he did his voice became so gentle and soft that you would have never guessed it was him speaking if he wasn't there smack in the middle of the classroom, high above everyone else on that creaking platform where he always sat or stood, when he wasn't parading through the rows of desks with his stick.

I have no memories of my mother calling my father anything. Maybe my mother did call my father "dear" or "amore," but I never heard those words, or any others, so I don't know what she called him.

I did ask Mammarosa what she called my grandfather, Papagiuseppe, though. I had never heard Mammarosa's voice call out to Papagiuseppe either, because I was only seven months and getting ready to leave my mother's womb when Papagiuseppe died. I never heard Mammarosa call him and I never heard the sound of his voice reply. Although I don't know how and why, sometimes I hear a faint voice as of one struggling to speak, mumbling a prayer, I think. And when I hear this gentle, soft voice I see myself not on my mother's lap but inside of her, by Mammarosa's bed where once Papagiuseppe also rested and slept.

I asked Mammarosa if she ever called Papagiuseppe a devil. There was a silence. I ventured further, plainly asking her if Papagiuseppe was a devil like the husbands of the women on Piotta's patio. Mammarosa thought for just a little while as if she had to sort through a tall pile of something before she spoke. "No, no," she finally decided. "He was not a devil, he was an angel; though a fallen one, he was still an angel." And then Mammarosa whispered in my ear that she didn't always think Papagiuseppe was an angel. "There were times when he was so angry he couldn't sit still. He kicked and he fussed and he thrashed about." What else could she think except that he was a devil, no different than the husbands of the women who sat and embroidered on Piotta's patio? I think these must have been the times before Papagiuseppe stood tall, before he changed, when he crawled and squirmed, more like a worm than a butterfly. Mammarosa said that during those periods she mumbled and cried a million times, "Why, why, why?" until one dark night, and a strange dream.

Mammarosa said that on that night, as soon as her eyes became heavy with sleep, she felt a new weight added to each of her shoulders. She ran her hands up and down her arms and felt a smooth feathery softness. It was the same softness that ran past her fingers when she caressed her favourite little hen every evening in the coop. Mammarosa said that she looked to see and sure enough, she too had feathers. She had soft feathery wings attached to her shoulders! And when she tried to walk in her dream, the wings fluttered with each of her steps, until the faster she walked the more they fluttered, and soon they fluttered so fast that they lifted her whole body off the ground.

Her feet, being accustomed to moving whenever her body moved, tried to keep pace and hurried their steps until Mammarosa tucked them under, because she decided she would much rather fly than crawl in mid-air. Mammarosa flew across the valley where her vineyard blossomed, and there from a distance, far above the trees in the valley, she saw someone in trouble. Someone was creeping, inching along the ground by the side of the road. She folded her wings and landed with her feet precisely next to this creature, who was hurt and bleeding.

His face was so contorted by pain and anger that although it looked very familiar to her, she was confused and couldn't make out who it was. Yet she was not afraid. The creature was tall and strong, yet he could not stand because someone, something, had bruised him and inflicted deep wounds. Ones that would certainly leave deep ugly scars on his wings. He could not fly, he could not even stand. She saw him struggle and try, but all he could do was crawl.

Mammarosa tried to lift him by his wings to help him but he kicked and fussed until she too was wounded and bleeding. Without wanting to, she found herself wrestling with this stranger who had fallen by the wayside. But for some strange reason, she was drawn to him. She was drawn to stay by his side until he could heal, get off the ground, stand tall and perhaps even fly. And then Mammarosa's dream ended. But all through the morning she could not stop thinking about the creature she had wrestled with and stood by all throughout the long long seasons that winked by so quickly, as they do in dreamtime.

She saw the creature's familiar yet unrecognizable face in front of her as she stepped down from her bed. She saw his reflection in the water in the basin where she washed her hands and face. She saw him, still consumed by anger and by pain, still crawling on the ground, right before her with every movement and every turn her body made that morning, as if he was part of her very self. Mammarosa said that it was later that same day that she saw the fallen creature's face clearly. It was around the time of mid-morning mass, when she set out down Via Roma to buy a bouquet of fresh basil from the merchants at the piazza, that she heard a great commotion.

There was a whole crowd of people rushing out of the church, running after Don Antonio, the priest, and my Papagiuseppe was at the very front, ahead, even ahead of Don Antonio. Mammarosa said she came to a sudden stop. Her eyes blinked and blinked, trying to erase the scene that appeared in front of her, but it was no use. The crowd got bigger and the noise got louder. Don Antonio was shouting "Devil, devil," and Papagiuseppe was yelling "No, no," and Don Antonio shouted "Fallen, fallen," but Papagiuseppe still yelled, louder, "No, no." Papagiuseppe had dared to stand up and say no right in the middle of the sermon just as Don Antonio was waving his arms here and there and everywhere, trying to burn into the minds of those present the importance of telling him all about their wretched deeds, even the very thoughts of them, each and every one, every day. Don Antonio was calming himself down, doing less waving about and breathing a little easier when he said that he would do his part and sit there faithfully, inside the wooden box. Then suddenly his voice became like nearby thunder, warning that he would keep track, and for sure those that did not conform would never, ever, have a seat in the pews of paradise. He would see to it! It was then, after Papagiuseppe had sat there and listened and listened to Don Antonio say things like that, day after day, after he crawled in his pew, after he boiled and boiled, that he stood and spilled it all out: "No, no."

When Mammarosa arrived at the piazza Don Antonio was chasing him out of the church and that is what the commotion was all about. And the crowd, Papagiuseppe's very friends, were not on his side at all.

They said he should have known better and they laughed and whispered and they joined Don Antonio as they ran out of the church crying "Fallen, fallen, devil, devil."

But Mammarosa looked from the distance and she did not see a devil at all. She looked and there he was, Papagiuseppe standing tall. And she searched and searched his face as if it was the first time her eyes ever saw him. She looked and looked and she thought it resembled—no, no, in fact it was—the face of the creature that she had wrestled with all through her dream. Right there, where she stood in the piazza, Mammarosa closed her eyes, and smack in broad daylight, she was in her dream. The feathers had grown back and the scars blended into what are the normal lines on the face, on the arms and on the wings of any creature's body. She saw the wings flutter and flutter until they lifted Mammarosa's angel off the ground and she saw him fly high above the vineyard, even above the tallest of trees that grew there, shouting "No, no, no."

Yes, he was fallen, Mammarosa said, but he was not a devil. She was sure of it that day in the piazza and never did she doubt it since. There would be no more kicking and fussing and thrashing about. He was an angel.

Ricotta

Follow the cheese recipe and add more milk to the remaining liquid in the pot

Heat to 200 degrees

Now add a few ounces of vinegar and water (slowly)

You will see small pieces of ricotta floating

Gather and collect in a colander

Ricotta may be sweetened with honey or sugar and used to stuff cannoli shells

Or it may be mixed with a little simple sauce and used to stuff cannelloni shells

Paradise

CECI THRASHED AND KICKED and pushed and didn't care who he hurt or whether anyone bled on account of his thrashing about until another letter from America arrived. My father said in the letter that soon he was coming to San Giovanni—alone. He was coming as soon as he could get the documents in order and book a seat on a train to Halifax and a cabin on a ship to Naples. I interrupted my aunt with what I saw in my head as she was reading. I told her that I could see my mother, flying softly and gently, her wings spread out like a beautiful butterfly. But my aunt told me to hold the nonsense because for sure my mother had better things to do than chase the wind. I turned around to see if Ceci was laughing at me but he wasn't. Ceci sat quietly. He didn't move, he didn't even stir. He sat peacefully, staring at a blank spot in the air of the room, and listened carefully to every word. He didn't laugh once, he didn't even try. I couldn't believe this person was the same Ceci that I knew.

And at dusk the very next day, again I couldn't believe what my eyes were seeing. From far away I looked and squinted to make sure. It was only when he walked up the stairs and came real close to me that I believed that this dirty, sweaty, grey-covered body was Ceci's.

My aunt too was surprised. She too squinted and strained her eyes, even when Ceci stood right in front of her face. Ceci's shirt was a terrible mess, all covered in grey dust and crusts that clung to his shoulders. I thought my aunt would start to rattle off warnings to Ceci but surprisingly she didn't.

Ceci sat next to her at the top of the stairs on the threshold of our home on Via Monterosa and he didn't say a word. He didn't even flinch when my aunt peeled off the shirt, the blistered skin, and gently washed the leftover cement out of the raw exposed flesh of his shoulders. I saw my aunt take a deep breath as if something was welling up inside of her. I thought she would blurt it out, but she didn't. She just kept on peeling and washing Ceci's skin. I knew what was mulling in her mind. If she was going to say something it was going to be about Ceci's shirt. "At least you should have come home to put on an old shirt," she would have said. But she didn't blurt out a single word. She even stopped taking those deep breaths when Ceci handed her a little roll of paper liras, announcing that in the morning he would be off again, to carry buckets full of cement on his shoulders up and down the stairs of the new house being built at the new development at the basin of the mountain.

Could this be Ceci? Could this have all happened because of a simple letter from America that promised my father's arrival in San Giovanni? Maybe yes. Maybe that is all it took. Because ever since that letter Ceci did not laugh quite as strangely and my aunt was calmer. She didn't slap her face quite as often because the sausage count was always right, now.

Ceci had changed. I remember on the day another doctor (not Dr. Rafaelino) said I was going to die, Ceci didn't laugh either. Instead he looked quite kindly towards me. Yes, when the doctor looked into my eyes and shook his head because my heart was skipping and said I was going to die, Ceci offered me some of his canned Simmenthal meat and tomato salad. I thought I even saw a tear in his eye. He asked me to sit next to him and he filled up my plate with the meat he had bought at Mancuso's store with his own money.

Too bad my mother did not shout "No, no" to my father before, long before, when Ceci was little and didn't know that unless your boots were the right colour you couldn't stand in the front row. If my mother would have stood and argued and shouted and said no before then, my father would not have been in far-away America and Ceci would not have stood alone the day Mr. Ficosecco laughed at him and told him to get out of his picture. No sir, my father would have gone up to Mr. Ficosecco and looked that devil straight in the eyes long and hard, so hard that he would have gone blind. And then, not Ceci and not any other person would have been pushed out of the way on account of the wrong colour anything: boots, hair, skin or even dress.

I had always thought until now that Ceci was a devil, not half a devil like the rest of us because we were not christened, but a full real devil. With real horns coming out of his head, because that is what my aunt and everyone else said about Ceci. Now that I think about it, there were no horns on Ceci's head. In fact, I think Ceci may have been left too long on the side of the road, with his wings broken and hurting, just like Mammarosa's dream angel. In fact, if it wasn't for the chattering of the white-breasted swallows chasing after each other right by our window the morning my aunt was reading the letter, I'm sure I would have heard clearly the sound of wings courageously fluttering—Ceci's wings.

I have asked myself what gave my mother the courage to stand up. At first I thought it was the threatening letter that my aunt wrote to America but then I remembered that my mother's letter about her yes and no arguments with my father arrived only a few days after that serious letter from my exasperated aunt left San Giovanni. My aunt mailed that letter herself. I saw her lick the flap and pound it shut with her fist and I heard her say a million times to the man at the post office wicket, "Registered mail, registered mail . . . don't forget it is to go registered mail." I watched, standing a little ways from where my aunt was, as the man first rolled his eyes, then threw up his arms and squeezed his temples hard between his hands. "Oi, signorina, my head, please! Any more of this registered mail, registered mail and I'll have to be transferred in a straitjacket!" And after all that, he reminded her patiently that registered mail took longer to arrive in America. But my aunt didn't care. She had said registered mail and not even thunder and lightning were going to change her mind.

But I'm sure my aunt's letter didn't help my father's case at all when it finally did arrive. In fact, I think it probably cemented my mother's stand and weakened my father's position. That letter was of no help on any front and now that I think about it I should have done some shouting of my own. "No, no, please no," I should have shouted when my aunt first picked up pen and paper to carry out her threat. I should have assured my aunt with a million convincing words that Ceci would never eat sausage again.

And as for me, I should have pledged right there and

then, before she sat down to write, never to allow candies or sweets or even sugar to ever touch my lips again. I should have sworn it to her and hoped to die, as long as she would not have written. I should have pleaded, "Anything, anything, but not this! Please don't write to America. If they find out we are bad they will make us leave. I want to stay here in San Giovanni. I don't want to go to America." I should have asked my aunt to pull my hair. I should offered every one of my long curls, laying them on her lap where she sat to write. I should have asked her to slap my face and punish me. Maybe I should have pulled my own hair and slapped my own face. Anything, anything, as long as that letter had not left San Giovanni. My father was coming home but he was not coming to stay. He was coming to make preparations, sign papers, so we too could go away.

I never thought we really would have to leave because in every letter, up until lately, my father promised that soon he would be back. And I believed him. My aunt didn't believe him. When she read his first letters, she did. She did and I saw her shake her head, sighing that we would never make it to America if my father didn't stop writing nonsense. Nonsense like telling my aunt to greet his homeland—his land of exquisite tastes where soft and warm the sweet breezes murmur over the gentle rolling hills and rugged peaks that since time have stood immortal. But ever since those kinds of letters dwindled she knew we were going. She knew my parents would not come back.

Why else then when Mr. Volpe tried to sell her a gas stove did she say no? Why else were our walls bare and why else did we still rip the flesh off the back of our thighs on the old rush-woven seats when even Piperella had new smooth, modern plastic chairs? It was because she was preparing to go to America. And I believed her until one day I heard La Casinise say something like "They go, they go. You stay, let them go." And I saw my aunt cry because she didn't know what to do about going to America!

What!? My aunt didn't want to go to America? Well, I didn't want to go, but if I had to, I certainly wanted her to come along. It had never occurred to me that she wouldn't, that she shouldn't. How could she even have allowed the thought of staying in San Giovanni to find a place at the very back of her head? Why, America was like paradise, even if there were a lot of children in paradise, for sure I thought my aunt wouldn't mind going there. So I got in front of La Casinise, looked into my aunt's tearful eyes and reminded her that America was like paradise, a promised land that flowed with milk and honey and bread and wine. "Bernardo told me," I said. But I lied. Bernardo had never told me anything about America even though he had plenty of jars and tins with sweet and fine things in them that were from America. Once I saw him drop a spoonful of ground coffee in a cup of hot water and presto—just like magic—the whole house smelled like fresh espresso and there was no espresso machine in sight. Well, it wasn't really a full lie when I said that Bernardo told me that America was paradise. You see, once I had heard someone say that America was a land of milk and honey and another time I had heard Bernardo say that paradise was a heavenly Canaan, a heavenly promised land where milk and honey freely flowed, so I put the two together to better convince my aunt about America.

But my aunt turned away and said as if in pain, "Oi, oi, a moment alone, a moment of peace, peace and quiet, please, please." I don't think she really wanted to be alone. She just wanted to keep on talking with La Casinise, and that is just what she did. No sooner did she ask me for a moment alone and for peace and quiet than she was cheek to cheek with La Casinise, wailing all over again about staying in San Giovanni or going to America. "What you don't want is what always ends up sprouting in your garden. It's always like that, it never changes," my aunt said. La Casinise told her that unlike herself, who was old and frail, my aunt was still young and strong, and she could weed whatever sprouted voluntarily and plant what she wanted to in her garden. My aunt was having a hard time with this weeding and planting suggestion, I could tell, because some of the finest and most beautiful things, like dandelions with petals of the shiniest gold and thistles clustered like royal purple crowns, came up on their own.

My aunt knew that. I heard her say her heart wouldn't give her the go-ahead to uproot her garden. "I am torn," my aunt said. I understood my aunt. If she was going to come to America (to paradise) with us, the only sure promise was nothing but children, children and more children—seven times children for the rest of her life. But I could have convinced my aunt that dandelions and thistles that sprouted voluntarily were also beautiful. "Just look at us. Just look at me, in fact." I would have to admit that I was obnoxious sometimes and gave her no rest, like a thistle thorn stuck in her flesh, but I was still beautiful, wasn't I? If not, why did she, all these years, call me bella, bella? Had she lied to me that I was her bella? I would have said it and convinced her, I'm sure, if only La Casinise did not insist on staying so close to my aunt.

She sat there with her face next to my aunt's ears, telling her that she should uproot what she didn't want and start a new garden from scratch. "Don't water a thistle, don't water a thistle," she kept on whispering. "It will give you nothing but thorns in return." She told my aunt right in my presence (as if I was stupid and didn't understand what she meant) not to water a thistle.

The Ave Maria bells had rung and it was past the dinner hour.

The broadbeans in La Casinise's lap had all been shelled and she should have been thinking about cooking the beans and throwing the shells to the pigs in the sty under her own stairs because they were squealing. Not to mention that her husband would soon appear, bouncing from one wall of Via Monterosa to the other, full of wine. But no, she kept on whispering instead. La Casinise should have been minding her own business but she wasn't.

I am convinced that not only did she enjoy seeing my aunt cry, but she wanted to see her shake with fear. She started to tell my aunt about Alfredo the old blacksmith, how he may as well have watered a thistle when he followed his son because he almost got ripped apart by thorns. "But thanks be to Providence, he didn't," she said. He didn't because Alfredo was able to pull the thistle right from its roots, just in time. "Their mother wants you, the children want you, they want you because of what they can get from you. They will squeeze and squeeze until you will have been squeezed and pricked and choked right out of your own garden," La Casinise said with her long nose stuck into my aunt's ear.

La Casinise didn't know what she was talking about. What did Alfredo the blacksmith's life have in common with my aunt's? If La Casinise was Sara's age and not an elder, I would have slammed my hips against hers and sent her flying a mile. There was no way Alfredo could have known if his son was genuine and really cared and wanted him. There was no way Alfredo could have known if it was a thistle, a dandelion or a head of lettuce that he was tending in his garden. Alfredo was rich and my aunt was not. What was I, or any of us, going to squeeze out of my aunt?

The other day she took me to Maria Pia's sister, who is a seamstress, and she let me choose a lovely green piece of linen for a new dress for the occasion of my father's arrival. I heard her tell Maria Pia's sister that she would pay for it later, when she had sold her last remaining sack of potatoes. Alfredo had potatoes, tons of them, and he had money too. How was Alfredo to know if his son wanted him, all ancient and consumed, just for himself or for what he had?

My aunt had nothing. All she had were the holes in the pockets of her skirt. That's what she showed me every time I asked her for twenty liras in the summer when Sara ran around licking cone after cone of lemon "gelato." My aunt would dig in her pockets and pull out the torn lining. That's what she had. She had nothing. I didn't want her to come to America because of anything. I just wanted her to come, that's all. But no one would listen to me. My aunt was busy crying and La Casinise was too involved in this Alfredo story. As if we didn't know Alfredo's story.

I remember Alfredo. Everyone knew Alfredo. Alfredo agreed to go with his son one day. They were not going far like we who were off to America, they were just going to a lawyer's office. But it was still a ways off from the piazza in San Giovanni where Alfredo lived now that he had sold his blacksmith shop. On the way there, when the road became rocky and Alfredo lost his balance, his son held him by the elbow, gently yet tight, and insisted he climb on the donkey that was loaded with things like a flask of wine and a good cured ham for the lawyer. When the donkey heard Alfredo's son shout "Ha, ha, ha" he knew it was time to resume his clip-clop up the hill and he did with the old man on his back.

But not poor Alfredo. Alfredo didn't know what it meant when he heard all that "Hahahahaha, hahaha haha," all through the time the lawyer wrote on the long sheets of paper. It sounded to him like plain old smiling and laughing between father and son and a trusted friend. It was all sweetness and laughter, that's what Alfredo thought it was, until the long list of possessions was all recorded, squeezed on a few sheets of paper, and until he signed them all over, everything over to his son. While he drew a cross at the bottom of the pages along a dotted line he heard the same "Hahahahaha, hahaha hahaha."

But all the way on the descent towards home when the stones on the hill started to slip and slide under Alfredo's feet, he heard nothing. Alfredo waited for his son to stop the donkey and offer him a ride and be kind like he was on the way up when he agreed to follow him, but the offer didn't come. Alfredo heard nothing except the echo of that "Hahahahaha, hahahahahaha" in his ears.

The old man stopped walking and said that he was very tired but the offer still didn't come. So Alfredo asked if he could mount the donkey but the son replied that the beast too was tired and then the "Hahahahaha, hahaha ha" in his ears got louder.

La Casinise told my aunt that it was a good thing that what happened to Alfredo happened so soon after he had signed the deed. It gave him time. He asked his son to go on ahead and promised that he would catch up with him later. The son and the donkey did. They marched right on ahead and left the old man behind. The old man turned around and went back.

Alfredo pulled up a chair in the lawyer's office and even if his hand was shaking some, he still was able to make another cross along another dotted line on another long sheet of paper that gave him all his possessions back. Then he headed back down the hill slowly because he had lots of time. "As long as he was worth something no one would push him," La Casinise told my aunt, and then she also said for my aunt to take her time. But what did La Casinise know? My aunt didn't have time, my mother had already sent a letter saying that we should go to Veltri's Photo on Via Roma next to the butcher shop to have our pictures taken. Also, a long sheet of paper requesting my aunt's signature had arrived just the other day in a brown shellacked envelope from the Canadian Embassy in Rome.

Of course my aunt didn't have time. I started to get real close to my aunt's skirt. I didn't mean to push my aunt or anything, but if she was going to spend too much time with La Casinise she might have to rush in the end and do the wrong thing. She might listen to her advice about gardening and, in her hurry, pull up everything. My aunt hadn't said a word while La Casinise told her the absurd story of the old man who followed his son. But now, as my body brushed against hers, I heard my aunt take a breath, a deep breath. I thought my heart would jump up right through my throat and end up on La Casinise's lap, still full of empty broadbean shells.

"My heart won't do it. I can't do it. I can't just rip things up," my aunt said. And as she did I felt my own heart return to its beating place. Now that I knew my aunt would sign the papers and get her picture taken and come to America I pushed my hip against hers, just so that her ears would be out of reach, away from La Casinise's mouth before she had a chance to say again, "Don't water a thistle, don't water a thistle, rip it, weed it out."

I was trying to get my aunt's attention when I pushed my hip against hers, so I could smile at her and let her know that I was happy she was coming to America, but she turned the other way and gave the bucket, all full of pigs' slop, a violent kick that sent it flying several yards. I didn't mind. I wished I could have sent a bucket of pig slop flying. It wasn't that I didn't feel like it, oh no, it was having to run up Via Monterosa and up the whole mountain with my aunt at my heels that stopped me.

I wasn't happy about leaving for America either. I really didn't want to go. Mammarosa wanted to go but she said she couldn't. "They won't let me," she said. "I'm feeble and old, I would never pass the health tests and the X-ray exams." I told Mammarosa that if she didn't go then for sure I would never leave either. Mammarosa knew that I was not just saying empty words to be polite. She knew that if she couldn't go, no one would. Even my mother and my father knew that. We were to move together, as one body, and never ever again be divided. So I kept on telling Mammarosa that if we really had to get this going-to-America thing done, she too must agree and come along. But she kept on saying no, no, no. She said that she must stay where she was and we were to go to America because we had waited long enough. She said we were to leave without regret, because in America we would blossom and grow just like the figs on the trees at the vineyard, even after that terrible storm. And then Mammarosa was quiet. As quiet as always when a storm raged in her insides. She sat for a long while at a time in her little child's chair by the fireplace.

I couldn't understand why we could not blossom and grow here in San Giovanni right where we were planted. I couldn't understand why the wind, the rain, the lightning and the thunder had to rip gaping holes all through the mountain's side. Why they had to beat, consume and strip naked the trees to their very roots. And then the thought came to me like lightning in the middle of darkness: "I will never leave, I don't have to."

Yes, they could make me go but I didn't have to move. They could pull me and drag me, but I would hold my ground and hold on tight. Just like the roots of my tree on the ravine, I would be flexible and elastic. That way, when I would be pulled halfway around the world I would not break but stand firm, right where I belonged, on the sunrise side of San Giovanni's mountain, next to my own tree on the ravine.

Suddenly I thought I might not mind at all going to America. In fact, I think I would have been happy about the whole adventure of going halfway around the world now if it wasn't for Mammarosa, who insisted that she must step out of our way because she was a roadblock.

Every time when I said she must come along she always came back with that horseshit about not passing the health test and about no one ever making it to America without a satisfactory X-ray and health exam. One day I shouted, "You are wrong, America is not like that at all." I even told her that I had the proof. I told her about Maria Pia's postcard, the one her father had sent, the same one she brought to school. I told Mammarosa that I did not remember reading on that postcard anything that suggested America was the land of the perfect, the young, the strong and the healthy. I told her that I remembered seeing clearly on Maria Pia's postcard these words in big bold letters: "America: The home of the brave and the land of the free." "See, did you hear what I said? The land of the brave and the free. You can come, of course you can come."

Mammarosa smiled, but then she turned away, towards the flame that burned hot in the fireplace, and she mumbled. There was no winning. It was of no use to reason with Mammarosa over this issue. She had become as unyielding as the grave. From my pillow, late into the night, I saw that she mumbled and I fell asleep knowing Mammarosa still mumbled.

Now I know, but I should have known then, what the silent words that moved her lips were. Then I, too, could have done some mumbling of my own. I could have shouted and cried and pleaded and I could have given God a million reasons why Mammarosa would not have been in our way. I would have asked God not to pay attention to what she said. I would have argued that she was not a roadblock—oh, no, not at all! She was like the first rays of sunlight on cobblestones after a dark night. I would have asked Him not to listen to her, but I didn't because I slept.

There are two things I will never forgive myself for— ever. One, for not stopping my aunt from writing that letter, and two, for sleeping through Mammarosa's mumblings.

Brodo

For once leave the hen alone and put a nice
rooster in a big pot of boiling water

When the scum surfaces remove it all
with a spoon and discard

Now you can throw in celery, onions, parsley
and carrots and let it cook for a long time

Strain

Clean the meat from the bones
and add it to the brodo

Slice carrots and return to the brodo

Drink as is from a bowl or add pasta
and eat with a spoon

Happiness

MY AUNT TOO COULDN'T FORGIVE HERSELF, although I don't know for what. It was a hot day, there was no doubt another summer had circled around the world and now rested on San Giovanni's mountain. I remember my aunt standing there by Mammarosa's bed with her hands over her face, crying and saying, "Forgive me, Mamma, forgive me." I saw the tears stream right through her fingers, down her thin wrists. There was panic in her eyes and they were the deepest blue, like the sea waves tossed by the wind far from shore in a storm, even a summer storm. I had the feeling they would stay blue for a very long time. My aunt was sad—as if Mammarosa had refused to forgive her. But Mammarosa didn't say anything. She just lay there quietly as I had seen her many times before in the evenings when she sat by the fire. I remember how I tried many times to break into her quietness, but she stopped me. She stopped me with her fingers pressed against her lips. "Shh, you can't hear the heart beat unless you are still and silent," Mammarosa told me a million times, but I always forgot. My aunt kept on crying while she hurried about the house. Mammarosa was never going to hear her heartbeat.

I could hear Mammarosa's heartbeat, I could see it even now in the veins beneath the transparent veil of skin on her neck that shook and trembled. But Mammarosa didn't tremble as she lay there weak and helpless with her mouth half open as if she had been thirsty forever and there was no hope of water around, she did not tremble.

Mammarosa had left early that morning, as usual. She had taken her little black pocket knife and a burlap sack because she had planned to pick dandelions and chicory along the way to the vineyard.

It was almost mid-morning when I saw her coming back, labouring up the incline towards Via Monterosa. She was weak but walked on, stubbornly, dragging her sack. In it were a few handfuls of the bitter greens, enough for one minestra. I watched her from a distance, from the threshold of our house. I looked on with my mouth half open, thirsty for words, but they did not come. And now Mammarosa lay there in bed.

Soon Bernardo arrived and was there by her side, shaking his head. Then the doctor came and he too shook his head. "Nothing, nothing, there is nothing that can be done. The ulcer has burst, it has gone too far. How old? Seventy-three? No, no. She won't make it to the hospital. It's too far to the city." He looked down at his pad of paper, scribbling something all the while he spoke. When he finally lifted his head he tore a slip off his writing pad and handed it to my aunt. "They will make her comfortable. But it will not be long." These were his final words.

I sat in front of the spent fire, squirming on Mammarosa's little chair, wondering if he would have been so quick to speak and write if it had been his mother and not Mammarosa lying helpless on that bed. Where was Dr. Rafaelino? My aunt should have called Dr. Rafaelino. He would have looked into Mammarosa's eyes and said, "It is nothing, nothing, it is only an ulcer. How old? Seventy-three? No problem. We will have her in the hospital in two hours. In fact, I will send my driver with my car and it will take even less time." That's what Dr. Rafaelino would have said. But no, this jackass who stood by Mammarosa's bed whispered loudly, without discretion, in my aunt's ear, "Nothing, nothing, there is nothing left to do."

And then to make matters worse Tata arrived. When she came in through the door, a wave of panic ran from the top of my head to the bottom of my feet. My heart moved. Mammarosa heard it for sure, even through all the commotion. When Tata stepped over our threshold my heart fluttered like swallows' wings when their nests under the clay tiles of our roof were threatened by the vampire bats who arrived punctually every day at dusk. I thought for a moment my heart would stop, I thought this was the moment I was destined to die.

Tata was bad news. She had been at our house before, and really I had not minded, but it did not feel right to see her there just now with Mammarosa sick in bed. I just wished that she had not come.

I had put it together some time ago. Everywhere she went something bad happened. She was there, like the white flag of defeat, at every disaster, every accident, every revolt and conflict, but mostly at sickbeds. She was the first to run out onto the street and shout "Earthquake" the night of the hottest day last summer. She just happened to be walking through the ravine when the miller's truck overturned off the road. And it was Tata, of course, who pulled his broken body out of the wreck while stronger men looked on. She was there at the piazza, marching and shouting, showing off her red petticoats and waving a red scarf, inciting the crowd at the last election. When things got out of hand and the police shot at random in the crowd—they missed her! It was as if Tata had received a divine ordination to pave the way for the angel of death. That is why I didn't want her there.

But whether I liked it or not, Tata came in every day, several times a day, after Mammarosa lay in bed day and night. She whispered things in my aunt's ears. I did get close so I could hear but Tata was not like the donkey who examined Mammarosa, she whispered for real. So I heard nothing. All I had to go by was what I saw.

One morning I saw Tata take a little packet out of her skirt pocket and empty it in the water of my aunt's washtub. The water immediately became black and thick like the inkwell of my desk at school. I watched as my aunt dropped her dress, blouses and the few other clothes she had in the black water. Then she stepped aside while Tata stirred them round and round with the stick of the broom. Mammarosa just lay there in bed and said nothing. She should have. They were painting the world black before darkness even came. They were stripping it of every colour. They were turning off the lights and the sun had not set yet.

The sun's rays played hide-and-seek with the water that flowed over the rocks in the brook at the basin of the mountain. Mammarosa had come here often with her jugs to get water and sometimes even to wash clothes. I too went there. I went there on that black day and picked vibrant red poppies, deep purple pansies and pure white daisies from among a patch of tender grass alongside the stream. I picked them bright and I picked colourful, just for Mammarosa. I held them tightly by their stems but they cried. They cried and cried and soon my hands were wet with tears that flowed down to my wrists.

By the time I handed them to Mammarosa they had surrendered and died. They were all flopped over, the petals bruised, and the stems, drained, no longer held them up. There is nothing beautiful about death, I decided as I handed Mammarosa the lifeless bunch. But Mammarosa said, "They are beautiful, oh they are sooo beautiful, my bene!" She slowly caressed each one. She held them close to her face and inhaled deeply, as deeply as she was able to. "Mmmm. I smell the river. You have brought me the sun!" I was going to say that they were disgusting, but I didn't.

I remember once I did say that to Mammarosa. It was the day she took me to the wheat fields. It was in the fall. We had taken the little train there, a proud little green wagon that whistled loudly before every tunnel and showed off its impressive F.S. (State Railways) insignia affixed with gold nails at the edge of its every window.

I remember that as soon as I got to the field I ran off to trample, skip and hop all over the black earth. If my aunt had been there she would have shouted a few threats but not Mammarosa. Mammarosa took me by the hand and held me still by her side as she knelt on the ground and with her hand uncovered the earth. I couldn't believe what I saw. In the dirt were seeds, little grains of wheat to be exact. Some were just opening, some had thrown off their shells, just like the snake who had shed its skin and left it hanging from the peach tree. Some looked rotten, attached to a little pale yellow remnant, and yes, there was a stench coming from the ground—that is why I said they were disgusting with my nose tightly held between my fingers. But Mammarosa shook her head several times and said "No." "No," she said. "You should be happy, not disgusted. They are beautiful and come June they will indeed be a sight to behold, tall, blond and as good as gold." But I didn't see gold just then. All I saw was an ugly mess of dirt and rot, not beauty and certainly not a reason for happiness, or for jumping up and down with joy, for sure.

Beauty and happiness, I still saw not one or the other as I stood next to Mammarosa by her bed, holding on to those dead flowers. Mammarosa knew I was not happy. She knew because she knew everything, and even now, when she could hardly turn around to look at me, she knew and saw. In her mind, she saw me still standing there on that wheat field with my nose turned up, saying, "Ughhhh, that's disgusting." Mammarosa always told me that when I turned up my nose and pouted I was not beautiful. While I stood next to her I was aware that I was really pouting. So I made an effort to smile, to erase the pout, just for her, because once I heard her say that happiness on the lips makes the whole face beautiful.

Once when I was all alone, when I had the house all to myself (and that was not often) I looked in the mirror of the dresser, trying to figure out the best pout possibility so my lips and whole mouth might look plump and thick like Maria Pia's. I wrinkled my nose and turned and twisted my lips in every possible direction but the more I tried the worse I looked. In fact, the more I pouted the more I struggled just to breathe. It is truly a struggle to pout and turn up your nose and breathe at the same time. I remember having to take such deep and strong breaths through my upturned contorted lips and nose that I almost passed out. This pouting business had threatened my very life even if it was only for a short little while in front of the mirror.

Once I did see a man really struggling to live. I was walking alongside Mammarosa on our way home from the vineyard, crossing the Neto River bridge, when a wave of courage came over me and I reached and stretched to look over the cement wall that banked the narrow passage. I expected to see the river peacefully flowing, because it was a nice day with no wind at all, but instead I frantically pulled on Mammarosa's skirt and pointed below because there was a man in the water, thrashing about. He looked quite ugly with his eyes bulging out of their sockets and his mouth, open, gasping for air as he went up and down and in and out of the water.

Mammarosa was ready to yell, she had already taken a long breath and was going to let it out, when out of nowhere I saw another man, a stranger, throw himself in the water and drag that miserable wretch to safety on the bank of the river.

"Did that stranger not care about his own life?" I asked Mammarosa. But Mammarosa did not answer my question. She had one of her own. She wanted to know how it was that I was certain that the men were strangers. For all we knew, she said, they could have been brothers. "What if someone saw the two of us together and thought, Oh, there goes a strange old woman taking a strange girl home." "Very well, then," I said to Mammarosa. "But why would anyone, stranger or not, give their life away, why?" "Because love is stronger than death," Mammarosa replied. "It gives and gives and is never afraid. It gives until there is nothing left to give, until there remains not even a spot of flesh for itself to live."

This giving and giving didn't seem fair to me. It was not right that after one gives and gives there should not be even a tiny little spot left for herself. It was not fair that one should lose one's own place to live. I remember Mammarosa saying that giving up your spot and place to live didn't mean you stopped living. She said that when all the flesh is gone, you just move on and go on living without it. Mammarosa said it was a little like going to America—travelling a long way to find a better place.

Mammarosa gave and gave. She even gave what no one asked her to give. She had convinced herself that we had to go to America at all costs. The way had to be clear and now she had convinced God of it too. She decided that she must give it all up and give it now, I know she did, otherwise what was she doing languishing in this bed day and night?

I tried not to pout, I tried to smile for Mammarosa and be happy and look beautiful but I couldn't. As a matter of fact, I was starting to breathe heavy and hard, because I was angry. I had not yet decided with whom: my aunt, my father, Mammarosa, the jackass who looked in her eyes, myself or maybe God for giving in to Mammarosa's argument over not going to America before I had a fair chance to say what I thought about it. I was not happy and I was going to pout for a long time. But I was curious to know what was in Mammarosa's heart. Mammarosa once said that if I was still and silent, and listened carefully enough, not only would I hear the beat of the heart but I could actually weigh it. I had sat still and silent enough times, but had never really listened that well, because my mind wandered in the dense maze of the silence when Mammarosa and I sat at night by the fireplace.

If I listened now I would know. I wished and wished for a pair of scales where I could weigh, on the one side, our departure for America, and on the other side, Mammarosa—then I would really know if she was really happy in that bed.

I remember once, when Mammarosa could talk longer and louder, asking her about happiness. I did because that day Mr. Ficosecco had gone on and on for a good hour on the subject, and by the time he finished, I didn't know what was heads and what was tails about happiness. He had me all mixed up and confused.

It didn't take Mammarosa an hour, although she had to think a little when I first asked her about happiness. "It is nothing more than a line, a simple line," she said slowly. Mammarosa could not read or write very well yet but she could draw a line, a little crooked, yes, because she was old, but still it was a line.

She drew one on the hearth, with a piece of dead coal that she had picked from the ashes, and when she was finished she pointed to it and said, "This is happiness." She said it was really a fence, that line, for capturing dreams. She said that if they were not captured and kept within the line, dreams would run away and disappear altogether. "You'll chase the wind and embrace nothing but a mirage if you don't draw a line," Mammarosa said.

I remember trying to embrace a mirage once. I didn't know then that it was a mirage. To me it was wave after shining wave of water rolling across the freshly paved road in the dense heat of summer. I ran and ran to catch the waves of water, but the further I ran, the further they moved away from me. I chased and chased after them until the sun no longer shone bright and the waves of water stopped their game of rolling on the road and disappeared. I remember standing there crying because not only had I lost my game, but I had also lost my way back home. In fact if it wasn't for Filomena, the poor devil, who worked in her mother's fields until late and was just then walking home carrying her child on her hip, I too would have disappeared. I could see the importance of what Mammarosa said, but it is not easy to draw that kind of line. Mammarosa knew it was not easy. She had tried to teach Peppe because Peppe, although he was the best, always cried.

It was a rite, this crying thing of Peppe which he performed every day punctually at the dinner hour. I remember, without fail, right after Nina said thanks, he looked around the table and with his eyes made a stop at every plate. He stopped at Nina's, at Ceci's, at Julia's and at mine, and then, no matter how much he tried to suppress the sobs and the tears, he broke down and cried. He didn't care if my aunt slapped her face or pulled her hair, nor did he consider that one of these days she might injure herself seriously on account of his crying, no never, not Peppe. Even after my aunt came up with the brilliant idea of serving Peppe's portion at dinner in a big bowl so it looked bigger, he still cried sometimes.

I remember the day Mammarosa decided she had had enough of Peppe's unhappiness and tears. That was the precise day that she sat him down beside her on the threshold of our house and showed him patiently how to draw a line. "It's not a big thing, this crying thing you do," Mammarosa said to Peppe. But she also said that tears were like the raindrops. One at a time and a little at a time they wash mountains and tear down walls. Whole villages had disappeared, she said, because of tiny little raindrops, as tiny as Peppe's tears. She asked Peppe to imagine for just a moment what his tears, which flowed and flowed incessantly because of his unhappiness, could do to our delicate little fences, those little lines of ours that we draw. But he didn't answer. (I think he was ready to cry again.) "Before you know it, while you are still going about pouting and crying, you look around and find that your dreams and all the special things of your life are not there, because the line has been washed away," Mammarosa said to Peppe.

Mammarosa showed Peppe just how to draw his line and keep it safe. She told him that starting that very evening he must say to himself, "I will not cry if I get one piece of sausage, I will smile and be happy. You see," she said, "then if you get two pieces you will be extra happy. Now should you get a half piece, then you must remember the times when you had none, and then again you will be happy. And if indeed, God forbid, the day will come when there will not even be a half piece of sausage in your bowl, then think of the fields full of chicory and dandelions that also are good to eat. They are free and easy to digest and that too should make you happy because you will have spared a pig and your body a whole lot of trouble. Pork is hard on the liver, you know." But Peppe didn't want to know.

Even now from her bed Mammarosa summoned my aunt to her side once in a while. "Peppe, be patient with Peppe," I heard her whisper. And my aunt nodded and didn't shout. Not even once since Mammarosa lay in bed did I hear my aunt shout. In fact, I have seen her go about whispering all day long, sometimes in angry frustrated whispers that made her pull not only at her hair but tear at her clothes too, but nonetheless whispers.

One morning after Tata whispered something in my aunt's ears that I could not make out, I followed them as they both hurried down Via Monterosa. It looked like they were going to the little market in front of Mancuso's store. It was early Saturday morning and the out-of-town merchants had already set up their tables with their wares.

I ran, because if my aunt was really going to the market, then I really wanted a new pair of shoes. Maria Pia came to school a few days before with a new pair of shoes, and not only were they new, but they had a heel, a high heel! So now Maria Pia no longer walked ahead but sideways too, with her hips going here and there, as if it was necessary, this swinging of hers, now that she wore heels. I wouldn't know if it was necessary, but I sure wanted to find out. I was going to try anyway.

I had tried already, a few months ago, when I saw my aunt wandering through the tables at the same market. I remember pulling at her skirt and pointing to a mountain of shoes but she said no. There were millions of men's shoes and children's shoes but mostly women's shoes on that pile, and the women's shoes had high heels. "Please, please, they cost no more than a chocolate bar, please," I pleaded. But my aunt shook me off and looked at me as if I had committed a crime. Goodness, I had just asked for shoes! "I'd rather you go barefoot than wear those shoes," she whispered. As we walked away from the market she told me that the reason the shoes were so cheap was that they were stolen. Some were stolen from the living, but mostly from the dead, during the war, and mostly from Jews, she said. I don't know what a Jew is or what one looks like. I have never seen one.

My father has seen a Jew. Many Jews. While he was marching behind other soldiers during the time of the war, he saw a huge dugout with soil scattered over a whole pile of bodies fed to the earth like unwanted mouldy bread, castoff crushed grapes. "Until one day," my aunt said, "when the earth would have her fill of bread and wine and throw up the slain." "Jews, Jews," the captain of my father's company said. My aunt said that's when my father, in the middle of the night, snuck out of his campsite near Pisa. He left because he did not want to ever have to take part in something he might later regret. "Better dead," he said, "than dying with regret." So he ran and ran and hid among the corn and the wheat in the fields and he slept surrounded by thick trees where the wolves howled at night.

My father didn't always run. My mother and Bernardo once begged my father to run but he wouldn't. It was in church at a time when the voices of war were growing loud. It was during one of Bernardo's heated sermons. No sooner did Bernardo begin to read his text—"Give to Caesar what belongs to Caesar and give to . . ."—than my father rose from where he sat and stood in the middle of the congregation on the men's side and just as heatedly replied, "Give to Caesar a "calcio in culo," that's what belongs to Caesar, because Caesar has no business in Palestine!"

Aie! A "calcio in culo"? A kick in the ass to Caesar! Bernardo wiped the pearls of sweat with a swipe of his thick hand across his brow while my mother's head sunk deep into her lap. They cried "run" but my father wouldn't.

He ran now, all alone. He hid and ran until, near Rome, at a crumbled railway station where he had spent the night, he felt a strange hand shake him. The gentle hand was that of an African who woke him. The African spoke in a strange tongue. My father did not know then that it was English, but he didn't care, so he followed the African because they were not enemies, they were friends.

I have seen an African but I have not seen a Jew. I saw the African in a picture that Professor Ciano's sister received in a letter from her husband who worked in Eritrea. Africans have plump lips, way thicker and fatter than Maria Pia's, and of course I liked that, but I didn't like their noses. I don't know why I didn't, outside of the fact maybe that my aunt herself had big nostrils and a flat nose and she always said that it was not the best part of her face. Once I even heard her say that she hated her face because of her squished nose and big nostrils. And oh, yes, Africans have black skin, much blacker than Peppe, who sometimes we called African because of his dark complexion.

There were a lot of people in San Giovanni with dark skin. The men of San Giovanni called any woman with dark skin a "bella mora." Peppino the Gypsy, every St. John's day, collected one hundred liras for each time he sang his "Marina, Marina the Bella Mora" song. The song was about a much-loved woman called Marina, a dark woman, as dark as the mora berries, who sends men's hearts beating a thousand miles an hour.

We had a "mora" bush at the vineyard. Its blossoms became the blackest berries and everyone said they were beautiful, but the women of Piotta's patio who crowded around the photograph from Eritrea looked sad and shook their heads. "Black, black," they said. No one looked sad and shook their heads when twins with hair and skin as white as death were born to a "bella mora" in San Giovanni. Mr. Ficosecco said that they were albinos.

I have seen albinos but not a Jew. I don't know why I have never met one. I should have. Mr. Ficosecco said that it was quite possible that Jews lived right here in our own town on account of San Giovanni being that famous "ius asyli" a city that guaranteed the right to refuge, a title received smack right at the same time when Jews were told to leave the countries of Spain and Portugal. The last time Mr. Ficosecco said that he looked straight at me. But I stared at him right back for a very long time and then I gave him a good rolling of my eyeballs. I didn't have to worry, though, no one would want my shoes. Why do you think I kept on pestering my aunt that I wanted new ones?

I looked at the pile from far away and thought that whoever or whatever Jews were they couldn't have been too much different than me because there among the millions of stolen shoes I spotted a pair that would fit me just perfectly. I had asked my aunt for the shoes before, and now, a few months later, even after what she said, I was still running towards her and going to ask again. I don't know what made me think that she would change her mind about that mountain of shoes on the ground in front of Mancuso's store. I ran to meet my aunt but when I got close I stopped running. I saw her and Tata nodding and pointing to some very fine linens at a merchant's table. I saw my aunt reach into her pocket and count and recount her money while Tata argued with the merchant. Then I saw both Tata and my aunt talk while they turned up their noses at the sheets, but the merchant didn't seem to care, although I did see him throw his arms up in the air. He seemed to me quite angry while he pretended to fold the sheets and put them away.

When I saw them standing there I forgot about my shoes because I saw in my mind a mountain, a whole mountain, as big as San Giovanni's, full of women in their pretty shoes. I saw them swaying on their tall delicate heels, going round and round, walking, shopping and driving merchants mad, and then they all fell down and even the mountain shrank, it was nothing but a pile of stolen junk on the ground in front of Mancuso's store.

I saw my aunt cry all the way home, not because she couldn't buy the linen, oh no, she settled with the merchant and carried the beautiful sheets under her arms. But she cried because for the first time in her life she bought something beautiful and no one was going to be happy about it. Death was going to steal the linens with Mammarosa in them and only the grave would enjoy their beauty.

But my aunt was wrong. She did not know about Mammarosa. She did not know how well she could draw a line. As a matter of fact, Mammarosa smiled and looked happy when my aunt spread the sheets on the bed for her to see. She was thrilled that she should be wrapped in beauty and go with such dignity too.

They were indeed beautiful, those sheets, of the finest pure-white linen, with angels embroidered from one end of them to the other. Even the pillow where Mammarosa's head would rest had angels on it, all in a row, wing holding wing. There were angels on the sheets and there were angels on the pillow but I didn't see angels next to Mammarosa and she didn't either, because she just lay there silent, every day more silent.

The women of Piotta's patio, the old and the ancient, all came. They came to say good-bye. I saw them come up the stairs and they took a very long time. "Consumed, consumed with one foot in the grave," they would have replied if I had been respectful and asked "How are you?" I didn't ask, but they said it anyway. "Consumed, consumed with one foot in the grave," they cried as they approached Mammarosa's bed.

I heard them remind Mammarosa of the hard life she had, of the hard times she had gone through and of the hard work she had done, as if she didn't know. They whispered among themselves how quiet Mammarosa was. They said she had not flirted with regret, ever. That is why she lay there peaceful, they said, because her good works had followed her all the way to this big bed where she lay. I saw them, the ancient ones bent over telling Mammarosa secrets that only those like Mammarosa could be told. "Consumed, tell him I am consumed. It won't be long, I'll see him soon, tell him I'll see him soon." "Tell her she left me in a fine mess," a man said out loud and angry by the side of Mammarosa's bed. I don't think he cared that his message was not a secret. Tell him this and tell her that, the ancient and consumed whispered in Mammarosa's ears, and each time she nodded and agreed that she would. But none of the messages, I noticed, were for angels.

Had they forgotten that Mammarosa was about to go on a journey with angels? Had they nothing to say to those who had made them smile after birth's long journey? Although of mine I remembered nothing. They came and they left, Mammarosa's friends, and nothing of what they whispered was for an angel. All the messages were for those who had gone before and waited on the other side. Even Mammarosa must have forgotten. Not once did I hear her speak to her angel, or any angel for that matter, and I was there, sitting, standing or lying by her side a lot. I couldn't understand why this was.

I was going to America, not heaven, and although I did not know exactly when, I had already bought a second-hand book of English phrases so I could learn to speak. I practised those strange words, I even pretended to speak with those foreign people in that far-away land on the other side of the great sea. I was starting to think that maybe my aunt had been wrong about angels, that she had made it up just like a fairy tale, how they follow us through life, invisible, until death, when they show up again just like at birth, to help us. I was starting to think that maybe they were not there at all. That maybe they had left us on our own. They had accompanied us here to the earth to live and then they went away so we might learn to die—to live and to die on our own, without help.

It seemed fair to me, we had forgotten about them and they had forgotten about us. And then one night in the deep darkness I woke suddenly, as if someone had shaken my body and whispered, "Hurry, hurry, wake up and hurry." In fact I still felt the brushing of someone's soft hand on me when I opened my eyes.

My aunt, too, awoke at the very same time as if she too had been shaken out of her sleep. I turned to my right, as if an invisible finger had pointed and ordered me to turn in that direction, and there burning bright on the night stand I saw a candle. My aunt too looked, puzzled at the sight of that candle. I had no idea who put the candle there. Ever since the advent of that electric bulb in the middle of our room, ages ago, I had never seen a candle on the night stand.

The last time the wind and the rain ravaged San Giovanni and suddenly day became night, my aunt lit potatoes, not candles. I remember carving the inside of my potato half with Mammarosa's pocket knife and my aunt filled it with oil. Then I put a short piece of twine in the middle of the oil, and when my aunt lit it, the potato burned bright and longer than any candle.

This candle on the night stand burned for a very short while and then went out suddenly as if someone had blown on it to be spiteful. It was then when the light of the candle went out that my aunt cried, "Mamma, Mamma," and rushed out towards Mammarosa.

Just then I turned towards the light, but the candle was no more, and out of the stillness of that dark night came a faint voice. "Though I walk through the valley of the shadow of death," Mammarosa whispered faintly and then stopped as if she had forgotten the rest of the words. "I will fear no evil, Mamma, no evil," my aunt said as if to refresh Mammarosa's memory, but Mammarosa did not reply.

The angels had come. It was they who had blown out her candle. She was gone. Her mouth was half open though, and so were her eyes, as if she wanted to say one last thing to me. Come to think of it, it may have not been to me at all that she wanted to speak. It was more likely, under the circumstances, that she wanted to finally acknowledge the angels. It could be that she was trying to apologize to them for a lifetime of silence when she parted her lips for the last time. But she didn't. They didn't give her a chance.

They took her by the hand and snatched her away as if she was a brand they had come to save out of a fire. They rushed off with her.

But Mammarosa was going to have plenty of time to say all she wanted. It would be a long long road, longer than the long road to the vineyard, past, way past the cypress fence that enclosed the holy grounds. Mammarosa could talk and ask all the questions she wanted. She always let me ask and talk all I wanted. She had always held my hand and showed me the way on the long, long road, on the cobbled streets, even through the dark forests of San Giovanni. She had walked with me and I was not afraid.

Mammarosa was gone before the first sight of dawn. Like the moon she had stepped out of the way, so that the sun could rise bright and get on with the new day.

In no time at all Tata had Mammarosa washed and dressed and laid among the angels of beautiful pure-white linen. There were just Mammarosa and the angels in the white linens in that box. She had asked for nothing. She left empty.

Before noon, the ancient and the consumed, Mammarosa's friends, made their way back up the stairs of our house on Via Monterosa. I saw them waving wide handkerchiefs across their faces as they cried, as they called out, "Maro', Maro', where are you Maro'?" as if they didn't know! "Blessed are you Maro', the fire that consumed you has burned out. Blessed, blessed, blessed are you Maro'," they chanted as they wiped their faces with the handkerchiefs. But I saw no tears. They were not real.

Mammarosa lay there cold and still. She did not seem real. Soon the angels on the linens were no longer visible. Mammarosa was covered in a sea of bright perfect flowers that did not cry. Their petals were not bruised and they were not flopped over because they were not real. There wasn't, and had never been, life in them. They were cold and dead and still.

For a moment I thought my own life had disappeared.

I looked deep, very deep into the depths of my being, I searched up and down the chambers and walked through the corridors of my mind and found nothing. I felt nothing. There was nothing. Not even a word to speak, not one. What words would have changed death's mind anyway? None, not one.

But wait! I could make a fuss about it. Yes I could. I could kick and scream and fuss because there was no way I was going to let Mammarosa go without a good fight. In fact, I determined that as soon as I was alone I would do just that. I was going to let God hear how I felt about His decision to send angels to take Mammarosa just now.

I thought I should do it right and shout and cry out loud when I made this fuss so I decided to walk up to the basin of San Giovanni's mountain, and there by the stream, where I picked flowers, I would ask why. "Why, why?" I would scream. "Can you at least tell me why?!"

I was going to remind Him, in case He had not noticed, that Mammarosa was in the middle of learning how to read and how to write. Two more letters, the R and the S, and she would have fully written her name, Mancina Maria Rosa, with her piece of coal across the hearth of the fireplace. I was going to ask, why now, when we were almost ready to leave for America. Oh, if only I was a swallow!

I had seen an airplane fly across San Giovanni's sky once. Its wings were spread out and its belly was pure white like that of the swallows who nested and hid their young in the tiles of our roof. If I were a swallow I would have flown Mammarosa on my wings to far-away America and hid her. No angels and no death would find her there. If I were a swallow I could. But I wasn't so I walked and walked up the incline of San Giovanni's mountain thinking and thinking of things to say, well shout, when I came to a halt.

My feet had stumbled on something. I looked up and there before me was my tree! I had stumbled on my tree! I had tripped on its roots, which were still naked and exposed. And there, out of the blue, and into my mind (that same mind I thought lifeless and empty), came these words: "A thousand years is one day and one day is a thousand years." The words sang over and over again. "A thousand years is one day and one day is a thousand years." I was worried, after hearing these words a while, that soon I wouldn't know the difference between one and one thousand if this kept up.

Yes, I remembered those words. I remembered the day I hid them, the day they took up residence in my mind. I even remember Bernardo standing on the pulpit, with his face all pink, and his cheeks and extra chin jiggling and shaking all about while he repeated, "A thousand years is one day and one day is a thousand years." I should have paid attention when Bernardo spoke, but instead I turned around to laugh with Ceci who had just whispered "Bernardo is a big fat pig" in my ears, and that was the end of that.

So much for what was going to follow about the mysterious riddle of a thousand years and one day. Now I could only guess the riddle's meaning. Maybe Bernardo was trying to say that God couldn't tell time, I thought. But nah! I had learned how to tell time even before my aunt bought that first and only clock of ours. But whatever it meant, I knew for sure God did not have a clock.

I walked and I thought, and the more I thought, and the more I walked, the more it seemed pointless to fuss about this why-now thing. If a thousand years were indeed one day then how could I argue? What could I say? Was I going to be angry and argue over the fact that God had taken Mammarosa one hour before He took my mother and two hours before He took me and three hours before He took Lucrezia? (Lucrezia is the name I will give my daughter when I will have one because I have asked my aunt a million times to change my name and call me Lucrezia but she hasn't.) We were all going to be called on the same day, it seemed, Mammarosa, my mother, Lucrezia and me, so I realized that it would be petty to make a fuss and kick and scream about it. It would not be right. Although it wasn't right, either, that someone should jump for joy over it.

That's right, jump for joy. I remember Bernardo once said that the angels in heaven make a big celebration and jump for joy every time someone dies. There was nothing mysterious about those words. They meant just what they said. The angels were smiling and laughing and having a celebration while Mammarosa's body would lie and rot there in the ground just like the seeds of wheat she had shown me in the field that one fall. Oh well, it was going to be a long day, this thousand years!

I walked and walked until I was at the basin and there in the dirt by the stream I drew a line. I remember it was curved and it followed the horizon blue and clear across the sky. Beneath that line and very close up to it with my fingers I wrote "Mammarosa," and right there and then I decided to keep Mammarosa and everything about her safe within the confines defined by the line I myself had drawn.

I was not going to fuss and I was not going to cry, lest my tears like the rain would break through the line, and then who knows, I might be left with nothing but a mirage of her and embrace nothing but the bitter wind. No way, fussing was not a good idea.

I didn't want to be like Mr. Ficosecco, who thought of himself only and fussed about everything all the time. Like the time, a long time ago, when I drew that picture of myself and went out of my way to draw a detailed tree with roots in a vineyard, a cluster of grapes and even bells in the corner of the page, but no, he wasn't happy. He took all my work for granted, as if it got there on the page on its own, as if it didn't take time to draw every line and colour it too. Mr. Ficosecco was not happy, I remember, he wanted the drawing to be of me, me, me, and only me. And that is why he went on to fuss about petty details, like the way I drew my hair and the way I drew my ears and things like that. And just as I thought of Mr. Ficosecco, I felt embarrassed and it occurred to me that it would be appropriate, in fact, if I apologized to God for my intention to make a fuss in the first place. But then I remembered that He knows everything, even my thoughts, so I didn't. I just thought it.

And that was all right. With God you can do that. It's not like when you say something offensive to a friend, even a best friend. They sulk and take forever to forgive. No, He is not like that at all. He is not at all like Sara. I remember Sara once pouted all day just because I called her a donkey when she couldn't get a math problem solved after I went over it with her at least ten times.

Now that I think about it, Sara would like heaven. Math is not complicated there at all. A one is a one no matter how many zeros are attached to it. Anyway, I remember that I said I was sorry to Sara but that wasn't good enough. Oh no, not for her. Sorry was not good enough, she still would not talk. I sent her peace messages through friends, but her answer was still a cold silence, and not until I sent her all my pretty coloured marbles that my mother sent me in a package from America (including my big multicoloured beauty) was she satisfied and smiled at me again.

I remember hearing my marbles go click clock in her pockets and I asked her to play but she didn't want to. Sara was a donkey, there was no question about that, so

I had to follow her everywhere that day, just in case she decided to play with someone other than me, and then for sure I'd never see my marbles again. I remember finally after the Ave Maria bells had rung that she decided to play and I remember that I won everything back, even my big beauty. I had given Sara my marbles but I hadn't offered God anything, not that He had asked.

So I thought and thought and then came up with the idea that I should give Him a clock. That would have been a fine idea if my aunt didn't guard ours so. She had reason to. The last time I had the clock in my hands I was taken by a wave of curiosity and set out to find what it was about the tick tack tock of the clock that made the sun and the moon go across from one side of the sky to the other. I was about to place the blade of Mammarosa's black pocket knife on the screws at the back of the clock and find out, when I heard my aunt shout. I was startled. It was the last time I saw the clock that close up. So now I had nothing to offer. I was alone, left with nothing but my thoughts. I heard a stirring among the grasses. I turned around from where I sat by the brook at the basin and almost shouted. I looked and realized that I had no reason to be startled, it was only Margarita.

I had seen Margarita sit there by herself on a clump of grass by the stream often when I came to the basin to pick flowers. I had always wondered what she did there alone and silent. I wondered no more. Margarita knew who I was. I used to play with her son Davide. I remember Davide, he was tall and fair because Margarita listened to Dr. Rafaelino when he said "No coffee in the milk." She had listened and done all the right things and yet one day a little fire began to flicker inside of Davide. Soon it was a raging fire that turned itself off and on and on and off, leaving Davide burned out of all of his strength. Dr. Rafaelino looked in Davide's eyes and said that it was nothing, but it wasn't. So Margarita spread her wings and flew away, like the swallows, she flew to the east and she flew to the west, to the deepest south and the furthest north. As far as the wind's habitation Margaret flew with her son to hide him. But everywhere she went, the angel of death followed her, actually he got there first. It was as if he waited in ambush there for her, because each time, and in each place she went, just when Margarita thought she had Davide safely hidden, when she thought her running was over, the angel of death would light the fire and Davide burned hot all over again.

Until one day Margarita said no. She no longer wanted to run and hide so she took Davide home. I remember the day they came home. It was the same day Mammarosa and I came back home from the wheat fields. Margarita sat across from me with Davide in her arms. They sat on a double-seater in the little green train wagon and Davide's eyes were closed except for when the little train whistled its warnings before the long dark tunnels. I thought I saw Davide look at me for a brief moment while Margarita was turning his limp and weakened body in her arms to make him comfortable, so I smiled.

That same night the angels came but Davide refused to go. Not until Margarita, who had stepped out briefly, came into the room did he smile, close his eyes and agree to leave with them. Tata was there at Margarita's house when she brought Davide home and of course she washed him and dressed him when he died. I remember Margarita bent over, moaning, while she held Davide's cold hands. "My breath, my breath, the air that I breathe."

These were the only words that came out of her mouth for the longest time. People came in and out of the house all through the day. They all whispered nice words in Margarita's ears and to all she replied, "My breath, my breath, the air that I breathe," and even then, as she sat by the stream, I thought I heard her say again, "My breath, my breath, the air that I breathe."

Margarita wouldn't live long without breathing. If soon she wouldn't take a deep one, she too would die. She was chasing the angel of death. She had gone too long without taking a breath, I could tell. Her face was already looking paler than pale, and her once yellow hair, yellow as a daisy's heart, had turned all white.

I moved over a few rocks closer to Margarita and kept silent. I was thinking about showing her how to draw a line like Mammarosa had shown me. I was thinking about asking Margarita to forgive the whole host of heaven for not being able to tell time. I was thinking of a million excuses to tell Margarita, why the angels had come too early to take Davide away. I was going to tell her that there had been some mistake that couldn't be helped, and that happened sometimes, because in heaven there are no clocks.

I was thinking to tell her about my secret words, the mysterious riddle of life, "A thousand years is one day and one day is a thousand years." I had it all figured out in my mind as I sat there on my rock next to Margarita. I would hold her hands gently in mine and I would sweep back the hair stuck to the tears on her face and then I would embrace her and whisper all my thoughts in her ear. But I didn't. I said nothing. We sat there in perfect silence and listened, I to her heart and she to mine.

When the bells rang, Margarita walked down San Giovanni's mountain by my side. By the time we reached my home on Via Monterosa Bernardo was already there. "God be with you till we meet again," they were singing. I tried to join in the chorus but each time I tried, I felt as if something was stuck in my throat, something that stubbornly refused to descend and would not allow singing to come out. So I just moved my lips. I didn't sing.

I remember that Mammarosa didn't sing much. Once I asked her to sing but she said she couldn't. She couldn't, she said, because her soul was heavy, and I noticed that it was when her soul was heavy that she mumbled.

Her soul was not heavy now that she had flown away. Nina had closed Mammarosa's mouth shut just after her soul became as light as a feather and she left with the angels. Her mouth was shut and she was not singing. But as the chorus sang, as I strained my ears, I heard a faint echo. "Till we meet again." It sounded far yet I know it came from a place just a blink away, a place where there are no clocks, there is no time and a thousand is the same as one. I still couldn't sing so I mumbled. "Yes," I mumbled, "till we meet again, I will wait till we meet again. I will wait and it will not be long. Time goes fast when in a day you have to cram a thousand years."

It was night now, but the dawn was sure to come. The horizon behind the mountains would stay pale for only a moment and then it would turn to the brightest gold. And when this day was over, this mysterious day, the bells would need not ring to herald in the night. Unlike any other it would stay forever noon and the sun shine forever bright.

It was evening and the bells rang when we crossed over the Neto River bridge and walked through the cypress fence, where we left Mammarosa to rest in the holy grounds. Tata came back. She came back that very same night with a huge basket covered in a red and white checkered tablecloth. She walked through the house and went round and round, as if she had work to do and little time to do it in. She opened drawers and dressed the table, the same table that Mammarosa not long ago lay on! And she went around ordering Ceci and Nina about: "Get me this and fetch me that."

She spoke smiling and sometimes even laughing while I was crying. Even if no one could tell I was crying, I was. Tata poured marsala in little liqueur glasses in a tray and passed them around to the women of Piotta's patio, the ancient, the consumed, the old men, the young, and to all who had come to say nice things about Mammarosa. They drank sweet liqueurs and smiled and some laughed too.

If Tata had brought brodo in her basket instead of pastasciutta with meat and strong red wine for us to drink, I would be asking "Where is the baby? Can I hold the baby?" That's right, you would think it was not the house of sorrow, the house where the angel of death had lingered until it got what it wanted, our house that evening. You'd think it was a celebration of new life taking place, as if an angel had lit another candle and smiled with a newborn. It was as if a birth and not a death had occurred, the way everyone went on. Tata went around ordering everyone to eat and be strong. "Life marches on, life marches on," she said, as she added more food next to the food that already sat on my plate. "The journey is hard. Eat and be strong. Life must go on, life must go on," she kept on saying all night long, as if she had been commissioned, as if she had received some divine ordination to ensure that life indeed went on because there must always be enough life for death. Death and the grave had not said "enough" yet.

I realized that I was being petty. It quickly came to me that I was, in fact, fussing, so I held out my hand and accepted the strong espresso that Professor Ciano's wife brought because I had said to myself, not too long ago when I drew that line by the stream at the basin of the mountain, that I was not going to fuss. I held up my cup until Piperella's wife, who followed behind Professor Ciano's wife, topped it up with strong drink she had brought. I allowed Barbara, who followed after Piperella's wife, to stir in lots of sugar, and I even reached for one of her sweet biscotti. I was going to ask if all this sweetness was a peace offering sent through these kind women by the angel of death, but I caught myself in time and didn't. Besides, who would I ask? Not Mammarosa!

In the morning as soon as the new sun came up from behind the mountains, La Casinise walked in with a basketful of fresh eggs. Catarina, Carletta's mother, didn't. She brought a bottle of sweet liqueur because her eggs had hatched. I had seen eggs hatch. I had watched as the chicks struggled and wrestled to peck their way out of the shell. I remember being surprised at how much energy they had left, even after all that pecking. They went on struggling and crying and going round and round, as if they had to get somewhere, and get there fast. If only they knew they were destined for brodo!

Spezzatino

Sauté in a large pan olive oil, onion, garlic, tomatoes and hot, hot peppers

Add small chunks of liver, heart, kidney, lungs and strips of washed and cooked tripe

Continue to sauté, splashing several times with white wine
(at this point you can also add potatoes)

Add a little water when needed

Simmer until tender

When almost ready throw in lots of fresh basil and parsley

Eat with stale, hard bread

Wanderers

EVERYONE SAID THAT WE WERE destined for great things. They said that we were lucky because lady luck herself, as blind as she was, had found Via Monterosa in San Giovanni and out of all its numbers she picked number fourteen. I don't know why lady luck decided to pick on me. I never got picked. Maria Pia and that new girl Lucrezia were always in charge of picking players for games at school. I was always picked last. Once they even argued, "No, you take her." "No, you." So I should have been happy that someone finally picked me even if that someone was blind.

We had been picked, we were the lucky winners of a stamp that would say "Immigrant"—landed and rooted, ready to be transplanted. We had received free admission to America, paradise, and everyone said they wished it was them, that they had been this lucky, but I didn't believe them.

Once everyone called Piperella lucky too. He had

won the Totocalcio lottery and that day for the first time I saw Professor Ciano and Dr. Mauri smile and say good morning to him. Piperella's ticket number was indeed a winner and Piperella was so enraptured by his good fortune that even if he wouldn't know for a few days just how much he had won, he paid for drinks for the whole crowd that gathered around him and he even gave away his pick, hoe, and his shovel.

I remember that morning. It was the morning the seamstress delivered a new flannel nightgown for my aunt, who was preparing a few luxuries to pack in her suitcase. A new flannel nightgown was no small thing, not to my aunt anyway. She was so excited and delighted, one of the few times I saw my aunt in a blissful state such as this, that she put it on and all the way across from her door Piperella's wife saw my aunt prance like a ballerina around the floor. She saw my aunt hold the soft warm flannel against her cheeks and smile. That very evening the seamstress delivered a nightgown just as soft and just as pretty as my aunt's to Piperella's wife, who had ordered one just because of their good luck.

A few days later, when Piperella found out that his winnings amounted to much less than what it would cost him to buy a new beret, he got drunk. And that evening on his way home, he didn't apologize to the walls he crashed into as was his custom. In fact he bashed his body against doors and stairs and carts because he was determined to find that blind bitch called luck and crush her to pieces. "Bitch, bitch, filthy bitch," he called out to her. He was angry because he had spent money, given away his tools and had nothing to show for it, while his wife, on the other hand (thanks to my aunt), had a beautiful new nightgown to fondly remember the occasion when they almost got lucky.

When Piperella arrived at the top of the stairs he was

even angrier because he had grasped and grasped and bashed and bashed, and he still hadn't had the pleasure of having lady luck within his hold, for just a little while, only a little while, enough time to wrap his hands around her neck and squeeze. That would have been enough, but with his luck, all that Piperella squeezed between his hands was air, as usual.

As he stood there at the top of the stairs wandering to the left and wandering to the right, trying hard to locate the knob of his door, he turned in our direction and by chance caught a glimpse of my aunt, who was quietly trying to go unseen by gently closing our door. Piperella must have thought he saw lady luck when he saw my aunt because he started to shout, "Bitch, lousy bitch, there is the bitch, she's been busy running around town showing off her new nightgown."

But my aunt wasn't lady luck. My aunt didn't even believe in luck. Once she told me that luck was not a lady at all. She told me it was nothing but a worm, a maggot to be exact, that lived on the carcass of expired hope. Although lately I was worried that maybe she believed in luck after all. I couldn't help but think that, the way she went around giving away things, like her pick and her shovel and our winter canopy. I saw people come into our house empty-handed and leave with their arms full of things that my aunt had given them—every day—as if she too had won the lottery like Piperella. Especially since my father had come from America and signed all the papers and paid for our tickets.

I remember the day my father arrived in San Giovanni. He just showed up. Every day for the last week Ceci and Peppe had hung around the train station because, give or take a few days, that was the week he should have arrived. And he did. I saw my aunt, Ceci, Nina, Peppe and Julia run. I heard people shout, "The

Americano, the Americano," all along Via San Francesco and Via Monterosa, and in no time every balcony and window was full of people wanting to know who the Americano was.

I knew who the Americano was. I saw everyone on Via Monterosa gather around him. I heard them laugh and cry and ask a million questions, every one of them at once. I heard them from behind a niche formed by two walls that jutted onto the street across from Piotta's patio. I stayed there for a long time. It must have been a very long time in fact, because my aunt came looking for me. I tried to make myself small against the wall so she wouldn't see me, but she did. I fought with her but she won. She pulled my dress up and I pulled it down and she pulled it up again and in no time she had slipped it off and had me all dressed in that new green linen suit that Maria Pia's sister had made me, but no new shoes. My aunt pulled my arm until I was inside our house, and there, sitting by the fire, for the first time I saw my father.

I remember when I first saw his face. I was right. The picture of that man on the dresser by our bed was not of him. My father's hair was thin on top and he was not tall and slim like the man in the picture. But the smile, only by the smile was I almost fooled into thinking that they were the same. I remember that when I stood there in the distance he smiled without his eyes. I couldn't tell by that smile whether he was sad or happy, just like the man in the picture by our bed whose lips suggested a forced show of happiness, encouraged perhaps by some man behind a black box who told him a million times to look at the light and smile, smile.

My father reached for me with his arms stretched out but I didn't know what to do. When my aunt saw that I was taking too long to do what I was supposed to do she gave me one good push. Only once did I feel her hand flat and strong against my back and then there I was, smack in front of my father. And this was the moment when I knew I had been right all along. My father was not the man in the picture on the dresser by our bed because now he was smiling with both his eyes and mouth, his whole face, in fact even his ears. My father put his hand on my head and held it there for a little while and looked at me and all the time he was smiling.

My father's hand!

It was just as I had imagined it time after time when I saw Don Antonio, the priest, rest his hand upon the children who ran to him for a figurine of the Madonna and a blessing. I knew better than to go for a figurine, but I do confess that once or twice I was tempted to run up to Don Antonio and get one and kiss it to pieces, just so I could feel his hand on my hair. Yes, my hair, only my hair and not my head, that's how gentle I imagined it was. And it was! My father's hand made even my unruly hair feel gentle.

There was such a confusion and so many people in our house when my father arrived! Tata shouted at Peppino the Gypsy to come back another time when he tried to squeeze himself in, crying, "A dollar, a dollar, a lucky song for a lucky dollar." My father didn't shout, he gently said, "Let him in, let him in," and I saw him give Peppino a dollar.

After Peppino the Gypsy finished singing his song about Marina the bella mora I heard my father ask him if he knew how to sing Verdi's "Va Pensiero." I knew Verdi's "Va Pensiero." Even Piperella's wife knew it. I had heard some of the women of Piotta's patio sing it while they embroidered and knit, and I heard men sing it while they tilled the land. Mr. Ficosecco made us sing it at school so I knew every line.

Go, thought, on golden wings;
Go, rest yourself on the slopes and hills,
Where, soft and warm, murmur
The sweet breezes of our native soil.
Great the banks of the Jordan,
The fallen towers of Zion.
Oh my country so beautiful and lost!
O memory so dear and so fatal!
Golden harp of the prophetic bars,
Why do you hang mute on the willow?
Rekindle memories in our breast,
Speak to us of the time that was!
O as with the fates of Solomon
You make a sigh of cruel lament.
O may the Lord inspire you to a song
That infuses suffering with strength!

Once Mr. Ficosecco said that Verdi's "Va Pensiero" almost became the national anthem but it didn't. I didn't know why.

Peppino knew Verdi's "pensieri." He knew only too well those immortal "thoughts," and when he sang them, suddenly it was as if I had never known them, and was faced with thinking every word through, as if I heard them that day for the first time.

Maybe it was the way Peppino the Gypsy suddenly composed his whole body when he first started to sing them. He didn't shake his limbs all around and dance and look for women with dark complexions in the crowd to sing to, like he did when he sang the "Marina, Marina the Bella Mora" song. Oh no, as soon as my father even mentioned Verdi's "Va Pensiero" he stood tall, his body didn't sway once, and his eyes longingly looked towards the open door; towards the sky he sang, and to the wind he released the words and music of a longing heart and soul.

As I heard Peppino the Gypsy sing, a thought came to me and suddenly I knew why Verdi's "Va Pensiero" could not have become, ever, the national anthem. It was because this song was not a song of the nationals, it was a song of the wanderers. And Peppino sang it so well because he knew all about wandering. He was a poor Gypsy in a strange land, travelling with his caravan from town to town, yet he sang. Peppino's harp hung silent from the willow, yet he sang and sang.

My father was home in his own land but he couldn't sing. He wanted to sing along with Peppino, I saw him, but he couldn't. I think there was something stuck in his throat that refused to go down every time he tried, and wouldn't let him. I too was here still, on my own mountain, but I couldn't sing.

In fact I stopped singing the day I saw things, things that I had never given much thought to, like our winter canopy the colour and texture of ripe pomegranate, being carried out the door. The winter canopy collected our breath in the winter and kept us warm, but sometimes our breath was not enough, and I remember shivering through many nights.

I stopped singing when I saw the wooden quart that my aunt used for measuring wheat being carried out the door. I remember that my aunt measured precious wheat in that wooden quart and sold it when she really should have kept it because she really needed it to make bread. I don't know why I couldn't sing.

"Papa, is there a fountain on Fountain Street where our big beautiful house in America is?" I asked. "Papa, do the women gather there to wash linens, and Papa, what if an earthquake should spit San Giovanni right off of the mountain the day we leave because we dared to cross the abbot's forbidden boundary?" Papa told me only the brave dare to be free.

I should have been singing because I was going to America where women no longer had to scrub their linens until their hands were red and swollen. They had their own washtubs in their own homes. Tubs of steel, my father said, a new American invention, that twisted and turned all about, and the linens came out clean and bright without ever a woman's hand. But I still couldn't sing. And although my father had dared, although he had crossed the boundary and travelled to the land of the free, he could not sing.

I don't know why we couldn't join Peppino the Gypsy when he sang Verdi's thoughts. I looked around our four peeling bare walls. Was it the toilet that hung there behind the flimsy curtain next to the front door or was it the shutters that trembled in the slightest wind? I don't know.

I remember that Mr. Ficosecco once said that Verdi asked "why" a lot. I remember that he wrote all the words to Verdi's song on the blackboard one morning, along with a new word underlined and in bold letters. "Nostalgia," it read. And then he spent a lot of time talking and describing this willow that Verdi's harp hung on, so by the time he was finished I didn't know what was head and what was tail about nostalgia. A disease, I thought, by the time he erased the blackboard, that affected trees, uprooted trees only, perhaps.

When I asked my aunt about nostalgia she thought I had said neuralgia, and before I could correct her she was already rattling on and on, "Oh, Professor Ciano suffers from neuralgia. I told that donkey, his wife, that he had neuralgia, but no, she insisted on calling every doctor in San Giovanni hoping they would say he had something incurable, but every one of them said neuralgia. She should have listened to me, I said it was neuralgia from the first. I knew, your mother had neuralgia. . . ." She went on and on, saying that it was a disease that affected the facial muscles and sent pains straight through the temples to the whole head, and there was no way of stopping my aunt until I finally shouted, "Nostalgia, nostalgia. I asked about nostalgia, not neuralgia."

"Oh, nostalgia. Then why didn't you say nostalgia? All these years of school and you can't even say 'nostalgia,'" she said. "Nostalgia, now that's worse."

My aunt said that nostalgia was a useless pile of horseshit, a fantasy nursed by the mind, a far worse form of neuralgia. It was a brain disease, a disorder in fact, that started at the head and travelled through the whole body. It worked like a magnet, or better, like a mud pit, she said, and it prevented those affected by it from moving forward.

All my life she had told me to pay attention and listen and observe and remember because it was so important. "Who knows where on earth God might lead or pull you and then you might need to remember." And now, just because we had packed our bags and secured them with double-knotted twine, she was telling me that remembering, recalling what I had listened to and observed, was nothing more than being stuck in a pile of horseshit, a mud pit at best. "Water that's gone by can't turn the millstone," she said, and that was that.

She would say no more. That's what my aunt left me with as a clear explanation of nostalgia. Then she pointed to my books of English phrases and basic grammar on the table and told me to get going. She urged me to get moving, as if in those strange books was the real answer to nostalgia.

Where was Mammarosa?

Well, I was going all right, but not to the books, not for long anyway, I was going to run up the mountain, and as soon as she was gone, I left to do just that.

I ran and ran because I wanted to get to the ravine where my tree was at the basin of San Giovanni's mountain. I wanted to get there fast, but I found myself making so many stops that I was nowhere near my destination and it was almost the time for the Ave Maria bells to ring.

I stopped by zu' Michele's house because I thought I should hear just one more story. And I stopped to play with Sara and I stopped to pick up Biasi's plaid blanket that had fallen off his wheelchair and I stopped to watch the fornaia push more kindling into the fire of her oven and I stopped to hear the women of San Giuseppe's fountain wash their linen and I even stopped to play with Filomena's boy who was kicking a ball all by himself shouting, "He runs, he runs, he runs and he scores!"

I wanted to run but couldn't. I moved slower and slower after every stop. Soon I was having to take long, long steps, one foot carefully in front of the other, as if something was holding and pulling my whole body down. It was as if the whole mountain was charged by a great magnet, as if it was one big pile of mud and I was stuck in it and couldn't move forward. I struggled and struggled and as I inched along, holy shit! I bumped into Don Antonio's big belly. He looked at me and lifted his hand. I thought he was going to cross himself on account of his body coming into contact with me, a half devil, but he didn't. He must have thought that I was an angel. Yes, that's what Don Antonio called his children, he called them angels. He must have, because he rested his hand on my head for just a little while and I think he blessed me, as if he was sent to, as if he were an angel too.

They were all angels, all of them, the whole of San Giovanni's mountain was inhabited by angels, I concluded. Even Maria Pia was an angel. I remember that she saw me inch up the slope. She looked at me, she stared from far away, but I didn't care. So what if she was going to tell everyone that I couldn't move, that my feet were stuck as if in thick mud? I remember thinking that she could tell whoever she wanted, what she wanted. I was leaving for America and that was far enough that I wouldn't hear or see anyone laugh at me.

From far away I thought I saw her laughing already. I saw her swaying to the right and swaying to the left in her very Maria Pia way with her hands behind her back. But soon I realized that she was moving towards me and she was not laughing, she was just smiling, and she smiled even more when she handed me something from behind her back. I couldn't believe it! She opened my hands and then wrapped them around her beautiful globe, the one that her father sent her from America with the whole world, every mountain and every ocean, on it, the one that went round and round on its own golden stand! Maria Pia gave it to me and smiled like an angel. I didn't know what to say. She kept on smiling while she turned and went her own way.

Now I just thought and thought with this globe, the whole world, in my hands, as I inched up the mountain. And by the time I stood next to my tree, that gigantic, naked yet proud pine that I encountered so long ago on my way to school, at the basin of the mountain, I was exhausted. My head was spinning and I was feeling faint. My feet couldn't move and that's when another thought came to me, that perhaps I had been infected by that strange disease, the one that struck only trees, uprooted ones, the one Mr. Ficosecco spoke about the day he wrote Verdi's thoughts on the blackboard.

Thoughts and thoughts and nothing but thoughts. It all started when I saw those insignificant things like baskets and blankets and canopies and measuring quarts go out of my door into smiling people's arms, and now as I struggled up the mountain it was worse. They struck my brain like lightning, they struck and struck against it, until my body was short-circuited and I felt like that lonely lightbulb in the middle of our room when suddenly it stopped shining whenever a storm hit San Giovanni's mountain.

My head started to spin and I felt as heavy as a millstone that had come to a grinding halt, and suddenly my limbs were unable to move. They were as if planted deep, as deep as the naked roots of my tree, deep into the ground, and I could not go on.

If my aunt was right about nostalgia being horseshit then I was in a big pile of it, as big as Verdi may have been. Although I didn't speak to trees and idle harps like he did as I stood there next to my tree, I thought I heard the wind howl and blow as if a storm raged through the mountain. I felt the very earth shake and move beneath my feet as if the very elements were conspiring against me, and yet the day was beautiful and the sky was calm and clear. I heard the wind, and felt it pull and pull, and mostly it pulled me. It pulled me around the mountain and it pulled me across the sea, around the world it pulled me. On its journey it took me and then suddenly it stopped. I did not hear it howl and I did not hear it pull in the deep silence that followed. I heard nothing. I saw nothing, except my bare feet still planted, deeper, into the ground, right where I had been and would always be, next to my tree on San Giovanni's mountain.

When the sun was barely up over the hills of San Giovanni, before the birth of the new day, before the break of that one cold morning that could have been the dead of winter or the birth of spring, the day we turned our backs on Via Monterosa for the last time, the only thing I heard was the wind. Invisible, like the angels my aunt had told me about, yet there. I heard only the wind.

At the railway station it threatened to rip the sign that read "San Giovanni" right off the hinges it hung by. All of Via Monterosa was there on the platform waving and crying. We were huddled together like a pile of dry leaves brought together only to be scattered and tormented by the wind. I am sure that they said we were lucky, lucky, lucky a million times, but I didn't hear any of that. All I heard was the flapping of their handkerchiefs in the howling, ripping wind. It sounded like the fluttering of wings, angels' wings, struggling. I saw them, all of San Giovanni's angels, with their feet stuck to the earth as if a magnet held them back. They fluttered and fluttered, hoping the wind would help them get off the ground, but they didn't. They couldn't.

I stood silent with my face pressed against the glass of the little train's window. Soon they would become no longer visible. There, yet invisible.

I saw the kerchiefs torn by the wild gusts, I saw them like fluttering wings. I saw them until the train wailed and entered a dark wide gaping hole in the side of San Giovanni's mountain, and then I, too, became invisible.

There, always there, yet invisible.